Seal Woman

Seal Woman

A Novel

SOLVEIG EGGERZ

GHOST ROAD PRESS

Library of Congress Cataloging-in-Publication Data.
Seal Woman
Ghost Road Press
ISBN   (Trade pbk.)
13 digit 978-09796255-3-4
10 digit 0-9796255-3-x
Library of Congress Control Number: 2008920343

This book is a work of the author's imagination. Any
resemblance to persons dead or living is purely coincidental.

Ghost Road Press
Denver, Colorado

ghostroadpress.com

Author's Note and Acknowledgments

During the late 1940s, 314 German men and women arrived in Iceland to work on farms by arrangement of the Icelandic Agricultural Association. Most arrived on June 8, 1949 with the Icelandic ship, Esja, which transported 130 German women and 50 German men to Iceland. The rest arrived by trawler. The association provided a one-year contract at 400 Icelandic kronas a month for women and 500 a month for men. The farmers who hired the Gemans paid their passage from Hamburg to Reykjavik. Of the original 314 workers who arrived in Iceland, 48% of the women and 42% of the men married and settled in Iceland.[1]

The Seal Woman is an entirely fictional account, inspired by the experiences of the German workers described above. From interviews I learned that the Germans' arrival had an invigorating effect on the countryside where they settled. Icelanders considered them hardworking individuals who contributed to the social fabric of the countryside where they settled. I was told by several sources that the Icelanders, out of consideration for the workers' privacy, did not ask the Germans about their experiences in Germany.

I would like to express thanks to my agent, Sandra Bond, and to Sonya Unrein and Matthew Davis of Ghost Road Press. For encouragement I am grateful to Margot Livesey, Ann

1 Statistics are based on a thesis by Pétur Eiríksson, entitled "From Memel to Melrakkasletta: the origin, fate, and adjustment of German agricultural workers brought to Iceland by the Icelandic Agricultural Association in 1949, University of Iceland, September, 2006.

McLaughlin, and Susan Lescher. For research assistance I thank Hildur Stefánsdóttir, Soffía Stefánsdóttir, Hólmfríður Gunnarsdóttir, Guðrún Þórarinsdóttir, Kristín Þórarinsdóttir, Þorbjörg Björnsdóttir, Erika Einarsson, Hjálmfríður Þórðardóttir, Halldór Stefánsson, and Pétur Eiriksson. For close reading of drafts I am indebted to my Holey Road writing colleagues: Bert Brandenburg, Susan Clark, Catherine Flanagan, Bob Gibson, Phil Harvey, Frank Joseph, Katherine Lorr, Linda Morefield, Leslie Rollins, Joye Shepperd, Wayland Stallard, David Stewart, and Paul Vamas.

To my father, Pétur Eggerz

1. At the End of the World

Charlotte stood on the black sand. The surf swirled around the toes of her boots. Columns of hardened lava rose from the water like wading trolls. Fulmars quarreled in the cliffs above. Her desire to speak the forbidden names was overwhelming. She raised her head and directed her voice to the line where ocean and sky met.

Max. Lena.

She shouted again. When her throat grew sore, she pulled the hood of her jacket over her head and turned away from the ocean. Beyond the sea grass on the dunes, a gravel road passed alongside cliffs stained white by generations of birds. A black Ford pick-up approached. Ragnar was already back from the village to fetch her. Why did he always rush her?

She'd asked him to see if her oil paints had arrived from Berlin. Her mother wrote that the lids had been screwed on tight. Twelve years and the paints were still good. He walked towards her now, swinging his plowman hands. He didn't like her near the ocean. He'd made her promise two years ago never to go into the water again.

That seaweed in your hair. So horrible.

Why not, she'd asked, wanting more than the obvious answer. He'd described the horrors of drowning. *You feel like you're suffocating.* When he was a boy, a friend from the neighboring farm had thought he could swim in the North Atlantic. He hadn't returned.

Ragnar had breathed that story into her neck the first time they'd made love after she went into the sea. It wasn't until early morning that he gave her the right answer.

Because I love you.

After ten years of marriage, he'd finally said it.

Now his disapproval made her throat tighten. Easing her voice around that feeling, she addressed him in his native language—farm talk.

"Did they have the grain?"

He started to speak, but hesitated, and she grew impatient, hating herself for it. The other farmers didn't wait for him to finish, just gabbled on about wool and prices. But she was his wife. She had to listen.

"Two bags," he said at last.

She took his hand. He pulled away, but then gave in to her. People didn't hold hands, not after they were married, he'd said. People would think they—they what? Inside the truck, the silence thickened between them. The rumble of the motor came as a relief. He ran his hands over his thighs before grasping the steering wheel. His overalls were threadbare from the frequent gesture.

"Any mail?"

He shook his head. Disappointment stung her. All these years on the island, she'd used colored pencils or watercolors. Suddenly she'd wanted the paints from her old life. She leaned her head against the dusty leather and sighed. Eventually the paints would emerge from the hold of the ship in Reykjavik, and the bus would bring them to the village, but would she still need them then? A headache crouched at her temples. Dust swirled up through the floor of the truck. Bulging sheep eyes watched from both sides of the road. The wooly-barreled bodies bore tiny heads with delicate nostrils and a thin mouth curved into a tentative smile. Charlotte often gagged on farm life. Humans weren't meant to live among moss and heather, climb rocks, and freeze in summer snowstorms. That was for sheep. And men like Ragnar.

Halfway up the hillside, Max would have worn her out with talking. Odd how Ragnar's stolid silence still made her think of Max's restlessness. In the rear view mirror, the gray sky blurred into the black sea. The car groaned as its tires gripped the rutted road for the last part of the ascent.

Suddenly she remembered why he'd gone to the village today.

"Did you get the new blade?" she asked.

"No deliveries this week," he said, his voice furred with disappointment.

Of course not. The blade was in the hold of the same ship that contained the paints from her mother.

"We're at the end of the world," she whispered to the sheep.

His shoulder shifted defensively. "But it's better than Germany—right?"

The hillside was better, better than the Germany she'd left after the war was finally over—no work, nothing to eat, the best people dead or gone. But she didn't like hearing it from him. Sometimes they didn't talk for days. He lived at the center of a world warmed by cows and sheep while she clung to its periphery. She fed the chickens in a daydream of her favorite German painter, David Casper Friedrich. How did he gnarl his trees? How did Rembrandt pock his noses?

Farm chores kept her focused on eggs and milk. Penciled reminders on the calendar dictated their lives—May, manure grinders at the cooperative store. June, grain shipment. July, barbed wire.

But memories often eclipsed the calendar. Last winter, treading the snow rut between house and shed to milk the cows, she'd seen her old life. Max stood beside her in the cold classroom at the academy, pointing at the model, then at her painting.

Her breasts aren't pink. They're really green and yellow. Thighs are purple.

Thanks to Max, today she still measured everything, even the distance from then to now. But she didn't want to be like

Lot's wife, looking back over her shoulder. She hated how memory ate the edges off her real life, how images of *then* were brighter than scooping out the gutters in the cow shed. She'd be listening to Henrik, her island child, when Lena's voice from years ago would break in. *Mamma.* It was Henrik pulling her ear. But she heard only Lena talking to her bear under the kitchen table. Sometimes she'd stop work and fight it. She'd chant the days of the week in Icelandic—*sunnudagur, manudagur*—until the memories broke into little pieces.

In the ray of light that streaked through the dirty shed window, she would hold up thumb and forefinger and, once again, measure the fateful distance from point to point, until she would decide to give her child away. This mental geometry often caused her to drop her rake, to cut the sheep she was shearing, to miss the last drop in a cow's teat.

The child might not be dead.

Just last week she'd perched on the greasy stool, stroked Skjalda's warm udder, and told the cow about Lena, the story that Ragnar didn't want to hear. The cow had turned to look at her with round brown eyes, extending her rough purple tongue towards Charlotte's cheek.

Mornings when Ragnar heard the chickens cackle, he placed his feet on the cold floor. No other world existed. A courageous man, he would walk into a blinding storm to find his sheep or climb the mountain path while the gravel rolled downhill under his horse's feet. He often rode along the glacier rim, where a misstep meant certain death on jagged rocks in a crevice.

But he feared Charlotte's past.

Talking was not his strength. When she first arrived at the farm, he'd scattered words at her, and she'd pecked at them. Later, she'd learned to enjoy his stroking at night, his murmuring about new milk filters and fence posts.

Back then she hardly understood him. Picking her way among the tussocks behind a cow's swinging udder, she'd moved her lips searching for phrases. Ragnar had named things and made her repeat the words. But once he'd established her basic farm vocabulary, he'd gone quiet. Back then, it hadn't mattered so much. She'd been moving forward into a new life. That was before she realized how time looped back on you and knocked you down with things you'd rather forget.

Charlotte had been without a man for a long time that summer when she met Ragnar. Their solemn promises in the shadow of the minister's ruff gave them rights to one another. And during that fall and winter their bodies slid together hungrily at night. The nighttime heat left a residual warmth that drew them to one another during the day. Furtively, she stroked his arm, his thigh when the old woman, his mother, wasn't nearby.

But soon the touching wasn't enough. The novelty of his quick couplings wore off. The less they talked, the more uncomfortable she felt as her memories backed up inside her. One night, the silence between them felt heavier than his long leg lying across hers.

"I want to tell you—" she started.

He pulled back his leg.

"About Berlin—"

"Don't like big cities."

"During the war, a lot of people—"

He placed his finger on her lips, shushing a noisy child. Afraid to upset him, she kept quiet, focused on breathing in a calm, even manner.

At last he spoke.

"We need a new outhouse."

"Of course, but—"

She placed her hand on his chest, felt it rumble under her palm, knew he was preparing to speak again. He rose up on his elbow.

"A husband needs his wife in the fields, not just at night," he said, then rolled onto his back, apparently exhausted by his own rhetoric.

She welcomed the pledge of friendship. Its restrictions dawned on her later.

The night Ragnar imposed the talking ban, her memories formed a knot inside her. What she'd lived long ago felt like a creature—perhaps a dragon—that slumbered uneasily within her. A light sleeper, the dragon sometimes woke up suddenly. On those nights, Ragnar found her shivering outdoors, talking through blue lips. Why? he asked. She didn't know why.

She and Max had been so sensual together. Her fingertips, the sides of her feet, the backs of her knees—every part of her—had desired him. They'd lingered over one another, languidly naming things—colors, painters, landscapes, sunsets. She had relished the slow build-up of desire, the sudden explosion of pleasure.

Ragnar never wasted time. In the village, he bought his grain quickly. In bed, he was efficient. *Slower,* she'd pleaded with him those first nights in bed, placing her hand on his, guiding his stroking of her. His face in the midsummer light had been contorted with embarrassment. Later, he'd spoken.

"She—"

He rarely mentioned his other wife, a woman who had grown up on the hillside. His mother had given her consumptive daughter-in-law lichen milk three times a day to clear her lungs, and still she'd died. He'd made a bad choice.

During the day, Ragnar helped Charlotte with such words as dog—*hundur.* Sheep—*kind.* Phrases like pass the fat—*réttu mér flotið.* He never labeled what you couldn't see and knew little of what she saw. He especially disliked the Berlin ghost who crept under her blanket while he slept.

Sometimes when the cold air from the outside wall touched every vertebra in her back, he appeared and warmed her. But after he was gone, questions arose. How many flour bag aprons, strung together through the years like paper dolls holding hands, would she wear out in this place?

Her union with Ragnar had grown from need, not love. Too many women had left the hillside, he'd explained—gone to work as maids in Reykjavik. For money. For running water. Germany had women. He'd advertised. And she'd been a woman without a man. Funny. She'd always thought of herself as an artist, one who could live without a man.

As the truck ascended the hillside, she stared straight ahead, determined to match his silence.

2. A Gift

The boys stood on the steps waving, reclaiming their parents at last. Eleven-year-old Tryggvi, named for Ragnar's father, strode toward the car on long, lean legs. His unwashed brown hair stood up stiff as a crow's feather. Henrik, five years old, ran down the steps towards her. Trails of earlier tears marked his cheeks. Pale-skinned and small-boned, he looked as if the cool summer breeze would break him in two.

When the midwife—a heavy-hipped woman from the foot of the hillside—had laid the squalling infant on Charlotte's chest, her father's name, *Heinrich*, had come into her head. But even as she rolled her shoulders in pain under the baby's hard gums on her nipple, she'd changed his name to Henrik. It would sound better on the hillside. Being the son of the foreign woman would be hard enough for the child.

Henrik's eyes held an accusation.

"Why didn't you tell me you were going?"

She stepped out of the car and caressed his fragile shoulders. Every time she went on an errand, he behaved as if she'd left him forever. Secretly she liked his fear of losing her. It tied her to the farm in a way that Ragnar never could. It matched her own fear for the safety of these pups born to her in middle age. Tryggvi bristled under her caution, but Henrik absorbed her fears, made them his own.

Now he hung on her leg.

"Silly," she said, tweaking his nose.

She must discourage this nervous hugging, help him grow up. Three years old the day they found her on the shore, he'd seen the waves washing over her. After that, she'd promised them. No more climbing on the rocks. Just a little whispering into the waves.

"We'll make pancakes," she said.

Henrik released her and ran into the house.

Tryggvi's features curled into indifference. She wanted to kiss him, but he wouldn't allow that, not since he'd begun to swing a scythe with his father. He rolled up his sleeves, reached into the back, and pulled out the bag of grain. Watching him struggle with it across the driveway, she felt a rush of pride.

Before entering the house, she glanced toward the sea. It was her favorite time, that moment of indecision in the ocean when the tide turned.

The old woman sat in the living room, knitting. Above her hung the three oil paintings Charlotte had brought with her. An old man looked tenderly into the eyes of his young son. The boy returned the gaze. The old man held a metallic glint in his hand, indistinguishable as a knife unless you knew how Abraham had hesitated to kill Isaac.

Before their first Christmas together, Charlotte had hung up the painting of Lena as a baby, her face merging with vinca and violets. In a certain light, her eyes sparkled with laughter. But when you stood in the door and looked at the painting sideways, you glimpsed a sadness. Charlotte always faced the painting straight on.

The third painting had stayed longer in Charlotte's suitcase. She was already pregnant with Tryggvi when she hung it in the corner, away from the sun's rays. It depicted a market place crowded with carts and peddlers. A figure ran towards the viewer. On its white cloak was a red dot. Each painting was signed. *Max.*

The old woman plucked a loop of wool from her needle.

She gestured with her chin to a small table covered with an embroidered doily. On it was a glass of water that contained two scarlet, white-spotted mushrooms. The stalks of the umbrella-like heads were snow white.

"Beserk mushroom—found it this morning," she said.

Charlotte saw the gleam in her eye and wondered if she'd sliced a bit of it into her chamomile tea. Hadn't the mushrooms' muskarin and atropin inspired a hallucinatory courage in the Vikings, helped them rip out the hearts of their enemies? Trying occasionally to dose down her own dreams with the mushroom, Charlotte had created bloody nightmares instead. In the kitchen she reached for her apron and tied it so that the threadbare section was on her side, not over her belly.

Clicking her needles, the old woman sang.

Covered with old and gray moss
Grass and green heather grow into our wound.

3. The Deepest Landscape Painting

That summer of 1947 Charlotte had wanted to get back on the boat and return to the ruins of Berlin. But she'd smiled tightly at the other women, then boarded the dusty little bus.

The bus ascended hills, crossed heaths, then ground its gears descending back down onto the sands. Charlotte saw how the rain transformed the moss from gray to green. All around her the women chattered in German. The newspaper advertisement that brought them here had been terse.

Farmers in Iceland seek strong women who can cook and do farm work.

As the bus rattled along the gravel road, she looked for faces in the moss and in the wildflower clusters. The tundra painter had taught her to look for human beings in the grazing land that fingered its way up the side of the mountain, to imagine the shape of bodies in the brown and gold lichens, to see profiles carved in the rock. In her suitcase, she had his book, picked up at a bookstall on the Potsdamer Platz. His wildflowers, lichens, rocks, moss-covered lava made her hungry for this place.

She touched the card in her pocket. It bore the name of her farm, Dark Castle.

The driver stopped.

Sheep's Hollow.

Silence. Each woman checked her card. The dust billowed through the half-open windows, and Charlotte felt the grit in her teeth. Finally, a short, broad-shouldered woman waved her card.

"It's me."

Applause as if the woman had set a new record on the pole vault. From her window, Charlotte watched the lone figure pick her way along the path.

Gisela sat next to her. She was a brunette from Berlin with curls parted and pinned back. Her face dimpled when she laughed in a way that men probably liked. She was from the Wedding district of Berlin, the place where Max had looked for trouble and found it.

"Mine's called Stony Hill," Gisela confided.

On the ship, crossing the Atlantic, the two women had walked the deck together, holding their coat collars high at the neck against the North Atlantic wind. Each day as the ship drew closer to the island, Gisela added details to the hair color of her future five children.

As the bus bounced over the ruts in the road, Gisela leaned against her.

"Remember what I said about a husband?"

Charlotte registered mock surprise.

"I want one," Gisela said. Chirpy as a shopper, she recited her list.

"And three boys and two girls, just like my mother had."

Would it work for her too? Could new humans replace old ones? Charlotte was still pondering these things when the driver stopped.

Dark Castle.

Gisela followed her out.

"You'll write me?" she asked, lips trembling.

Charlotte nodded, watched her only friend on the island disappear inside the bus.

Mountains, meadows, and ocean rolled towards the horizon. The same wind that flattened the grass tingled on Charlotte's cheekbones. Rocks with jagged features, like those of big-boned people, studded the foot of the hillside.

She ran her hands over her hips and looked up at this new sky. She was thirty-nine years old and still alive, a solitary figure in the deepest landscape painting she'd ever seen.

Up ahead, high on the hillside against a gloomy purple mountain, stood a liver-colored farmhouse. She picked up her suitcase, bulging with sweaters knitted by her mother, and walked up the gravel road. Stones stung her feet through the thin shoe soles. As she drew closer to the farmhouse, a small dog with a curled tail emerged from the bright green grass.

At the window, a pale figure lifted a curtain. The door opened, and a man with thick brown hair appeared on the steps. He extended a calloused hand and rolled the r's of his name.

"Ragnar."

She said her own name slowly, wishing she could explain how her mother had named her after Sophie Charlotte, the elector of Berlin's beloved wife who had died young. Usually, the explanation helped her get to know people. But her dictionary was at the bottom of her suitcase.

The dark hallway smelled of sheep's wool and rain gear. She slipped off her gritty shoes and left them next to the pile of rubber footwear. Above the door to the kitchen hung a driftwood painting of a three-gabled farmhouse. Ragnar padded across the floorboards in his socks. Looking too big to be indoors, he said things she barely understood.

Wife's dead. No children.

In the awkward silence, she heard the rub of cloth against the wooden wall. A third person was breathing in the dark hall.

"My mother," Ragnar said.

An old woman with narrow shoulders offered, and quickly withdrew, a slender parched hand, then moved along the wall into the kitchen, her sealskin shoes swishing over the linoleum floor. Ragnar picked up Charlotte's suitcase. She followed him into a small bedroom, dark but for the light from the small window. A chest of drawers stood against the window. A child-sized chair separated the two beds. On it stood a candle next to a book. *Egilssaga.* She and the old woman would take turns undressing in the narrow space.

When he set the suitcase down on the bed, the comforter made a sound like a person exhaling. At the foot of the bed was a wooden box full of uncarded wool. A carved plank bore words about God's eternal embrace. It hung on the paneled wall above the bed. Making rocking gestures with his arms, Ragnar explained.

From my father's boat. Dead.

Everyone but the three of them seemed to be dead.

The floorboards were splintered and the window casement warped. Above the old woman's bed hung a small oil painting of a farm with a chlorophyll-green homefield, next to it a photograph of an ancestor with a stiff priest's ruff.

"Coffee?" he asked.

When she nodded, he looked relieved. Through the thin walls, she heard him talking in the kitchen. A wave of loneliness washed over her. Until this moment she had been moving constantly, caught between then and the future, but now she felt the finality of having arrived. She felt alone like on the day her mother had left her at the new school.

Beyond the open window, earth and sky met at the horizon. She was sealed in. She'd wanted to leave Berlin, not slip off the edge of the earth. But it was not so much a matter of geography as of time. The years of her old life had run out. She swallowed hard.

Here, not *there.*

Under the neatly folded underwear in her suitcase, she found her old address book and brought it to the window. The names of her classmates were written in a childish script. Her eyes blurred over those who had not survived the war.

Folded up between the pages, she found the advertisement and read it again.

Farmers in Iceland seek strong women who can cook and do farm work.

No mention of companionship. That could not occur with this ungainly farmer. Still, his hesitating manner and his stained gray sweater suggested a pleasant humility. Perhaps he'd be more at ease outdoors. She placed her clothes in the chest of drawers. At last there was nothing left in her suitcase but her paintings. No place to hang them in this bedroom.

A shuffle of slippers, and he was back. Smiling awkwardly, he beckoned her to follow him into the kitchen. He seemed to have forgotten about the coffee. Fish sizzled in a pan, and potatoes rattled in a pot. He gestured towards the two place settings. The rest of the table was covered with stacks of bills and receipts. He placed these on the floor, opened the cupboard, and brought out a cracked plate. She sensed this would be her own special plate until it broke or she left.

The old woman gestured towards the steaming fish and potatoes. Then she drizzled a wooly smelling fat over her food. With their eyes on her, Charlotte did the same. Mother and son chewed the saltfish in silence while Charlotte had the feeling she'd interrupted a conversation begun long before she arrived.

There's a hole in the fence out by the main road. That chicken isn't laying.

The old woman dropped her gaze, and Charlotte studied the thick gray braids, looped against her sun-dried neck. The shiny hair appeared to have sucked the juice out of her face.

That night, Charlotte waited in the hall outside the bedroom until the swish of skirts stopped. When she heard the bed boards creak, she tiptoed into the room, slipped off her clothes, laid them at the end of the bed, and crept under the stiff sheets.

A sliver of moonlight revealed the old woman's stony profile, still but for the lips, vibrating with each breath. A cow lowed in the homefield. On the moor, a horse neighed.

But sometime in the night, her two worlds collided. She hadn't expected the ghost of Max—full of blame and love—to cross the Atlantic, to follow her up the hillside. His lean body pressed against hers in the narrow bed. He whispered about Monet's blues and greens. And she felt safe. But he wouldn't stay the night. When he slipped away into the mist, tears slid down her cheeks and into her ears.

4. A Creature Going Ashore

The sunlight drifted through the panes of the little window. Facing the old woman's empty bed, Charlotte dressed slowly. A burlap apron hung on a hook. She tied it around her waist and went to the kitchen. A rust-colored cat sat hunched over a saucer, picking at fish bones. Somewhere outside, milk pails rattled.

Between the kitchen and the cowshed, she made her plan for hitchhiking back to Reykjavik. Getting off the boat, she'd seen smoking chimneys in the town. They'd need maids—maybe German tutors—in those big houses.

A lamb grazed on the shed roof. Charlotte ducked her head under the wooden frame of the door and entered a shed that was dark but for one small window. Unlit oil lamps hung on the walls of piled stone. Under her feet, she felt the grit of a dirt floor. Her lip curled at the stench of ammonia, and she nearly tripped over a tub of soaking overalls.

Ragnar stepped out from behind the wooden framework that separated the cow stalls from the wash room. In this setting he looked almost graceful, walking towards her, trailing his fingers along the cow's spine. Nourished perhaps by the warmth of the animals, his voice had a resonance.

"Good morning."

She imitated the greeting as best she could. A follow-up phrase came to mind, but the words knotted her tongue. She watched him pour milk from a bucket into a waist-high canister that stood in the center of the room.

The angular haunches of cows rose above the wooden framework that separated one stall from the other. The cows' tails were looped up with string attached to the splintered beams over their heads. The old woman wore a smock of burlap bags and a brown bandanna over her forehead. She sat on a stool tugging the teats, sending streams of milk crashing into the bucket.

"Skjalda," she said, introducing the cow.

Shifting her bound hooves, Skjalda sent a canary yellow cascade into the dirt gutter.

The old woman cheered like a Berlin soccer fan, picked up her bucket and spun it away from the downpour of pee. Nimbly, she lifted a jar from the shelf and held it with both hands under the flow. When the cow had squeezed out the last drop, the old woman carried the jar back to the shelf, placed a lid on it, and reached for the milk bucket again. Other jars lined the shelf, each one full of yellow liquid.

Ragnar led Charlotte to the next cow. He tied the cow's hooves together and greased her teats. Then, holding one in each hand, he milked a bluish beam into the bucket. When it was her turn, the rubbery flesh swelled in her hands, but no matter how hard she squeezed only a tiny dribble hit the bottom of the bucket. To relieve the pain, she spread her fingers.

The next day, the milking went better. But later, when Charlotte was pulling up weeds around the yarrow in the garden, her hands hurt. Alone in the kitchen, she held up her right hand, counted the fingers. How many ways could you use a hand? She'd brought her little box of colored pencils. Drawing moss wrapping itself around lava rocks could keep her here.

That and a man's voice—if only he'd use it more.

The old woman entered the kitchen. She handed Charlotte a dirty smock and a pair of work gloves. Back in Berlin, she'd avoided the Imperial School for Secretaries, dreading the short skirt and nubby sweater uniform that typists wore.

Now she slipped her arms into a uniform stiff with filth.

A wheelbarrow stood against the wall of the shed. The old woman grasped the handles, and rolled it to the shed door. Charlotte stepped over the high wooden threshold into the winter residence of Dark Castle's sheep. The fresh manure squished under the toes of her boots. Ragnar held the handle of a square shovel with both hands, leaned his weight into it, pushed down with a grunt, and sliced through the layers of manure that had accumulated during the winter. He dumped the dark wedge onto a pile in the front of the shed.

Humming again, the old woman bent over, arms extended, embraced a brown load, staggered towards the door, cleared the threshold and dumped the manure into the wheelbarrow.

The sharp, blue eyes carried a challenge.

Your turn.

Charlotte pulled her sweater sleeve down to the cuffs of her gloves, lifted the waste in her arms, and inhaled the intestinal pungency. In the sunlight, the layers of manure looked like an archaeological lesson on Germania under the Romans, the layered history of sheep cloistered in the dank shed from October to May, months devoted solely to chewing and defecating.

Pushing the full wheelbarrow to the smoke shed, sweat pearling on her upper lip, Charlotte felt a sympathy for the churlish Bavarian farmers her bureaucrat father had laughed at.

Sometime that week, the clouds pulled away from the sun.

"Drying Day," the old woman said, raising her hands towards the crack in the ceiling in a gesture of gratitude.

Charlotte heard the praise in her voice. They hadn't discussed religion yet.

Outside, Ragnar wrapped part of the scythe blade in a towel, grasped it, and cut the manure wedge in half.

But the old woman whacked her wedge with a whale bone

paddle. "That's how my mother did it."

With her scythe blade, Charlotte gingerly halved a wedge. Gradually she built up momentum until she sweated and the breeze chilled her armpits. Finally, the old woman demonstrated how to prop the wedges up against one another to dry. Soon the entire home field was brown, a tent city of manure.

At the end of the day, the old woman was bent double. She gestured for Charlotte to follow her to the cowshed. Together, they wrung out the overalls that soaked in the tub and dumped the granite-colored water into the trough next to the shed. Ragnar brought a pot of hot water from the stove, then more. They added cold water, and the bath was ready.

Several vials lay on the shelf next to the urine jars. The old woman took one. In the weak light from the steamed window, Charlotte saw the long stalk and tiny purple bloom of lavender sketched on the label. The plant grew in the garden behind the yarrow.

"Lavandula—makes you happy," the old woman said and sprinkled drops of oil over the water. Its fragrance edged into the animal odor.

The old woman lit a candle and undressed. A tiny splash signaled her immersion in the tub. Her eyes glistened above the water, like a pond frog's during mating season.

"Get in."

Charlotte stepped out of her clothes, held the side of the tub for balance, and climbed over the edge at the other end. Easing in, she felt the old woman's skin against hers. Her bathing companion made small sighing sounds as she soaped her shoulders and neck, then lay back, eyes closed.

For a moment, Charlotte dozed in the warm, sweet smell. Then she heard the splash of a creature going ashore. The old woman, bones jutting, stood on the floor next to the tub, rubbing herself with a towel. Ragnar appeared at the door, then turned abruptly and disappeared among the cow stalls.

Charlotte heard his shovel scraping up dung. She climbed out of the tub, dressed hurriedly, and hung their wet towels on the indoor clothesline. The old woman held the door for her. Turning, she glimpsed his large pale leg scaling the side of the tub.

5. A Weather-ruled Man

The script on the envelope was German, but the letter wasn't from her mother. The stamp featured the volcano Hekla erupting. *Stony Hill* was scrawled on the back.

Dear Charlotte,

"My" farm is a little primitive. We have only well water. But I like the farmer. He's nice looking—for a man of fifty. I like him better than his brother who chases me and grabs me!!! Of course, I smack the devil. That's the price of being beautiful. Ha. Ha. Ha. I'll marry one of them. You'll come to the wedding!

Gisela

Hungry for words, she re-read the letter. Ragnar hoarded words, saving them like the cans of peas and beets she and her mother had stored at the back of the shelf at the beginning of the war.

Sometimes Charlotte pored over the yellowed newspapers—some dating back to 1945—that the old woman tucked behind the kitchen bench, but she discovered that newspaper words in this language were long and hairy.

One evening, the old woman handed Charlotte a leather-bound book and a bread knife. The pages were still uncut. She chopped her way into the story and spent evenings in the big chair in the living room flipping through her dictionary, puzzling together the novel's parts.

A young woman sews homespun on sheriff's farm until her fingers grow blue. Her only source of warmth is the sheriff's son's body rubbing against her at night. When his mother learns that her son has spilled his seed into a hired girl, she sends the girl away. She gives birth in a cave where a vagabond cuts the cord.

Charlotte tried to repeat the plot. Misunderstanding, the old woman gave her some feverfew leaves for headache.

"Chew it, but if your mouth hurts, spit it out."

Finally the old woman had to give her an ointment for the insides of her cheeks.

Even when Charlotte knew the words, talking to Ragnar wasn't easy. His topics were sheep, cows, rake. Charlotte muttered them after him—*kindur, kýr, hrífa.*

In the cowshed, he grasped the cow's teat—*speni*, he said. "Don't squeeze it right away. Wait until the milk comes in."

But his favorite topic was rain—*rigning.*

"He'll hang dry," he said on good days. Or, "It's wet as a dog's nose," when it rained. On sunny days, he raised his arms towards the sun. *Sól. Sól.* One evening, he scratched his head and sighed. At last, he took a crumpled paper bag from the chest under the bench, smoothed it with his hands, and wrote a poem on it. With the help of a dictionary, she discovered a poet named Jonas referred to a weather-ruled man like Ragnar, who begged the goddess of drizzle to send him some sun.

And I'll sacrifice

My cow—my wife—my Christianity!

But on the few Sundays when the village church offered a sermon, the old woman did not attend. She did other things, like talking to the earth, rocking back on her haunches, waiting for an answer. On days when the wind died down to a breeze, the old woman stood on the farmhouse steps, pushed her shoulders back, raised her face to the sky, and sang.

One day that first summer, Charlotte heard a high-pitched warble. She looked up at the gable of the shed and saw a thrush moving its yellow, black-tipped beak. Below it stood the old woman singing back to the bird, begging it to deliver a message to a sweetheart.

O greet most fondly, if you chance to see
An angel whom our native costume graces.

In Berlin, with Lena wriggling in her arms, she'd recited the names of all the birds they saw. When she saw a winter wren scurrying across the ground at Dark Castle, she shrieked *mouse*. But the bird's upright tail became suddenly evident. She heard its high tinkling warble just before it flew off and recalled the tiny rodent-like bird from her picture book.

During breaks on dry days, Charlotte walked the meadow until she found a hollow. Lying on her belly and breathing in the moss in the sun-warmed thyme, she dreamed of escape. Part of her vision involved her mother holding out her arms, the same mother with whom she'd argued bitterly until the day she waved goodbye to her from a train window in the station.

Mamma.

Now she took the scrap of paper and a pencil from her pocket and began a letter.

Dear Mamma,

I love the hillside. The fog hangs over the meadows until midday. Sometimes the sun gets so hot you have to wear a straw hat. The farmer doesn't talk much, but I don't mind. The old woman brews leaves and twigs on the stove, makes teas for aches in the back and legs.

In the margins, she drew pictures of horses carrying hay bundles to the barn until her hand, the lower one on the rake handle, ached. She dropped her pencil and closed her eyes. When she opened them, she sensed that Lena's curls had brushed her nose.

6. The Second Time in Her Life

Each lady slipper that grew on the edge of the field contained a drop of water at its center that sparkled in the early morning dew. Sometimes Charlotte bent to touch the liquid with her tongue as she had seen Ragnar do. But today she walked, stiff as a robot, turning the hay with a methodical twist, counting *eins, zwei, drei*. By noon, her nose itched from the hay dust. She stopped and placed her hand on the small of her back.

Ragnar put his rake down and came to her. Working the last row, the old woman tilted her face towards the sun.

"Hold it like this," he said, gently rearranging her grip.

His warm voice soothed her. But the narrowest part of her back—the spot where the day's work settled—still hurt. Later, she struggled to pack the hay into bundles against the side of her foot. But she couldn't rake it tightly enough. He had a functional way of touching her. Kneeling, he caressed her ankle.

"Like this."

At night, she imagined his rough warm hands on her skin, his strong arms around her shoulders—strong enough to pick up a sick ewe. She'd seen him carry a sheep and croon into its ear.

One day towards the end of that first summer, Charlotte bent over the washtub in the cowshed. The sunlight from the open door played over her hands as she soaped Ragnar's long underwear and rubbed it over the grooves of the board.

Her eyes measured the contrasts on her hands, the shadows and their opposites, adjusted the angry red of her skin to a delicate pink, placed her hands demurely in the burgundy silk-swathed lap of a sixteenth century Dutch dowager, all without releasing Ragnar's underwear.

The door should have led to a courtyard in Delft. But it opened onto the lush green hillside, brighter than any color from a tube. It went dark as Ragnar's large body filled the door frame. He lingered there, gazing at her. She stopped moving her hands. He walked towards the tub, rolling up his sleeves.

"Can I help?"

Together, they twisted the underwear in opposite directions until the water poured out, thick and gray. Carrying the basket of wash with her to the clothesline, he said a few words, and she said nothing. But they both laughed at the underwear dancing in the wind between his pajamas and the old woman's socks.

He smiled shyly. "I was cutting hay—I want to show you—"

She tilted her head, closed her eyes. A concert—front row seats, with Max years ago. She nodded acceptance.

They walked in the bristly growth of the moorland without speaking. Ragnar bent to pick a small cluster of little white flowers, grass of Parnassus, that grew at their feet and held them out to her.

"Good for the liver—mother says."

Charlotte examined the five petals, marked with delicate green lines, and smelled the sorrel on his breath. He stepped back, as if retreating from a line he hadn't meant to cross.

She touched her tongue to the roof of her mouth, pronouncing her thanks just right. *Takk.* Every time Max had brought her red and white roses, she'd scrambled to find a pitcher to hold them. Up ahead, the farmhouse seemed very small.

"Here, on the hillside..."

She waited.

He pointed to a post.

"...we call that a *staur.*"

Words tumbled from him—*steinar, girðing*—rocks, fence. He opened his arms—*sol, himinn*—sun, sky. Repeating the words, she laughed at her own pronunciation. His ears reddened as if he'd said the words wrong in the first place.

Years later, after their conversation had calcified into monosyllabic exchanges or hand signals across the fields, she realized that their early verbal giddiness had resembled the bucking of the cows in the early spring—the tumult that preceded the dull grazing pattern of the rest of the summer—the rest of their lives.

They climbed higher, and the grass gave way to small pebbles. Charlotte was breathing quickly now. He lowered himself to the ground and pulled her down next to him.

"Smell the lamb's grass," he said, pointing to a tussock covered with tiny pink blossoms.

She buried her nose in the flowers. The earthy sweetness stirred a sadness in her. Just beyond the next knoll, the fog rolled like surf all the way out to the mountain. At last they found the place where he'd left his scythe that morning. He gripped the handle, so that the blade extended over his shoulder. They walked in silence to the farmhouse.

The next day, he taught her how to walk sideways into sheets of rain.

Rigning. Vindur.

Rain. Wind.

She moved her lips around the words, imitating the way he spoke, probing the speech pattern of the hillside. At night in bed, she strung together nouns and verbs. One morning, after weeks of this, she decided to say a whole sentence. She came up behind him in the cowshed, stood in the stall gutter, and spoke carefully.

"Will we rake the hay before the rain?"

He turned around and smiled. His pride warmed her. The old woman's eyes were on her, wanting something too. Charlotte hadn't had a real conversation since she'd traveled with Gisela. Things unsaid knocked about in her head. She thought for a moment, then pursed her lips.

"Skjalda's milk is blue today."

The old woman's face cracked into laughter.

That night Charlotte reached across the distance between the beds to nudge the old woman out of a snore. But she wasn't sleeping. In a voice of stifled laughter, she repeated Charlotte's words, "Skjalda's milk is blue today."

After that, Ragnar often walked with Charlotte, teaching her new words, sometimes touching her. She wrote to Gisela:

I've learned to milk a cow and rake hay. This is an interesting agricultural experience for me. But I'm still thinking of moving to the city even though it's very beautiful here, and I think the farmer's mother likes me. How's the farmer's brother? Hah. Hah. Please write. I can't speak properly yet, and I've never been so quiet in my life. Any word from home? Charlotte.

It was a sunny day, and she was in the tool shed, searching for a rake that had all its teeth. Through the sunlit crack in the corrugated iron, she recognized his overalls and boots as he approached the shed. He stumbled a little in the dark, and then his arms circled her waist.

"Let me help you," he said.

She placed her hands on his and leaned back against his chest. Somewhere between her shoulder blades, his blood made a thudding sound. Aside from pressing up against strangers in bread lines in Berlin, she hadn't been close to a man since—

Stepping out of the shed, she trembled in the warm sun.

All morning, they turned the drying grass, the old woman bringing up the rear. Each time they came to the end of a row, Charlotte tilted her face towards him, so that his gaze could brush her cheek.

During the dry spell, they worked furiously to get all the hay into the barn. Then, as black clouds scudded across the sky, they baled and bound the hay to the horses' backs. Holding the bridle of the lead horse, Ragnar looked ready for a long and difficult journey. The barn was ten minutes away. Charlotte saw the change in his face, like the trembling of the track before the train arrives. She waited.

"Is it alright then?" His look said he meant her—and him.

"Yes," she said for the second time in her life.

The buttocks of the last horse quivered as the hay bundles swayed on its flanks.

Next day, she sat on the milk stool, and he stood above her.

"Did you learn to rake hay in Berlin?" he asked.

The question made her laugh until she had to wipe away tears. When she opened her eyes again, he was gone and Skjalda was studying her. The swirl of hair on her flank blurred into a vision of the years of raking, digging, and milking that lay ahead.

7. Take it off, Petronella

When Charlotte entered the kitchen, Ragnar and his mother went silent. The old woman stepped into the pantry. Charlotte glimpsed her through the crack in the door, climbing up on the chair, stretching to the top shelf. She brought down the canister of bearberry leaves and berries. Charlotte knew the old woman used them to ease her straining over the hole in the outhouse. Several times a week, after dosing herself with bearberry tea, she'd disappear into the outhouse for an hour or two, old newspapers under her arm.

Ragnar's brown homespun suit lay in a rumpled heap on the table. The old woman emptied the canister into the big pot on the stove, added water, and fed the suit into the mixture.

Soon the simmering liquid resembled thin brown tar.

The old woman fished up a sleeve of the suit on a wooden spoon and shook her head. She took the coal bucket and a small shovel from behind the stove. In a few minutes, she came back, straining under the weight of the bucket.

"Ragnar—your suit," she called.

He emerged from the bedroom, his eyes puffy. Had he lain too long silently in the dark? Could she live with a brooder? He picked up the bucket and emptied the black clay into the pot.

The old woman peered into the pot. Occasionally she stirred the suit with a wooden spoon. When the bubbles in the thick black soup began to pop, she sat down, crossing one leg tightly over the other, wrapping a gray-socked foot around an ankle.

Charlotte placed her hands on her chest as if to protect herself from the old woman's scrutiny. A foreigner, was she good enough for her son? Later, the black suit frolicked on the clothesline like an imp out of hell. The bits of fleece on the barbed wire blew horizontally in the wind. Nothing was ever still here. Between shifts in the wind, she'd said yes. Now her dread deepened.

The old woman looked sideways at Charlotte. "And what will you wear?"

Not the black dress she'd worn the first time, so many years ago. Later, in the bedroom, Charlotte held up a wrinkled black skirt and a handknitted red sweater. The old woman batted the air and disappeared upstairs.

Minutes later, she returned, unfurling a yellowed bed sheet.

"This is what you need."

The old cloth smelled musty.

But the old woman hopped around the kitchen, chattering about sleeves and waists. Even on the hillside, mothers went funny about weddings. Holding the sheet against Charlotte's chest, she pinned the fabric and cut it with sheep's shears. Then, wedging herself between the stove and the kitchen table, she began to sew. Under her breath she sang about a blunt sword named Dragvendill:

My teeth solved my troubles
And tore out his throat.

Next day the sheet resembled a garment. "Try it on," the old woman said through the pins between her lips. Charlotte shivered in the dusty fabric. Her armpits hurt. The old woman stepped back. "Sleeves too tight?"

Then Charlotte saw the stains across the front of the dress.

How old was the sheet? Had the old woman and Ragnar's father come together on it in the ancient ritual of love? It was a fertility gown, the earth goddess's cast-off skin. The old woman dropped it into the big pot, took a handful of lichens from her jar, and strewed them over the liquid.

She looked up. "Yellow or red?"

Charlotte recalled Petronella, the top can-can dancer in Berlin, how the audience had sung *Take it off, Petronella* as her red dress whirled. In the same show, a young woman, perspiring under the watchful eye of a stormtrooper, had struggled to keep her crotch cover from slipping off.

"Red."

The old woman went to the cowshed and brought back a jar of urine. She placed it next to the bowl of lichens. Later that evening, she poured off the lichen brew, added the urine, and set the pot on the floor to soak. For two nights in a row Charlotte woke up to the sound of the old woman pouring off the urine, adding more, and setting it to soak again.

Three days before the wedding, the old woman left the farmhouse early in the morning. When Charlotte got up, Petronella's earth mother gown hung like a scarlet flag on the clothesline. By the time the fog had burned off the hillside, the old woman returned with her apron full of leaves, roots, and berries. A pink spot colored each of her thin gray cheeks.

"Makes good babies," the old woman said, pushing a bowl of grass milk at her. Her eyes crinkled in laughter.

Charlotte was warm with desire for Ragnar. But a baby? She'd done that already and misplaced it.

Singing to herself, "headache, rheumatism, bladder, and liver," the old woman minced motherwort, raspberry leaves, and seaweed then scooped the plant scraps up from the cutting board in her small, dry hand and dumped them into a pot of water simmering on the stove. A smell like sweet fish oil filled the room. Leaning over the pot, she washed her small, sunken cheeks in the steam. At last she poured the light brown liquid over a cloth filter into a jar.

At dinner, three envelopes lay on Charlotte's dish. Picking up the first one, she met the old woman's shy smile. On the back of the envelope was a drawing of a hand covered with warts. Inside were dried daisies, tree bark, and dandelions. The second one featured a freckled woman and contained a rosette of reddish basal leaves. The last one bore a sketch of a wrinkled old woman with scraggly hair. Inside she found a stalk of dried yarrow.

The old woman's eyes twinkled. "Everything you need for married life."

Free of warts, freckles, wrinkles, and thanks to this fragile knower of mysterious things, she'd be happy on the farm. Charlotte almost fell over her chair as she reached for the old woman. Embracing her thin shoulders, she caught a smell of moist earth.

On the day before the wedding, Charlotte went to the cowshed for more milk. She saw the flicker of an oil lamp in the window. Inside, she discovered the old woman stripped to the waist and leaning over the washtub, her hair loose, her shoulders bare. She was pouring urine on her head and rubbing it into her hair. A row of empty jars stood on the shelf. Remembering how the old woman had reached for a jar each time a cow peed, Charlotte filled her pitcher from the milk canister and hurried out.

Later the old woman sat at the kitchen table. Her long, gray hair shone under the lamp.

8. The Sound of a Horse Neighing

The church stood halfway up the hill above the village, cream-colored with a red roof against the moss-streaked rock. Inside, six carved wooden pews bore traces of green and blue paint. Christ in a red robe prayed in Gethsemane on the gold-rimmed pulpit. A miniature cathedral, Charlotte thought, recalling how she and Max had sat on folding chairs and eyed a potted plant in the lobby of the bank on Pariserplatz on their wedding day. Her mother hadn't wanted to attend. Bank lobby? Should she bring a deposit slip?

The hillside religion always confused her—Ragnar raising his head to the sky and the old woman singing to birds or conjuring powers up from the earth. And here was the familiar Lamb of God preparing to sacrifice his life for the old woman. Charlotte felt she'd known Christ from the start—all those paintings of the annunciation featuring the holy spirit riding a golden ray, directed between the Virgin's breasts. But that mystery no longer enticed her the way the secrets of the old woman did.

She ran her hand over her hip, as if the old sheet were something she'd just bought at Bernstein's, Max's department store. The hillside people sat in the pews—rubber-shoed farmers and their strong, pale wives, silver brooches rising and falling on their bosoms. The minister had a christening on a farm deep in the end of the valley. The wedding would have to wait.

A farmer in the back row was explaining bovine fibroid

tumors to his neighbor in a loud voice. Nonni from Butterdale's wife placed a hand on each of her thighs and turned
towards the back of the church. Charlotte withdrew into the
shadows. It wasn't too late. She could still flee. The daily bus
to town would leave in half an hour. She'd scramble to the
back, keep her head down so they wouldn't find her—just
another runaway bride.

Rubbing the goose pimples on her arms, Charlotte headed
for the steps and the indoor bathroom. Ten minutes ago she'd
seen a line winding up the stairs, heard that people were
flushing more than once. But now she entered the empty
bathroom, breathing in and out slowly. Holding everything
back, she grinned into the mirror until her mouth hurt.

You have such a pretty smile.

Her mother used to say it. The door opened. Gisela's taut
face appeared in the mirror. Her friend giggled, and Charlotte pictured Gisela's long winter of thigh squeezes under
the silent gaze of sheep. They stared at one another. Then
Gisela opened her arms. Charlotte buried her hot eyes in her
friend's shoulder, moving her trembling lips against the stiff
fabric of her dress.

"It'll be over soon," Gisela said, patting her back.

Arm in arm, they reached the top of the stairs too quickly.
Charlotte could see the old woman sitting in the front row,
a silk scarf with a rose pattern over her shoulders. A circular
cap of black silk lay on her braids. A silver serpent climbed
her tassel holder, warding off the evil spirits that threatened
marriages.

The minister had arrived. He stood at the altar, in a white
robe topped by a ruffed collar big as the moon. Nonni from
Butterdale's wife sat at the organ now, her hands held high
above the keys. The minister pointed towards heaven, and
the organist's fingers pounded out the hymn, *I am a lonely
flower in God's sight.* The old woman often sang the words
when she crushed yarrow between two stones. As if he'd

suddenly found Charlotte, the minister gestured towards her, and the fibroid tumor farmer jumped to his feet and grasped her arm.

Walking towards the altar on the farmer's arm, Charlotte sensed something leaving her, floating out through the window, and gliding over the dark green grass out to sea. When she married Ragnar, she would be taking the entire hillside into her arms, the wind in the tussocks, the rain that stalked you, the sun that burned your face at noon, then ignored you for a week, and the sea that insinuated its bitter seaweed stench into your dreams. And she'd lose something precious. She shuddered.

Eyebrows bristling, the minister began to chant words that everyone but she understood. *Obey or burn in Hell,* she thought he said. Ragnar mumbled something. Here and now, she told herself and thought about her red dress and Petronella preparing for the mating dance.

The minister raised his voice. Focusing on Christ's suffering, Charlotte nodded assent. She extended her hand for the ring and wondered what she'd promised.

Afterwards, at the farm, she and the old woman served coffee and rhubarb cake with whipped cream. The farmers sat in silence, examining their fingers for cuts. They nodded their heads for refills whenever Charlotte brought the coffee pot. At last, they argued about the poor yield from the winter fishing season.

"*Akurey* brought in nothing this year, just enough for Butterdale," Nonni said, sitting next to Gisela on the sofa.

Gisela did not respond.

"We lost our catch several times. Didn't survive the surf landing. Once the keel comes up in the surf, you lose fish."

She eyed him with interest. "And do you lose men?"

Nodding, he brought his head closer to hers, his shoulders level with his ears.

Her lips were forming another fishing question when he

placed his hand between his thigh and hers. Gently, she slapped his hand. Several of the farmers raised their chins from their cups. Charlotte made a diving motion, indicating the strip of sofa between Gisela and Nonni. Reluctantly, Nonni moved.

Gisela leaned against her. "I was afraid you'd run away," she said.

"I tried to, but the big farmer held my arm," Charlotte said.

Soon they were laughing and hugging each other. Nonni rose to his feet. The old woman followed him to the window and filled his cup.

When the guests were gone, and Gisela had climbed into the loft, the old woman nudged Charlotte and handed her a cup of raspberry-seaweed tea. Ragnar's empty cup was on the table.

"Honeymoon tea," the old woman said.

Charlotte blushed. The drink was the color of her dress. She held her nose against the fishy taste, and—her heart hammering from the coffee—drank it quickly while the old woman watched.

In the bedroom, the curtains were open. Outside, the daylight blurred into the summer night. Ragnar lay on his back in the center of the bed. He looked as if he were sleeping. She whispered his name. Like a big dog, he rolled over and opened his eyes.

She started to unbutton the dress. The old woman had spent hours on the buttons. A zipper would have been better, but the cooperative store hadn't gotten its shipment. When the dress finally sank to the floor, she remembered Petronella and kicked out her foot and raised the fabric with her toe, dropping it on the chair.

His gaze burned her skin. Travelers in the desert, they suffered from the same thirst. How long had it been for both of them? With a deliberate slowness, she pulled her slip over her head, enjoyed his eyes on the swell of her breasts above her brassiere. Max had loved this ritual. Languidly, she rolled down her stockings. She regretted she had nothing prettier than the big square cotton underpants that everyone wore during the war in Berlin. At last, she unhooked the brassiere and let her breasts fall forward. His eyes drew an arc under each breast, and her nipples hardened.

He lifted the sheet.

"Come."

She slipped under the sheet and rolled towards him. His hardness brushed against her thigh. When her breasts touched his chest, she felt his whole body quiver. Through the rush of her own blood came the sound of a horse neighing somewhere in the homefield.

Ragnar's voice was a ragged whisper.

"He's happy for us."

His large hands stroked her shoulders, her breasts, her thighs, the backs of her knees. She raised her body to his. He slid his hands under the small of her back, ran them over her buttocks, squeezed gently. She vowed to make love to him all night long. But suddenly he opened her legs and thrust himself inside her. It was over too quickly. She and Max had always dawdled, prolonging the stroking and caressing.

Ragnar lay on his side, touching her hair the way he did the lead horse's forelock before bringing it to the barn. Beyond his shoulder, through the window, she glimpsed the outline of the hillside in the gray summer night. For ever and ever. What had she done?

In the morning, Charlotte was startled when her arm brushed against his. Remembering the weight of his body on hers, she stretched her arms above her head and arched her back, wanted his hands on her breasts again.

The sound of chickens fussing in the henhouse broke through her desire. Another reality passed over her happiness. Had she rubbed the life out of the memory of Max? Forgotten Lena? She'd wanted to flee her ghosts. But now she mourned them and wished Ragnar would go away.

He reached for her. Pretending a daytime shyness, she pulled back and watched his fingers on her arm, how they clasped her like a rake. She had a vision of cleaning sheep pens and turning hay until she too slipped over that leaden horizon. How many aprons would she wear out with no reward but this man's hands on her at night? After he was gone, she swung her legs onto the floor, pulled on her work clothes, tied the old apron around her waist, and went to feed the chickens.

9. Jewish Jokes

In the fall of 1928 Charlotte was twenty years old, and Berlin felt tight as a rubber band. The Communists fought the Nazis on the streets. Nude women danced with midgets on the stage while couples in tuxedoes and furs laughed. Poor people rented out their own beds when they weren't sleeping in them.

Certain Germans, according to the Nazis, had less value than the rest of the population. Jews with thick lips or bulbous noses felt the knuckles of the brownshirts. But, like the center cyclist of three, blond, pug-nosed Jews went unnoticed. Max Bernstein was not one of these. In fact, his hawklike nose looked as if it had been broken and reset wrong.

At the Berlin art academy that afternoon students were painting quickly, taking advantage of the faint winter light that still lingered over their canvases. A model sat on a stool, her nipples dark and puckered against blue-white skin. Charlotte chewed the handle of her brush. She'd painted the model's arms thick as thighs. Her neighbor stood behind her and stared at her drawing. He made her nervous.

"Add some curve to the hips," he said, picking up a piece of charcoal and measuring the space between the crook of an arm and the waist. He rubbed out the original line and drew a new hip.

A stool leg squeaked. The model rose stiffly and wrapped herself in her robe.

"Maybe a bit of yellowish-green," he said, folding his arms and studying her canvas.

The instructor was in the front of the room, arranging bruised apples, brown bananas, and a wilted cabbage on the table. Charlotte didn't want to paint decaying food, and she needed to get away from this blue-eyed critic. Outside, scanning the dark, gritty street for her bus, she heard a voice in her ear. "Hardest thing is seeing the bones under the flesh." She turned to face her hawknosed classmate. He smiled and extended his arm. "Join me for a beer?"

When her bus arrived, she didn't get on. Her mother would be holding a bowl of steaming potatoes, waiting to discuss typing lessons. And she wouldn't be there.

"Max Bernstein," he said.

The name brought to mind elegantly dressed mannekins in the window of a luxurious department store. She'd stood under her mother's elbow, her nose on the cold window pane, studying Bernstein's dolls, the finest in Berlin. Her mother's voice had sounded metallic.

Too expensive for us.

"Sophie Charlotte."

"Goddess of wisdom?" he asked.

"Wife of the elector in Berlin. My mother admired her."

She wouldn't tell him about her waitress job.

The pub was packed with men in blue overalls. Sitting on a rickety wooden chair, she watched the waitress drop two coasters on the table, mark them with a pencil she kept behind her ear, lower the tray, and place two sweating glasses of beer on the coasters. Charlotte couldn't have done that. She'd have sloshed the foam on the customer's shoulder. Feeling like a little girl in the front row at school, she watched Max take a small square book from his backpack and open it to the photos of Rembrandt.

"See the red on the tip of his nose? How the painter matched it with the red in his eyebrow?"

He was a real painter. Why was he spending time with her?

"Watch the light. Does it land on the model's elbow? Does

it change the color of her skin? How many colors did Renoir use for each breast?"

He cupped an imaginary breast on his own chest, pointed to where the nipple would be.

"Pink, then yellow in beige, light green where the breast's connected to the body."

The door opened, and a cold gust blew across the room. A young man in a brown shirt and brown pants tucked into black leather boots entered. The metal in his heels clicked on the nails in the floor boards.

"Watch—no sense of humor," Max whispered.

The brownshirt approached the poster on the wall, an advertisement for a cabaret. A topless woman with spots of rouge in her white cheeks raised her leg. The brownshirt's hand shot out as if to punch the woman's breast.

"*Juden Dreck*," he said, tearing the poster from the wall.

The workmen at the next table froze. The brownshirt clicked his heels and walked out.

Max spoke out of the side of his mouth. "No sense of humor."

"Why Jewish dirt?" Charlotte asked.

"Whatever's wrong, it's the Jews' fault."

Her stomach clenched at a memory. She'd asked her father for coins to buy bread.

Go look in my briefcase.

She'd found a Nazi newspaper featuring a fat Jew sitting on a German bank, buttocks hanging like flaps over the eaves of the roof. A hooked nose the size of a squash dominated the face. She'd asked him about it.

Somebody gave it to me. One of those people who stand on the corner.

Max gestured towards the shreds of poster still tacked to the wall. The name of the cabaret, *Schall und Rauch, 44 Unter den Linden*, was legible at the bottom of the poster.

"Have you been there?" he asked.

Didn't walking past with her friend Lulu count? Two men in tuxedoes and a woman had been getting into a taxi. A rubber penis lolled from the woman's cleavage. A clown with black slitted eyes stood in the doorway, a thin line of smoke wafting from his mouth. He waved at the departing taxi. The woman waggled the penis at him.

"The cabaret mocks everyone—especially Jews," Max said.

She raised her glass, set it down again without drinking.

"You know *Don Carlos?*" he asked.

Attending Schiller's play—a class field trip—they'd giggled so hard when the wizened emperor approached his peach-fresh young wife that the teacher had taken them back to school during the intermission.

Max dropped his voice.

"My uncle's cabaret made Don Carlos into a Hebrew, Markwitz, a big-nosed cartoon figure who talks Jewish, but wears a tiny imperial mustache and gets baptized every ten minutes."

He laughed, but Charlotte didn't think it was funny.

"My uncle hired a famous director, the one who matches the scenery to the actor's mood. Yellow and green forests if the actor's sick. Blue and purple sky if he's suicidal. He made Jews laugh their heads off at hook-nosed little men in bathrobes, bowing at the Wailing Wall."

She indicated the torn poster.

"And the *Jewish Dirt* man?"

"I was there the night Mr. Blackboots showed up at the cabaret. He and his friends roared at the Jewish jokes. *Even the Jews hate the Jews*, they probably said. When the Nazis published my uncle's jokes in their paper, he understood. After that, no more Jewish jokes."

By the time they left the pub, Charlotte's neck ached from bracing herself against Max's truth. Some things she'd rather not know. At the Friedrichstrasse cigar shop, the poster gleamed in the street lamp—a woman with pouty lips, a monocle at her eye, held a midget to her bosom. He waved a white-gloved hand.

Max's breath warmed her ear.

"Cabaret?"

Excitement rose in her.

"We'll go as artists," he said quickly.

She saw the fun in his eyes and herself, a tiny figure mirrored there.

10. You're an Artist

A t Aschinger's, Charlotte balanced a tray, struggling to keep the curry sausages from rolling off the plate and the beer from sloshing over the rim of the glass. Sometimes she had leftovers. Today it was a half-eaten sausage. When nobody was looking, she raised her tray and bit into the other end. She never went to class on an empty stomach.

Later she stood in the back chewing a leftover fricassée of chicken and sipping a Bock beer without touching her lips to the rim of the glass when she felt a hand on her shoulder. She turned to face the manager.

"I saw you," he said and pointed to the door. His other hand went to her waist, wiggled a finger under the waistband of her apron. He wanted the uniform back. She went home wearing her coat over her underwear.

The next day she found a job in a bar with beer-sodden floors. Schoolboys with rouged cheeks and perfumed wrists unzipped the pants of middle-aged bankers in the back booths. One day she brought the bill to a fiftyish gentleman, slack-jawed with lust, squeezing the butt cheeks of a boy.

When Charlotte took the job at Café Rilke, she feared she'd run into Max. Artists met here to argue about Dada and expressionism. Else Lasker-Schuler read her poems aloud.

> *Sweet lama son upon sweet sultan throne*
> *How long will your mouth go on kissing mine?*

One morning, Charlotte was standing at the mirror when her mother's reflection appeared behind her.

"Your father and I—"

Charlotte tied the starched apron strings at her back.

"You're a waitress, and—"

"And—? I'm an artist who supports herself by serving coffee."

Her mother's eyes bore down on her.

"You've turned down an education at the *Handelsschule*. You said no to a respectable career."

Charlotte licked her fingers and formed curls next to her ears.

"Your father has struggled so hard to reach his position in the city government."

"Is filing letters better than cutting a cherry tart into eight slices?"

Her mother's shoulders sagged under her daughter's unconventional attitudes, but Charlotte knew that stapling papers and looking for a husband behind the filing cabinet was not for her.

Balancing a tray and smiling for tips, she was still an artist. In her imagination, the part of her being that grew even under pinched circumstances, she collected impressions, arranged shapes, and mixed colors. Walking to the academy, she held her chin high, a habit from the days when she'd still believed her mother.

Sophie Charlotte, think of yourself as royalty. Your father sits at the right hand of the mayor of Berlin.

Ten years ago, he'd written one dictated letter on City of Berlin stationery. Poor Papa.

The early morning coal smoke ranged from light gray to slate gray with blue at the edges. Burning coal blended its fumes with the smell of baking bread.

Bells at the top of the door jangled when Charlotte entered the café. Last night's smoke hung stale on the plum-colored drapes. Lulu, electric curls framing her head, swabbed the ashes off a round marble table.

"Pigs made a mess of the place again," she said, waving a gauze cloth at the tobacco-brown wallpaper.

Charlotte nodded towards a man seated at a table by the window. But Lulu kept on chattering about the customers, picking up beer glasses from the floor of the telephone booth. Her father was a trolley conductor, who'd suggested Lulu work as a waitress because of the nice uniform. Her mother sold tickets at the UFA films. On her day off, Lulu liked sitting up front on the trolley, laughing at the passengers.

Now she waved her cloth at a young man with a beard. A serious-looking young woman with spectacles and no make-up sat at his side. They were the kind of people Lulu called degenerates, unlike Lulu's boyfriends, who overflowed with life juices.

Every afternoon, I ached for him. We did it in the coal cellar, standing up. Fast—with all that homework we had.

Beer glasses in the crook of one arm, Lulu joined her at the back counter.

"Did you hear about the blind ones—bunny and the snake?"

Trying to shush her, Charlotte spilled coffee on her apron.

"Bunny says 'let's feel one another and tell what we are.' Snake feels bunny. 'Ears and a little tail. Furry. You're a bunny.' Bunny feels snake. 'Long and cold with no balls. You're an artist.'"

Lulu neighed with laughter. Charlotte eyed the door. Two unshaven young men entered. One held the hand of a woman with helmet-shaped hair.

Lulu rolled her eyes.

"Dead peckers—too many books in the lap," she said, rubbing a lipstick butterfly off one of the glasses

An arm went up for coffee. He wore a tweed jacket and a soiled shirt. He could have been Max but wasn't. Charlotte carried out a tray with a coffee pot and three cups. She lingered over filling each cup, slowly wiping the spout of the pot with a hand towel before filling the next cup, then leaned in between them to listen.

El Greco's bodies are sickly green—like withered leeks.

The woman looked up when Charlotte laughed.

The door opened. The sun backlit the new customer, a man surrounded by dust and loose threads. Max. Pressing the tray flat against her side, Charlotte glided towards the back. She watched him hang up his jacket. Underneath he wore a fine woolen sweater.

He looked around. Smiling, he walked quickly towards her. He took her arm and whispered in her ear.

"The gallery? Remember?"

Charlotte stepped back, perspiration in her armpits, blood hot in her cheeks. He moved closer. The pot slipped in her hands. Coffee drops smarted her skin. She'd say no. He'd only make her feel ignorant. But something stirred in her.

"Four o'clock," she said.

"Gallery steps." He led her to his table.

As his friends looked up, she pictured a million waitresses falling on their faces before gentlemen. Her mother had been right. She should have learned to type.

"Sophie Charlotte, a colleague from the academy," Max announced to his friends.

Nodding like a marionette, she felt their eyes on her, burning her. They introduced themselves, but she couldn't focus on their names. Before they were done, she began walking backwards to the kitchen.

Lulu looked gloomy as a cobweb. "Slumming with the degenerates?"

Charlotte refilled the coffee pot. She wouldn't tell Lulu about the art gallery.

11. Your Breasts are Your Best Credentials

Charlotte's trouble with her mother began when she was fourteen. Hormonal and itchy, she'd spent homework time drawing bats wings and birds feet. After that, she and her mother drank cocoa before her father returned from the bureaucracy, joyless and exhausted.

"I'd like to go to art school," Charlotte said.

Her mother reached across the table and took her hand.

"Nice long fingers, perfect for—"

"Piano? I don't like music."

"No. Typewriter."

Charlotte jumped to her feet. "I hate you."

"How dare you talk to me like that."

Hands on hips, Charlotte said it again. And again. The floor side of her mother's slipper stung her cheek. Now she had to attend art school.

In art class, the other students threw sponges or stabbed their thumbs with protractors and played with the blood that dripped onto the paper while Charlotte strained to catch the teacher's words.

Don't just paint what your eyes see but what your imagination contains.

Addicted to Plato's ideal foot or hand, Charlotte wasn't ready for that lesson yet. Tongue between her teeth, she examined her palm, turning it over, then sketching the square little fingers. Next she painted her father's thick red fingers, her mother's thin, blue-veined ones, the flesh-wrapped twigs that passed for hands on the pianist at Bernstein's.

Her art teacher held the paintings at arm's length.

"You want to be a painter?"

She nodded.

"Don't. You'll end up as a teacher."

His nose was red from a cold, and a half moon of dandruff covered the lower part of his glasses' frame. He was like her parents—part of the opposition that she had to defeat.

Walking home in the November rain, she kicked the wet leaves and planned how to do feet, hands, noses—how to capture what everybody saw. This included folds in a dress and dents in a toothpaste tube.

She painted the hair-thin lines in the sweet violet's petals, then closed her eyes, imagined the color of its smell and painted that. She depicted her father asleep on the couch as a series of under chins in shades of pink folded on his chest. She stacked the paintings behind the bed and the drawings among her clothes, smudging her white underpants with charcoal.

The day Charlotte turned eighteen, she found tissue-wrapped gifts on her place mat in the morning. Under her fork was a newspaper clipping—*Join the next class. Imperial School for Secretaries.* Crushing the advertisement in her hand, she smiled at her mother.

"I'll become an artist."

Her mother frowned. "Be independent—learn to type."

"People who type think they're independent. They just end up with some man."

"What's wrong with that?"

"I want to live without a man—just paint."

Something inside Charlotte's mind stepped back from the words and stared. Had she really said that?

The next day, she showed Lulu her application and portfolio.

"My father knows the director of admissions at the academy," Lulu said. "He sits behind the driver's seat on his tram every morning."

"So what kind of man is he?" Charlotte asked.

"Wears a silk scarf at his neck."

"So?"

"People who wear silk scarves are very sensual. They pretend to be studying your drawings and thinking about paperwork, but mentally they're stroking your thighs."

All those tram rides had muddled Lulu's brain. Still the prospect of meeting the director of admissions made Charlotte nervous. People got into the academy through connections, and she had none. Her drawings were good, but if she had to beat out the daughter of a countess or a bank manager—what would make the difference?

Lulu knew.

"Drawings are important, but your breasts are your best credentials."

She walked in a semi-circle around Charlotte, eying her breasts until Charlotte's cheeks burned.

"Or your legs. Wear a short skirt. Keep your knees apart. Think of your body as a package of promises."

Evenings, Charlotte's mother read from the telephone book the names of typing schools. But mornings, Charlotte was at the café, waiting for the call. Finally it came. The voice of the admission's secretary was like chipped ice.

"Your interview will be tomorrow morning at nine."

She hung up and turned to Lulu.

"They'll never accept me."

"Make them."

On the day of the interview, Charlotte got up early. She took off her nightgown, studied her breasts. One was even smaller than the other. Time to hook up the brassiere she'd bought in a tart shop on the Friedrichstrasse. The saleslady had sucked in her cheeks.

Shows the outlines of your nipples.

Charlotte's sweater was one size too small. It belonged to Lulu's teenage sister. She hooked Lulu's wide mesh stockings to her garter belt. Next came the short skirt, a little tight at the waist. She recalled Lulu's advice.

Breathe in a slow, relaxed manner. But let him hear it.

Tottering on high heels, she practiced breathing. In and out. If she failed, she'd have no choice but typing at the *Berlin Handelsschule*.

The secretary took her coat and opened the door to the director's office. The woman's sharp look traveled on cats' claws down her back. The room was drafty. Good. Her nipples would pucker.

The director, a lumpy man in baggy pants, extended a hand. His glistening nose was his most prominent feature. He wore no silk scarf.

That damn Lulu.

He gestured for her to sit in a large, comfortable chair. Her application lay on the small table between them. He propped her portfolio against his chair. Charlotte sat down, folding her legs, showing a little thigh.

He bowed his head and stared at her application. "So you want to attend the academy?"

She crossed and uncrossed her legs, then remembered to part her knees. But they were concealed under the table. "I've always loved art," she said, leaning forward.

He reached for her portfolio. She rubbed her knees together, but couldn't make the sound Lulu had mentioned. Soon her drawings of hands and feet were spread across the table.

His brown eyes shone. "You seem focused on particular body parts."

"Oh, those are just for practice," she said. "I can also do elbows, shoulders, knees."

He looked at her. Charlotte panicked. He was preparing to reject her. Crossing her hands over her chest, she felt her breasts shrivel. In the expanding silence, she heard Lulu's voice.

If he hesitates, take one of his hands, place it on your breast. Put the other one between your legs. Once his fingers are inside, force him to admit you.

He leaned back in his chair and brought his fingertips together over his chest.

"I've read your application carefully."

No was climbing up into his throat now. This was her only chance. She turned sideways in her chair and slid forward. He glanced at her thigh and blushed. At least she'd distracted him from rejecting her. She pushed her chair closer, arching her back, and opening her legs slightly.

He raised an eyebrow.

The door opened, and the secretary leaned into the room. Looking past Charlotte, she handed the director some papers. He glanced at Charlotte. "I'm afraid I must turn my attention to some other matters. I want to welcome you to the academy."

He rose to his feet and cleared his throat. Pearls of sweat studded his forehead now.

"One thing—when you come to class, just wear something comfortable."

On the way out, she stopped in the bathroom and rubbed the crimson color from her lips. Her nipples stood out hard and clear in the cold air from the bathroom window. She buttoned her coat up to her throat.

Her friend opened the door before Charlotte rang the bell. "Well?"

"It was just like you said. He had two fingers inside me before he said yes."

Lulu narrowed her eyes in disbelief.

12. A Taste of Anisette

The honeyed sound of a saxophone spilled out of a doorway. A knee moved languidly to the music. *Hallo Sweetie*, a voice beckoned. Glimpsing a high-heeled shoe and a fishnet stocking, Charlotte quickened her pace, but Max grasped her arm, made her stop.

"Did you see her?"

"Of course," she said, flushing under the woman's hard gaze.

"I mean *really* see her?"

Charlotte looked again.

"See how the light lands on her hair. Blue and purple. Mix the colors in your head now."

The woman opened her legs and raised her middle finger towards him.

"Can you paint her essence?" he asked.

"I'd have to run home and start painting without taking my coat off," Charlotte said.

"That's just it."

The woman's mouth formed an angry lipsticked hole. "Move along if you don't want a fuck."

Max nodded politely then turned to Charlotte. "Primary colors are much more convincing for flesh tones than pink."

"Asshole," the woman said.

On Museum Island, they mounted the broad staircase toward the statue of Kaiser Friedrich Wilhelm. His horse pawed the air, against the Corinthian columns.

Inside, Max stopped at a painting by Vermeer van Delft, placed his fingers inches from the canvas and traced the light's journey.

"Follow it from the kitchen tiles to the woman in the courtyard."

Charlotte noticed the charcoal under his fingernails. How would it feel to run her fingertips down the joints of his hand to the tiny hairs on his wrist? Could she paint this new feeling? They studied a sulky young woman drinking from a glass, a man at her side. How to paint the warmth of his body?

Max pranced forward.

"See how the light illuminates the folds in his cloak here. But his other side has an entirely different color. Let's say the window isn't there. Just a flickering candle on the table. What color would the girl's dress be?"

Charlotte noted how the light played on the soft wool of Max's sweater.

A woman stroked her pregnant belly while her husband stared into the distance, his hand not so much holding hers as providing it with a place to rest. Lonely together, Charlotte decided.

A pearl necklace caught the light from the window, and Charlotte felt the warmth on her neck. Examining how Cupid's thick fingers caressed Aphrodite's ripe breasts, and Baby Jesus' tongue licked Mary's full pink nipple, Charlotte felt pinpricks of pleasure. Was that what he meant? Feeling the color, the texture, the light on your own skin?

Later, they sat in a café at Potsdamer Platz. The door swung open. This time the brownshirt was shaking a can of coins.

"For Germany."

The man at the next table reached into his pocket. Max rose, took a newspaper from one of the hooks, and began to read an editorial, moving his lips. The brownshirt was at his elbow now, staring at him hard, all the time shaking the can.

Ignoring him, Max continued reading.

The boy pretended to read over Max's shoulder.

"Interessant, huh?"

Charlotte saw the angry look on the boy's face. At last, he walked out. Like the earth thawing, the noise in the café gradually expanded.

"Those people scare me," Charlotte said.

He leaned towards her.

"The only way to fight them is from the far left."

This was new to her. Her parents dreamed of elegance under the Kaiser. Lulu didn't talk politics, but Charlotte suspected she favored the little Austrian.

"My father would have given the boy money—"

Max looked at her gloomily, and she tried to soften the statement.

"Perhaps out of fear—"

Max thrust a wad of bills under his glass and rose to his feet.

Outside, Charlotte noticed a new ad on the poster column—a red and black drawing of a muscular man, a swastika on his belt, breaking a sturdy chain. Above his thick, coarse hair hung the words *Schluss jetzt! Wahlt Hitler.* End it now. Choose Hitler.

"Versailles again—resentment tastes sweet. But bitter when you bite into it," Max said.

At Unter den Linden, Max stopped at a large tan-colored house with Greek columns. He climbed the steps, drawing her along behind him.

"Last gallery on the tour—my mother's house," he said.

She draped an arm around one of the columns, drawing him back.

"I'm wearing my old sweater," she said.

But she followed him into the house. The marble floor shone under the light of the chandelier. A gaunt man bowed low and exhaled a greeting.

A woman with dark hair hanging straight to her shoulders glided down the stairs towards them. She wore a soft, gray dress, gold-rimmed spectacles, and a thumb-sized piece of jade in the center of a tarnished necklace. Didn't the rich polish their silver?

Frau Bernstein eyed Charlotte over Max's shoulder. Turning to her, she offered a small hand as if for safekeeping and drew back her lips. Her teeth were small and very white, like a child's.

"Don't forget the Liebermanns," she said.

How easily they spoke with one another, without the angry sparks that characterized conversations with her parents. And about such things—she'd never known people who owned paintings by famous people. On the sofa lay a small dog with a pushed-in face. His breath rumbled in his throat. The light sparkled in the stones that studded his collar.

Frau Bernstein jangled her bracelets.

"I wish I could have tea with you, but they rescheduled the meeting of the museum board for today—yesterday's unfortunate event—"

Charlotte recalled the shooting on the museum steps. The victim and the shooter had worn uniforms from different parties.

After Frau Bernstein was gone, Max and Charlotte stared at one another for a moment. The only sound was the dog's breathing and the clattering of dishes in a distant kitchen.

Red and brown figures drew her eye to a painting. The figures had their heads together as if haggling over a small green spot. The signature read Max Liebermann.

Max Liebermann.

"I'm named for him," Max said.

"Is it Berlin?"

"Jewish quarter in Amsterdam."

He approached, stood close to her now, and her longing for

him filled the room to the ceiling. Afraid, she pulled back. But the space between them grew warm as his fingers moved over her shoulders. His mouth tasted of anisette.

13. Wood on Bone

Charlotte rolled up her napkin and slipped it into the monogrammed silver ring.

"I'll be working late tomorrow."

Her mother's eyes narrowed.

"Lulu's sick again?"

In lusty good health, Lulu was Charlotte's perpetual scapegoat.

"Must be chronic," her father said. "Like my knee—"

Sensing his need to discuss the Great War and the Kaiser, Charlotte brought her plate to the sink, and hurried towards the door.

Outside, the clouds appeared tinged with silver. Before Max, she wouldn't have seen it. Like the world of fairies she'd read about as a child, a non-concrete world existed, and she was just learning to see it. Her eye traveled the space from the gable of a building to the rooftop of the next. She measured the spaces between the bars on grillwork, the inside of an arch, the emptiness between columns, the air beneath a cornice, the openings in a balustrade. Yesterday she'd sketched the ragged gap between a dog's legs.

At the Friedrichstrasse station, she peered at the bulge in the wrought iron balcony with the Prussian eagle in the center. Her gaze traveled downward to the cigar shop. Max leaned against the wall, reading a newspaper. Without saying a word, he folded the newspaper and took her hand.

In an entranceway on Friedrichstrasse a black-clad man held

a glowing cigarette between glossy red lips. The yellow light from the open door backlit his slicked-back hair. Brightly painted fingernails drummed his thighs.

An aroma of fried potatoes filled the air. A woman sat opposite a man in a snack shop, chewing a sausage. A fox furpiece bit its own tail around her neck. The man gazed at her, moving only to dab her cheek with a napkin when the red sauce strayed.

Charlotte stared into the window, fascinated by the glassy eyes of the fox. The woman stopped eating, and Charlotte stepped back. But later, alone in her room she planned to experiment with yellow and green for the glitter of fox eyes.

At the cabaret, Max mumbled something at the entrance. Charlotte caught the name *Bernstein,* and a man opened the curtain for them to enter the theatre. A pool of light illuminated the stage. A whining saxophone undulated between the legs of a small man.

A peddler, dressed in a gold and red striped caftan and a felt hat, pushed a cart onto the stage, all the time chattering in Yiddish. He picked up the saxophonist, dumped him onto his cart, and wheeled him towards the audience.

"How much for this one?" he called to the audience.

A prop manager brought a cardboard picture of the big bank on Pariser Platz. The peddler Jew dumped the little man in front of the bank. The two couples at the next table laughed.

Charlotte asked Max if it was funny.

"Just an old Jewish joke," he said.

She felt humiliated—for his sake.

The little man was back on the stage, this time with a buxom woman. During the dance, the little man disappeared under the woman's dress and came out squalling from between her legs in a simulated birth. The woman scooped him up and held him to her bosom. The little man tore open the woman's blouse. Out fell two rubber breasts. He scrambled across the stage, caught one, locked his mouth on the rubber nipple and lay on the floor, sucking noisily, his legs curled under him.

Waiters brought more drinks. At intermission, the curtain came down, and the audience applauded wildly. Out of the corner of her eye, Charlotte saw the waiter seating two uniformed men in the back.

"Time to go," Max said.

In front of the theater, everything smelled of beer. Alongside the wall, Charlotte glimpsed men in long-pocketed coats, cigarettes glowing at their mouths, arms crossed over their chests. She clutched Max's arm.

"How can you stand it?" she asked.

"I don't take those jokes personally."

"But they're about you—"

"No. They're about the East European Jews. I'm a German Jew."

She said nothing, but pictured her parents looking into their Prussian sky and seeing her on the wings of this exotic artist.

As a teenager, Charlotte had gone to Bernstein's after school with Lulu. They'd admired the glittering chandeliers, walked between columns decorated with carved golden grapes, had run their fingers over the mosaics on the floor, depicting the Greek goddesses—Hera, Aphrodite, and Athena. Screwing up their courage, they'd asked the haughty sales clerk to let them try on the gold and silver necklaces and earrings that gleamed in glass cases.

"You need to look at the store from the corner—so you can see both sides of it at once," Max said.

They crossed the street. He put his hands in his pockets and rocked forward on the balls of his feet, his eyes dark under the streetlight.

"I could be working there—I mean running it," he said.

She stared at him. It was one thing to refuse to type letters, but to say no to Bernstein's—

"My mother wants me to live with her and run the store. Instead, I paint and she dresses mannequins and pays the employees."

"But later—"

"I told her if I don't succeed, I'll run the store. So she gives me an allowance, and I pop into the store when she needs me."

The red brick building looked more like a medieval city hall than a department store.

"Sometimes I think she prays I'll fail—"

She sensed that his mother wasn't the problem. Everything else in the world was.

"We have a bathtub with golden ball and claw feet," he said.

"So?"

"In some places—Neukoelln and Wedding—they don't have running water. And my mother bathes in rose oil."

She'd heard about Neukoelln, how the rats ate babies right out of their cribs.

Charlotte thought of her father filing city documents for thirty years, heard his voice in her head, *Art school's for failures.* His one concession to art was the lithograph of Kaiser Wilhelm over the sideboard in the dining room.

"You're ignoring your mother for a nasty place like Neukoelln?"

Did she sound like her own mother?

Shouts came from the side street. A man ran past, his face a mask of terror under the streetlight. Two stormtroopers followed, clubs held high. Max put his arm around Charlotte.

At the edge of the pavement, the stormtroopers cornered their prey. Charlotte hid her face in Max's jacket, but she could still hear the stormtrooper's voice.

"Dirty Jewish Bolshevik."

The sound of wood on bone. A scream. Two policemen appeared across the street. Max signaled to them. They glanced at him, then sauntered away. The stormtroopers tucked in their shirts and disappeared into the dark side street. The victim lay still, the back of his head leaking blood. Max climbed the steps of a café, pushing past customers who were on their way out. Charlotte saw him through the window as he entered the glass telephone booth. His finger went round the dial again and again. Then he threw the receiver back onto the hook and came down the steps.

"I must be crazy, calling the police," he said.

"Yes."

"The dispatcher laughed at me."

Charlotte pulled a handkerchief from her pocket and turned to the victim. But two men already stood over him. They lifted him to his feet, draped his arms around their necks, and dragged him between them. His shoes scraped along the sidewalk.

14. Hues of Yellow and Lilac

Shouts came from the lake. It was high season at Wannsee. Max took Charlotte's hand, and they walked quickly down the dirt path toward the water. The bushes opened. The sun reflected off a silvery chute that trembled on stalklike rods against the tree-lined lake. In the muddy water at the foot of the slide, bathers raised their eyes to the young woman hugging her arms on the platform above them.

With a quick motion, the woman patted her bathing cap, then gripped the sides of the slide. Her face was marked with fear as she studied her cheering friends. Suddenly, she raised her chin toward the sun, swung her arms towards the clouds, and flew. With a crash, she hit the water and disappeared. Seconds later, she exploded upwards from the surface of the water.

That was the way to do it, just let go and fly into the unknown, Charlotte thought as she eased her way down the steps of the dock. At the other end, Max jumped into the water. She stroked the distance between them and swam into his open arms.

Afterwards, they sat wrapped in towels, their feet touching. Max picked a scraggly dandelion, slipped it into a salami sandwich, and handed it to her. She bit into it. The flower was fuzzy between her teeth.

"*Pissen lit*, the French call it. Makes you pee in your bed, but protects you from colds. My mother fed it to me."

Dandelions didn't sound like Frau Bernstein, unless she was

strewing poison dust on the weeds that grew along the sidewalk. Max picked a handful of dandelions and slit the stalks to make a necklace. He brought it down around Charlotte's head, arranging it over her collarbones and brushing the place where her breasts began.

"We used to make these at our summer house—my mother and I—when we were waiting for Herr Esch to call us in to lunch."

The valet again—bowing and serving, sneering and eavesdropping.

Her eyes went to his lips. They'd tasted like anisette. She stroked his cheek, moved her fingers to the back of his neck. His hand went to her breast, and she melted towards him.

Laughter crackled in the bushes. Charlotte sat up and covered herself with the towel. Through the branches, she glimpsed a man hunched over a bottle of wine, pulling the corkscrew. An extended arm held a wine glass.

In the tram, they sat close, his arm warm against hers. When the tram approached her stop, she prepared to rise. But he took her hand. She noticed that the blue of his eyes was as changeable as Monet's cathedral, painted at different times of day.

She settled back into her seat.

When he opened the door of his apartment, the smell of turpentine and rotting fruit greeted her. The photo of a dumpy woman wearing a flat veiled hat hung in the hall. The tiny black letters read, *Rosa Luxemburg with friends.*

In his studio, brown bananas appeared glued by their own juices to a small round table. From a distance, the canvas on his easel looked like bad weather. But up close, Charlotte saw the distorted lines of a woman's face. To the top of the easel, he'd clipped a magazine photo of an attractive actress.

"I paint what I see," he said, pointing to his head. "In here."

Suddenly, he pushed his sweater up over his head and stepped out of his pants. The curve of his back just above the buttocks was olive green in the studio light. He threw back his head and stretched his arms upwards in an arc, simulating a man dancing with a wriggling snake between his arms.

He held the snake with both hands, resisting its attempts to lock him in its embrace. Hadn't the soothsayer fought the snake that the gray-eyed goddess Athena had sent?

"Who am I?'

"El Greco's *Laocoon*," she said.

He grinned, clapping his hands. His chest was smooth, but auburn-colored hair surrounded his navel and bloomed between his legs.

"Your turn," he said, taking a book from the shelf and sitting down in a chair.

As a little girl, she'd loved being naked. A long time ago, even before she'd thought of painting, she'd pulled off her bathing suit and hid it in the bushes when her mother wasn't looking. Swimming the breaststroke, she'd imagined the lake water entering her body, coming out through her gills, somewhere under her arms.

She slipped her sweater over her head. Who would she be? Renoir's *Odalisque*, her eyes half closed, lounging languidly in gold-edged silken pants? No. He'd prefer a nude. She folded her clothes in a neat pile.

Conscious of his gaze, she eased herself onto the sofa pillows, tilted her body toward him, held her legs together, revealing only the top pubic hairs. She stretched her arms above her head, slid her hands under her head, felt her ribcage widen, and willed her breasts to spill to each side. She imagined the dark, secret places of the moist earth and the fertile female body. Men longed to unite with her.

"Goya's *Maja Desnuda*," he shouted triumphantly.

He rose from his chair, his eyes bright.

Suddenly embarrassed, she sat up abruptly. Where had she put her clothes?

But he lowered himself to the sofa. She lay back again, felt his warm thigh against her arm. The odalisque would have covered her soft hands with fragrant Indian oils and stroked him. Charlotte ran the back of her hand along his thigh. Leaning forward, he ran the tip of his tongue over the skin toward her breast, over the roundness of her nipple. She touched the back of his neck where his hair began. His finger drew tiny circles on her belly, then gently probed her navel.

"Monet. Manet."

He trailed his fingers over the top pubic hairs.

"Caravaggio," he said, sliding his finger inside her. Playing with the damp tendrils, he chanted, "Carracci brothers," now moving his finger in and out.

Bending over, he brushed his lips over her belly, and his voice came from between her legs.

"Delacroix."

Throbbing under his tongue, she reached forward to stroke his ears and grip his hair. He rose to his knees. With the fingertips of both hands, she stroked his erect limb. He groaned under her touch. The blood pounding between her legs, she guided him towards her.

"Van Gogh," he breathed, entering.

In a field of sunflowers and lavender, lilac and yellow hues washed over her in wave after wave of color and fragrance. Afterwards, she held his head between her breasts and relived muted shades of sunshine and periwinkle.

15. The Fault of the Jews

Charlotte and Max stood on the balcony of Frau Bernstein's house. Below, a group of elderly men carried black, red, and gold banners, the anti-Nazi colors. Charlotte glanced at her mother-in-law, who smoked in silence.

Suddenly, Herr Esch appeared and extended an ashtray. Mischievously, Frau Bernstein flicked her ash onto the balcony tiles. He rolled his eyes and withdrew.

Why did they keep the valet? Max had told Charlotte how Herr Esch had steadied him on his new bike when he was eight years old. But whenever Charlotte walked down the hall, the man pressed himself against the wall with a mock obsequiousness. Once, she'd looked back and caught him smiling to himself.

Max stroked her arm.

"Tomorrow's May 1," he said.

She'd seen the call for demonstrations on the posters, knew about the police ban on open-air assemblies and demonstrations.

"You'll get arrested," she said.

The Social Democrats had hired volunteer fighters from the Frei Korps to beat down the Communists. And the right wing Frei Korps would go beyond that. Killing an heir to Bernstein's would be a coup.

"It'll be a rout."

"I don't like dead bodies," she said.

By the time she went to sleep, she had a headache. Still, next morning she rode with him to Hermanns Platz. Men in frayed clothes stood in the square carrying signs.

Save the Workers.

Charlotte sensed the distrust in their eyes. Was it her hair? No Bolshevik bun for her. She wore it short and stylish, like in the magazines. Nodding to Max, the demonstrators formed a knot and sang the *Internationale.*

A woman crossed the square, her arms weighed down by shopping nets bulging with potatoes and onions. Lacy green carrot stalks hung over the top of one of the nets. She tilted her head, peered at the hand-lettered signs.

"May Day—for higher wages," Charlotte said.

It'll be hand-to-hand combat with press coverage as the ultimate goal, she started to say. Gunshots cracked across the square. People ran. A tram stopped, and passengers spilled out. A man with a briefcase and an umbrella scrambled up onto the sidewalk. A schoolboy clutched his cap to his head and jumped curbs to shelter. Police officers, clubs raised, surrounded the demonstrators.

More shots. The woman fell to the ground. Potatoes rolled onto the cobblestones. Max took Charlotte's hand. They ducked behind the abandoned tram, then crept into a niche behind Julius Meinl's furniture store.

Pleasure edged Max's voice.

"They're fighting back—"

He took a step towards the scuffle.

Charlotte grabbed the back of his sweater with both hands.

He shook her off but didn't advance onto the square. A layer of smoke crept over the woman's body where it lay on the ground.

"I want to go home," Charlotte said.

He took her hand, and they made their way down the side streets. Shots continued behind them on the square. Riding on the tram, he stood behind her.

"I shouldn't have taken you there."

But she knew he didn't mean it.

Later when she mentioned the dead housewife, he told her the police had been brutal. He didn't trust people in uniform the way she did—firemen, police, bus drivers. That was one big difference between them. She had two waitress uniforms, she told him, and was proud of the spare.

When Max wasn't looking for trouble, he pretended they lived in normal times. He invited Charlotte to the Scala to see Grock the clown and Rastelli the juggler. A pair of clowns stepped onto the stage and pretended to wrestle. One fell to the floor, then jumped up and draped his arm around the other. They sang:

If it thaws, or if there's a breeze, if it drizzles, if it sizzles,
If you cough or if you sneeze, it's all the fault of all those Jews!

On the way home, Max took her arm, drew her close, spoke quietly. "I'd hate to be Jewish."

"But you are."

He stiffened. She didn't understand him at all. On the Kudamm they passed broken windows of Jewish stores, places where Jews had been beaten up. Where did he fit in?

After that, Charlotte set up her easel in Max's studio. In yellow, red, and blue, she painted the police chasing the demonstrators over the square and the dead woman. Toning down the colors, she created an overall effect of yellow streetlights burning through the haze of fog and smoke.

Suddenly he threw his brush down, sauntered over to her easel, stood next to her, arms folded. Something prickled at the back of her neck. She wasn't in the mood for criticism.

"You made the demonstrators too big—the police too small," he said.

She glanced at his canvas, at the series of black jagged lines that gave his figures a look of perpetual motion. The police resembled gargoyles. He was glorifying people who ran across squares and got shot for a cause.

Her brush sucked up the red on her palette. She used it to paint the sole of the dead woman's shoe scarlet. Her bare foot she colored pink, as if her veins still carried blood to the skin of her extremities—as if she were still alive.

The Weimar Republic ducked but not fast enough. In October 1929, when the U.S. stock market crash set off a worldwide economic crisis, the wound to the struggling German republic was lethal. The Communists and the Nazis hugged the impoverished Germans to death. The Communists looked over the embraced lover's shoulder with an eye on the goal— a Soviet Germany. Nazis linked arms with Communists and mouthed slogans.

Free the working class.

But the brownshirts dreamed of a Third Reich free of the Communists.

Storekeepers in the Friedrichstrasse went bankrupt. They sold their wares from wooden carts. It became a song and dance number in the cabarets.

Shops on wheels, just like in America.

Charlotte's father developed a black humor that replaced his sulky longing for the Kaiser.

"If I lose my job, we can get horse meat at the soup kitchen," he said at dinner, talking about a man who fed his family at the soup kitchen. He'd gone to the bank for his money. When it was his turn, the teller had shaken his head, pulled down the iron lattice. Charlotte mashed a potato into her broth. Next time, she'd bring them something from Bernstein's to cheer them up.

On the Jewish holiday, stormtroopers popped up like mushrooms on a damp day. When worshipers spilled out of the synagogues in the Fasanenstrasse and Lehniner Platz, stormtroopers closed in on them singing their favorite song.

When Jewish blood spurts at the end of the knife.

The day after the attack on the synagogues, Charlotte went with Max to the girly review at the Metropol. They sat in the front row, holding hands in the dark.

On the stage, women—among them a few black women—danced nude but for the mandatory crotch cover. At first, the musicians in the pit played marching music. The dancers moved with an athletic bounciness, celebrating their strong, healthy bodies. Then to the drums, the dancers moved rhythmically. Suddenly the music stopped. In the silence, a man sang, *Take it off, Petronella*. Soon the audience joined in. The dancers undulated to the tuneless chanting. In the center, a chubby blond woman wiggled pleasurably.

A police whistle squealed. The dancers stopped, bumping into one another.

But the blond kept on dancing and humming to herself, eyes closed. She kicked out her leg, and her crotch cover drifted to the floor, revealing a chestnut-colored bush.

A stormtrooper approached the stage. He picked up the patch and waved it. Everyone laughed. He turned to the woman. She was giggling nervously now. Using both hands, he nudged the cloth back into place.

Like a wind-up toy, one of the officers swiveled to face the audience.

"He's perfect for the part," Charlotte giggled. But Max looked ready to leap.

"I smell garlic—must be Jews here," the policeman said.

This time nobody laughed. A shiver went up Charlotte's neck. The stage lights reflected off the officer's pot-shaped visored helmet.

"The dancer is in violation of the dance obscenity laws of 1926," the officer said.

A woman next to Charlotte got up and left. The stormtrooper who had fondled the dancer faced the audience.

"Be good Germans and go home. The police will shut down this swinish Jewish show."

Outside, the nails in a stormtrooper's boots clinked on the tram tracks as he crossed the street. In front of him, a small dark figure disappeared down an alley.

16. The Peddler

In the summer of 1932, street fights erupted daily. Charlotte and Max walked quickly, ducking down different streets, discussing Delacroix's influence on the French academy—pretending things were normal. They often crossed the city with sketchpads under their arms, stopping in quiet places to draw.

But there was one place Max wouldn't go—the Hacke'sche Markte, where Eastern European Jews, bearded people with skullcaps and black robes, sold their wares from carts. She wanted to paint them, but he wouldn't go with her.

"Those people make me feel uncomfortable," he said.

She rolled *those people* around in her mind, his strange attitude towards Jews. Once she'd joked about it, tried to formulate it in a way that made sense to her.

"You're a German department store Jew, not a Yiddish-speaking peddler's cart Jew."

He glared at her.

To celebrate her birthday, Max invited Charlotte to the summer palace built for Queen Sophie Charlotte, *Schloss Charlottenburg*.

They stood looking up at the statue of Friedrich Wilhelm, the great Elector. Max slid his arms around Charlotte's waist.

"He loved Sophie Charlotte so much. But he couldn't keep her from dying," he said.

Leaning back into his warmth, she felt a wave of melancholy at the sight of the blue green dome of the palace. She'd often come here with her mother who loved to talk about the beautiful Sophie Charlotte and the elegant life she lived in the seventeenth century.

"I'd rather visit the Hacke'sche Markte for my birthday," Charlotte said.

Without a word, he took her arm and walked with her towards the tram.

People spilled out of the side streets into the Rosenthaler Strasse. The air smelled of frying potatoes, onions, apples, and spices. Cart wheels creaked on cobblestones. Vendors shouted out their wares. Closer to the ground, dogs barked and children squabbled and sang. Something silky brushed against Charlotte's skin. A peddler with stained teeth held up filmy scarves.

He extended an arm draped with shoelaces.

She fingered leather shoelaces for boots. But Max gripped her hand, pulled her away, elbowing his way through the crowd, calling to her over his shoulder.

"Bad neighborhood here. Let's get a sausage at the Alex."

But the dark street narrowed, and the peddlers crowded in closer. She almost bumped into a cart piled high with coral necklaces and fabrics. She gripped the edge of the cart and picked up an amber-colored brooch.

Max was edgy, but she ignored him.

The red-bearded peddler held up a cracked mirror for her as she struggled to pin the brooch to her blouse. But in it, she saw the angry flush in Max's cheeks.

"I'll buy you jewelry on the Ku-damm," he said.

"But I like this one," she said.

Seeing the interest in the peddler's eyes, she was ashamed of the whine in her voice. Max abruptly handed the peddler a stack of bills, clipped together. The peddler offered him change, but he'd already turned his back. A mother and two children stared up at her.

Smells of salty and sour foods tickled her nostrils. Pickled herring lay next to pastries rolled in honey and sesame seeds. Women in long dark skirts, scarves on their heads, talked to friends, keeping a hand on a child's shoulder.

"Everything for your sewing needs," a peddler called, gesturing at cards of buttons, hooks and eyes, spools of thread, lace collars, and elastic bands of different widths for waists and legs of underwear.

Dresses hung on hangers across a wooden rack. A woman fingered a blue one with tucks at the waist. The peddler took it down, spreading the dress over his arm.

"Meine Dame."

Max stood in a small open area between carts and watched, as if he'd finally gained the distance he needed. Charlotte went to his side.

"Where do they come from?" she asked.

"Eastern Europe—the *shtetls* of Galicia."

A man with hands and arms like gnarled branches pushed a cart heaped with pretzels. Studded with quartzlike chunks of salt, they sparkled in the sun. A boy in a short shiny robe and an embroidered skullcap ducked under his cart, then jumped out again and ran alongside, holding a stick against the cart's rolling wheel. He laughed when bits of bark broke off the stick.

"*Oi vey, Junge. Bist du meschugge?*" the peddler called, slapping the boy.

"What did he say?" she asked.

"You crazy?"

"You speak Jewish?"

"My aunts talk *shtetl*."

The peddler offered Charlotte a pretzel. But then suddenly he noticed Max.

"You again," he said.

Max extended his hand.

"Bielski—"

Ignoring the proffered hand, the peddler embraced Max, then stepped back and looked up into his face.

"I've got to talk to you."

After some instructions to the boy, the peddler took Max's arm, led him to a doorway, set so low that Max had to duck to enter. Charlotte followed. In the dark, Charlotte felt her way along the table before sitting down. Without a word, a man in a stained brown apron brought rolled herring for Bielski. Gradually, Charlotte distinguished two bearded men in black robes seated at the next table.

Max placed his hands, palms down, on the table.

"What is it, Bielski?"

"I've missed you."

"I'm not in the mood for your story, not with Charlotte here."

Bielski's mouth sagged. "It's been a long time."

"She doesn't need to hear it."

"Rivka's begun to cry again at night—keeps me awake."

The peddler turned to Charlotte.

"Would you like to hear about my little daughter Rivka?"

"Yes," she said, averting her gaze from Max's face.

Bielski's eyes gleamed. "Know about the Cossacks?"

She'd seen pictures of men with big teeth and fur hats.

"We came to Berlin a long time ago when my daughter Rivka was young, but it seems like yesterday. Do you know why it seems like yesterday?"

Charlotte smiled encouragingly.

"Because she never got over it. It happens to her again every night."

Bielski cleared his throat.

"The Cossacks came to our village every time the price of bread went up in Kiev. Big men—ate lots of meat, grew up on creamy milk. Wore leather boots and fur-lined gloves. You could hear them laughing long before they got to the village. Laughed when they kicked in the doors. Laughed when they broke the furniture, tore up the bedding, dumped the winter grain onto the snow. Laughed so we couldn't hear our women screaming when they raped them.

"It was 1914 before Russia got sucked into the Great War. We were getting soft—hadn't had a pogrom for a while. Then suddenly in the middle of sunny winter's day, I hear the horses' hooves, and I know they're back. I see their big white teeth as they ride down the street. I run indoors, close the shutters, pray they'll pass us by. But then I hear the screams from next door, my brother's house. Isaac, the fool, must've fought back, I think. Later, I find him. They'd crushed his skull with their rifle butts."

Bielski stopped for a moment. He was breathing hard, as if he couldn't get enough oxygen to fulfill his mission.

"They come after us, eyes hot. First they tear up the mattresses. Break the plates against the walls. I know what they're after. We'd hidden her, but not well enough. Rivka. My beautiful Rivka—only fourteen. They laugh when they pull her out from behind the boxes in the closet. And what do I do? Do I rip the Adam's apples out of their throats? Do I give my life for my beloved daughter? Do I throw the doorstop at them? Kick them from behind to bust their kidneys? No. I put my hands over my ears to shut out her screams. That's what I do with my hands. Like a pet dog, I follow them outside until one of them picks me up and throws me against the wall of the house.

"When I come to, I lie on the ground and watch. But all I can see is the big legs and broad backs of those men. No sign of my poor Rivka. But I hear her. Good God, do I hear her. At first, her screams are louder than their laughter. Then I can only hear their laughter. That's worse. My father once told me laughter was the music of the soul. But if you don't have a soul, it's a cry for blood.

"Afterwards the swine pull up their pants, still laughing. They pass around a flask, throw back their heads to drink, wipe their mouths with the backs of their hands. At last they go. And the screams and laughter move down the street. Rivka lies still, her eyes closed, uncovered like a woman should never be, blood oozing from between her legs onto the snow. A neighbor helps me carry her back into the house. Finally, we hear the horses hooves, and the devils are gone again."

The peddler seemed to have dried up. Whatever fuel had driven him to retell this story was spent. His hands—small and withered with spread fingers—lay on the table like forgotten things. Charlotte touched the back of his left hand, stroked the cool, thin skin. Slowly, he came alive again.

"That night, I slept on the floor, praying for my brother's soul and crying for my daughter's innocence. We had to leave. We knew about the Jews in Berlin. They worked in factories or sold things off carts. So we came here. We had some distant relatives in Berlin. They took us in. The Germans are good people. They opened their arms to us."

The time between then and now lay like a lead ball in the silence.

"Last night, when she screamed, I was the little mouse again, the one who crawls into the wall and hides in the dark until the Cossacks are gone."

"If you had fought them, both you and Rivka would be dead," Max said.

This wasn't the first time Max had said these words to Bielski, Charlotte thought. She recalled his strange behavior at the cabaret. Something was pulling him in two directions. The peddler rose to his feet.

"That crazy boy of mine—he's probably lost everything off the cart."

Outside, Bielski disappeared among the carts.

Max, his hands in his pocket, walked away quickly, talking as if to himself. Charlotte strained to hear his words.

"People like Bielski love Germany even more than I do. But he and the others from the *shtetl* have always made me nervous. They walk about chattering like squirrels, bowing and scraping. Liebermann paints them, but I keep my distance—except for Bielski. And he came to me."

At the street corner, he stopped, leaned against a traffic sign.

"They're foreign, go to synagogue, talk funny. When I was a kid, I pointed at them—'Look at the strange people.' My mother smacked my hand. 'They'll soon be German, just like us,' she said. But I didn't believe her—still don't."

And how did Max fit in? Was he more German than Bielski? Jewishness and Germanness seemed like the medieval humors—blended differently in each individual.

The muscles in Charlotte's neck hurt from the pain of Bielski's story.

"It's the rabbi who makes them different. In the east it's 'Yes, rebbe. No rebbe. Lift your robe, so I may kiss your ass, rebbe.' They say it all day long in the *shtetl*. They come here, bring the *shtetl* with them. And they expect the rest of us to like it."

"But, they've suffered."

His eyes darkened.

"When I first met Bielski, he didn't guess I was a Jew."

The other day he'd insisted he wasn't a Jew.

"I came here once with a cousin," Max said. "Gerda still had one foot in the *shtetl*, wanted her fortune told. I was waiting outside for her. Suddenly this little man came up and starting talking, talking at me. I didn't want to listen, but I couldn't stop him. After that, I forced myself to come back. I promised Bielski. And I let him tell me things I don't want to know about."

"But it's the truth—"

"I don't need to know about that kind of hatred. Anyhow, at first Bielski just thought I was a nice, sympathetic German."

"And you are," she said.

The tightness left his face. It occurred to her that he might want to separate himself entirely from Bielski's world. Would she be the final act in Max's personal assimilation play?

They crossed the street and stepped onto the curb. As they put more distance between themselves and the Jewish market, Max's step grew lighter. Finally, he stopped and gestured towards a pub window. Inside two men were playing billiards. He raised his thumb and squinted, and she knew he was calculating the distance between a crooked elbow and a hip, transferring a portly body to his canvas, daubing a set of overalls with reds and yellows.

She was learning that a painter did not absorb pain directly but broke it down into parts, integrating it gradually into his soul, often blending it with his own pain, then giving it back—in oil—transformed.

17. Eating Porcelain

Charlotte wore a sweater buttoned up to the top and sat on a bench at the Friedrichstrasse subway. She sketched people quickly, creating balls of motion as they walked past her. Later, she'd fill in the detail—the slumped shoulders, the frayed clothes, the sad look. She added one dynamic element, the prostitute leaning languidly against a lamppost. At home, she'd fuss over the woman's army top boots, the unlaced peasant blouse, the leather skirt.

The clock struck noon. She packed her bag and hurried to visit Max.

He was barefoot, his hair uncombed, and his clothes rumpled. The kitchen table was covered with stacks of election leaflets embossed with the hammer and sickle. He'd been in the middle of stuffing them into his backpack.

"I think I've captured the mood," she said, opening her sketchpad.

He didn't look up.

"I have to finish these leaflets. We've got to beat the Nazis in this election."

She didn't want him to be political today. Hadn't disrupting Goebbels' speech been enough? His comrades had attacked the stormtroopers with brass knuckles and rubber hoses. She felt she was living between two armed camps.

"What's the difference between you and them?" she asked.

He looked at her, his eyes wide.

"Both sides wear uniforms and look humorless."

"I don't wear a uniform."

"I didn't mean you."

She dropped her sketchpad on the table, sending an unbound stack of leaflets sliding to the floor. Grumbling, he picked them up. He looped his arms into the backpack and swung it onto his back. She boarded the tram with him and watched him get off at Potsdamer Platz.

From the streaked tram window, she saw him join a group of men in tweed caps. They pushed leaflets at passersby who ignored them. A truck pulled up across the street, and stormtroopers jumped out of the back. As her tram moved forward, Charlotte craned her neck to see, but when it rounded the corner, she lost sight of them.

It was late. At dinner, Charlotte had ordered fresh trout in lemon sauce, and Max had gotten something French in wine sauce. Her mother, who struggled with new ways of serving potato, thought she was out with Lulu. She mustn't know about the restaurant.

On the way home, Max seemed preoccupied. Without a word, he went straight into his studio. He stood and gazed at a large canvas. He'd been working on it for days. Prussian soldiers, their grinning faces resembling buttocks, raised knives against a group of huddled young girls, whose mouths formed black holes of fear.

"I'll add another monster," he said.

"No room for hope?" she asked.

Even during dinner he'd been in a fierce mood. Charlotte knew that horses trampling corpses would be as close as he could get to painting something nice now. But he backed away from the easel. She placed her hands at his waist and stroked his sides. Sandalwood oil—wasn't that the balm that Asians used to calm agitated individuals?

Raising his sweater, she moved her lips across his chest,

sucked the nipple, and heard his groan of pleasure. Nuzzling his chest, she leaned into her exotic god, imagining his sweet spicy aroma. She closed her eyes, led him to the sofa, and envisioned his fragrant body on a silken bed, surrounded with rubies, sapphires, and emeralds.

Pretending to spread sandalwood oil, she stroked his entire body, her nostrils tingling at the imagined fragrance. Brushing his ankle with her lips, she heard him speak.

"Artemesia Gentileschi."

"You mean Mary Magdalene," she said.

"I like the baroque painter better."

By comparing her to the woman who'd painted the wildest version of Judith cutting off Holofernes' head, Max was making love to her like no other man could.

She slipped off her clothes, straddled him, gently took his limb into her hands, bent over it, and traced its length with her tongue. She moved her knees forward, felt the heat of his thighs between hers, and slowly eased him inside her, thinking the words that fired her senses.

Cinnamon. Cloves. Nutmeg. Cumin.

"If I am Artemesia, you are the Prince of the Spice Islands," she said.

"I was thinking of the gray-green plant with the lovely smell. My mother used to give it to Herr Esch to put in French sauces," he said.

"Your smell is sweeter, though," she said.

Afterwards, he dozed off. She reached for his bathrobe and slippers and went to her easel. She quickly mixed colors, then painted a ground that consisted of gray with splotches of orange and gold. With tiny brushstrokes, she made a cerulean sky that shaded into azure. Faces appeared in the seams where one color blended into the next. Her brush gave the faces bodies. She stood back, surprised. Where had she seen these faces?

It was the first time she'd painted something that she

couldn't recall seeing, something that only lived inside her. Suddenly she felt very tired. She wanted a bath. As the water tumbled into the bathtub, she undressed and stepped into the water. Immersing herself up to her shoulders, she enjoyed the ache in her thigh muscles, a reminder of her pleasure with him.

Eyes closed, she imagined a bazaar in Marrakesch, full of colorful carpets, soft silks, and sweet perfumes. The scratch of a pencil on paper reached her ears. Max was sitting on the stool next to the bathtub, drawing her.

"Who said you could come in?"

"I missed you. Don't move—I'm doing the nose."

"I was thinking of asking you to marry me, but now I'm tired of you. Next time I'll lock the door." She stepped out of the bath.

He kept scribbling.

"Your hair," he said.

She arched her back and toweled her hair furiously, then posed for him with her wet hair. He took colored pencils from his pocket, moved his hand in circles over the page. At last she turned to the mirror and brushed her hair.

The next day he showed her the painting, now on canvas. The face lacked detail, but her hair was a tangle of color— chestnut, amber, marmalade, and siena. Fingering the ends of her short brown hair, she realized he was as crazy as she was—in the same way too.

No, not in the same way, not as long as he insisted that the Red Front was the only answer to the chaos of the republic.

Charlotte sat in Frau Bernstein's parlor, admiring the gilded frame on the portrait of Frau Bernstein's parents. Frau Bernstein was talking about the collapse of the Austrian bank.

"Bad for Bernstein's. Bad for the republic."

Banking was not Charlotte's favorite topic.

"The German Danat Bank is next. Bank of England would have gone the same way if it hadn't abandoned the gold standard. England's the place to be," Frau Bernstein said, placing her cup onto the saucer with a stony click.

For a moment her gaze rested on her son, but then she turned to Charlotte and spoke in the hushed tone of a confidante.

"I don't mind his becoming an artist," she said.

Charlotte waited. This was only the prologue to her real message. Women who talked bank language didn't want their sons to be artists.

"As long as he pops into the store a few times a week," Frau Bernstein said, resting a knuckle on Max's knee, and leaning over him towards Charlotte. "But I don't like how he runs around with those ragged revolutionaries."

"Mother, we can't simply let the Nazis take over," Max said.

"Then support the republic."

"The world's laughing at this stupid little Weimar Republic. It's failed the working class. Families fight over one potato in the tenements."

"Maybe over a turnip, hardly a potato," Frau Bernstein said, picking up her silver cigarette case.

Herr Esch emerged from somewhere between the floorboards and extended a silver tray. On it were three ornate cigarette holders. While he lit her cigarette, Frau Bernstein kept talking.

"The crooks in New York destroyed the stock market. The money of the republic is worthless. We can't pay our workers," she said.

"Jews' fault?" It was Max.

Frau Bernstein rolled her eyes in the direction of Herr Esch. They sat in silence for a moment while Herr Esch finished pouring tea.

Max made a sweeping gesture towards the chandelier and

the paintings. Then he waved a hand at the glass cabinet. It contained seventeenth century engraved copper discs from the Safavid capital of Isfahan.

"We don't deserve this as long as people are starving."

Frau Bernstein blew out a smoke ring.

"Nobody willingly eats copper plates."

"Not funny," Max said.

"It's reality—like your thing about the potato."

Max dropped his tone.

"I'll help with the store, but I won't abandon the workers."

Frau Bernstein's fingernails clicked on the wood of her chair.

"If you want to help the workers, support the republic. The damned Communists are handing the whole package to Hitler. If they keep tearing the republic down, people will beg for a sharp kick in the ass at the next election."

Max slapped the top of his thighs in a gesture of concession. Frau Bernstein wagged her cigarette in his face.

"Laugh in my face. That's what boys do to their mothers. But don't make a fool of yourself."

The light from the chandelier glittered on Frau Bernstein's rings. She rose.

"Excuse me, but all these words are making me feel rather vague. I must write down some numbers—you know, add them up, then subtract them."

She allowed each of them to kiss a cheek.

The fragrance of honeysuckle and lilacs drifted in through the open window. Charlotte moved to the sofa and sat next to Max. He turned and placed his head in her lap. She stroked under his chin and over his cheek, ran her fingers over his throat.

"Your mother's right," she said.

They didn't hear the sound of feet at the door. Herr Esch, his eyes cloud-gray under bushy eyebrows, stood on the threshold. He carried a tray with two wine glasses of wheat beer, *Berliner Weisse,* tinged green from a shot of woodruff syrup. Blushing, Max sat up. Charlotte reached for a sticky glass. Herr Esch handed Max a plate of smoked *barbell* fish, arranged in thin slices, then placed the tray between his arm and ribcage and moved backwards, bowing crisply.

In Herr Esch's presence, Charlotte felt like an outsider at Unter den Linden. He was always testing her manners, as if to determine if she was worthy of his attention. He'd probably seen her through the window at Café Rilke, decided that she carried her tray under her arm just like he did.

Max leaned against her, and she could smell his body. She unbuttoned his shirt and slid her hand over his ribs. He stroked her forearms. Their lips touched, and the familiar flame rose within her. In the hall, Herr Esch hummed a patriotic tune. She pushed Max away.

18. Idealist

She didn't really want to go with him to the slums. Her father had said workers were people who didn't wash their hands. That's why they had nasty jobs in factories.

Still, she wanted to understand better, so at dawn she waited for him in front of her building, listening to a man in overalls scraping the sidewalk with a branch broom. The smell of hot granite filled her nostrils as the woman in the building next door poured steaming water onto her steps. A pair of horses snuffled their grain bags while their owner unloaded coal from the back of the wagon.

They rode the tram to Kreuzberg, got off at Jannowitzerbrucke, and crossed the canal. A copper green church dome rose above the squarish cityscape. Plaster peeled from the houses' facades, and torn curtains hung behind splintered window frames. The smells of oatmeal and animals wafted from behind courtyard gates.

The sign on the wall said *Koepenickerstrasse.* A steaming horse waited hooked up to a wagon while a man in patched clothes lifted baskets of produce into the back. He nodded to Max. In the courtyard, a woman wearing a headscarf unpinned socks from a clothesline.

The air was gritty with the smell of boiling potatoes. Like two different versions of the same symbol, flags featuring swastikas and the hammer and sickle hung from windows at every level. It was Monday, and unemployed men leaned against the walls. Fighting words were scrawled on the wall.

First Food, Then The Rent!

"Tenants strike. No jobs," he said crisply.

At the courtyard's center, a statue, an angel of freedom with wings high and unfurled, revealed a shapely leg between dress folds.

"Hope of the future," Max said.

"She wants the Kaiser back?" Charlotte asked.

"Don't you believe in Germany?"

She thought of the caricatures of thick-lipped Jews in her father's newspaper, of Frau Bernstein apologizing for the banks that wouldn't give your money back, of the Communists beating up the Social Democrats, of the Social Democrats hiring freelance street fighters to shoot at the Communists.

"No."

A small boy, green mucous at his nostrils and a school satchel on his back, was looking up at her. Charlotte reached into her pocket, brought out a handkerchief, and placed it under the boy's nose. He took it from her and ran away. The sound of bells came from the courtyard entrance. An organ grinder wearing a Prussian steel helmet decorated with tiny bells wheeled an organ decorated with golden dragons across the cobblestones, still shiny from the night drizzle. Like animals of different species squabbling, the sound of bells, drums, organ, and harmonica filled the courtyard.

A woman appeared in a doorway, wiping her hands on her apron. Charlotte glimpsed a tub of soaking wash behind her. The organ grinder shook his head so that the bells tinkled. The woman stepped forward and put her arms around her neighbor. Unsteadily at first, then dipping and twirling vigorously, the women danced across the courtyard.

Wir tanzen den Lichtensteiner Polka, mein Schatz.

Two girls in pigtails held hands and danced. More women appeared in doorways. They clasped one another and swayed to the music. A man in a tweed cap approached Max and handed him some papers.

Back out on Kopenickerstrasse, Charlotte gave Max a look.

"You signed something."

He looked around, seeing nobody on their side of the street but an old man with a cane, he spoke in a whisper.

"Remember how they cut the pay of the tram drivers?"

She recalled how the leftist parties had protested.

"We're going to strike against the Berlin Transit Company," he said.

"Do you realize the inconvenience?"

"It'll bring the city to a halt," he said happily.

She'd like to smack him, she thought as they walked to the tram.

He spent days painting signs and making lists of strike participants and their assigned posts. The day of the strike it rained. He didn't deserve to be fed, but at lunchtime she brought him a sandwich. At the depot, tram and bus drivers linked arms and formed a line that snaked around the building. Rain dripped from Max's ears and nose.

"You'll be sick. Let's go home," she said.

Instead he withdrew from his companions and took her to the train station at the Zoo. The line to buy tickets wound its way down the street.

"Chaos," he said proudly.

"What about the little grandma who just wants to catch a train to visit a sick grandchild?"

He looked at her as if she'd spoken Chinese.

They side-stepped puddles, passed parked trams and inactive subway stations. Finally, at the main station, shouts rang out.

Red Front. Heil Hitler.

Picketers surrounded the station. Two figures stood in front of the others. Charlotte recognized the little club-footed Nazi leader, Joseph Goebbels, arm in arm with a stocky man with a mustache. His picture was in Max's literature—the Communist, Walter Ulbricht.

Carrying Max's empty coffee thermos, Charlotte cursed herself for falling in love with a foolish idealist.

19. The Warmth of Acceptance

The Nazi press glowed with reports of the transport strike. Goebbels had given the voters the choice between Bolshevist anarchy and National Socialist order. Voters would choose a strong leader to put an end to the chaos of the republic.

But in the final election of 1932, only 720,000 Berliners voted for Hitler.

Frau Bernstein, with Herr Esch at her shoulder, paced the floor and smoked a pack a day of cigarettes. She mourned the republic even while it still lasted.

But Max was elated over the election.

"Both the Communists and the Nazis are calling the republic the enemy of the little man—seventy percent voted either for the Communists or Nazis."

His mother wasn't impressed. "Then you're both fools."

"We can work it out with the Nazis—we both stand for saving the working class," he said.

Charlotte hummed the song about Jewish blood at the point of a knife.

"Nazis are just a staging post on the way to a fair and just society," he said.

"Why don't you just paint?" Charlotte asked.

"Somebody has to save Germany."

Feeling guilty for thinking him a fool, she put her arms around his waist, laid her cheek against his, vowed to forgive him for his absurd idealism.

Later that week, at Frau Bernstein's, Max talked about the election, how they might have to sacrifice the republic for the tenement dweller who divided a potato five ways. His mother picked a piece of tobacco off the tip of her tongue and examined it thoughtfully. She turned to Charlotte.

"When Max was a boy, he begged me to let him visit a factory. So I took him to see my friend—his company produced tram tracks. We went in wearing goggles and ear covers. Max loved it—tugged on the sleeves of the workers. 'How do you like your job?' he kept asking. Imagine, eleven years old."

Max pulled a stray silk thread from the sofa's upholstery. Frau Bernstein went on.

"He stayed in his room after school, drawing pictures of workers demonstrating and striking. Wouldn't wear a suit to Bernstein's—said it set him apart from the workers."

The wedding was to take place in the middle of January 1933. *Much too cold,* Charlotte's old aunts said. But they disappointed Charlotte by promising to come anyway. She went over the guest list—friends and business associates of Frau Bernstein's, a few artists, some of Max's school friends, and girls from Charlotte's high school class.

Max wanted to get married in the French Cathedral on the Gendarmenmarkt, a refugee church, he pointed out. Expelled from France, the Huguenots built this church to look just like the one in Charenton that the Catholics destroyed in 1688.

Cheated out of playing a Middle Eastern princess beneath the majestic Moorish cupola of the New Synagogue on the Oranienburgerstrasse, Charlotte let Max know she'd just as soon get married on a tennis court.

"I've never liked churches or synagogues—except for the statues and paintings," he said. So Frau Bernstein had her way and reserved a bank lobby for the wedding.

The flower-decorated tellers' windows seemed a poor

replacement for a golden dome, Charlotte thought. Still Frau Bernstein arranged for paintings of the prophets Isaiah and Jeremiah to be displayed among bank interest rate charts.

On her wedding day, Charlotte's black dress slid like cold-blooded skin over her arms, settling into place on her body. Her mother stood in the doorway wearing a dark blue suit, wrinkled after a decade of hanging against the back of the closet. A black pillbox crowned the ensemble.

"You can't wear that," Charlotte said.

"Who cares—it's a Bolshevik wedding," her mother said petulantly.

"Bernstein's not Bolshevik."

"I won't go," her mother said.

"Nobody'll miss you."

Later, Charlotte stood by the door while her father, in woolen knee pants, called the taxi. A noise from the bedroom. Her mother appeared in a purple silk dress, familiar from the old photographs. She pulled her shoulders back and strode out the door and down the steps ahead of them. Her father clasped his wallet, letting them know as they sat pressed tightly against one another that it wasn't every day that they traveled by taxi to the Gendarmen Markt.

At the bank, the judge, a friend of Frau Bernstein's, greeted them. Men in dark suits and women in furs sat on folding chairs. Besides the Old Testament prophets, Frau Bernstein had hung paintings bought at auction—the annunciation, the nativity, and the assumption—all in gold frames. Daniel in the Lion's Den hung directly behind the lectern.

Charlotte's school friends looked pinched from poor food and guarded conversations. But Lulu, like a curly-haired cherub with bright red lips, wore a fitted coat that underlined her bosom. The bank lobby rang with Bach's cello sonatas played by members of the national symphony.

Then silence. A rubber shoe squeaked on the marble. Charlotte looked into Max's eyes. They were the same blue as the sky in the Munster-Eifel oil painting behind the lectern, part of the bank's permanent collection.

Afterwards, Max and Charlotte posed in front of the Schiller monument outside on the square, pressing against one another for warmth, her parents and his mother flanking them like off balance columns in a Greek temple. The old aunts refused to be on the photo, jumped instead into the first taxi.

"Always you and me," Max whispered in her ear. His voice sent a quiver across her belly. How would she get through the wedding meal without sliding her fingers across his navel? She longed for his smell free of the perfume of the relatives.

The Café Kranzler was brightly lit, and Frau Bernstein, red highlights in her hair, glided from table to table, extending an elegant hand, kissing a powdered cheek, smiling at a compliment.

Is the stuffed oxtail to your liking? The wine sauce piquant enough?

And when Frau Bernstein turned, Charlotte tilted her head to enjoy the warmth of acceptance on her cheek.

20. A Bright Red Dot

Under a blaze of torches the brownshirted stormtroopers and the blackshirted SS sang at the top of their lungs as they marched from the Tiergarten through the Brandenburg Gate. Max and Charlotte watched from the window of Frau Bernstein's house.

Frau Bernstein blew out smoke rings.

"Such fun. Follow the leader."

A short man holding a glass of whisky with both hands stood next to her. He opened his mouth and sang:

As long as Unter den Linden the old trees are bloomin'
Nothing can overcome us, Berlin is always Berlin!

"No, Rudolf." Frau Bernstein tapped the singer on the wrist.

Charlotte knew he owned the next biggest department store in the city, next after Bernstein's, and that he and Frau Bernstein often had dinner together. Max compared his mother to Queen Elizabeth I of England. She'd never give up her throne for a man. Like a poet studying a pond for signs of life, Rudolf looked into his glass, then up at Max.

"I don't give your Commies much time."

"No, Rudolf." Frau Bernstein's voice was sharp.

That night Max made fierce love to her, as if their lust could fend off the Third Reich. Afterwards, she slid her hands down his sweating back and held him until he slept. Her own inner eye—the organ that normally overflowed with colors and shapes for paintings—stared all night long at eager florid faces, distorted by blazing torches.

The next day, too tired to paint, she spent the morning prying wax from between floorboards. A knock at the door startled her.

The mocking expression was the same. Surrounded by Frau Bernstein's crystal, marble, and silver, he'd looked less menacing than he did now, standing in the dim hallway. Herr Esch handed Charlotte a box, then bowed so low that she could chart the furrowed terrain of his head.

"Madam thought you would like these."

Like an elastic springing back, he rose up quickly. Had she imagined the tiny click of his heels? Seeing him shift his weight, she set the box down and took a banknote she'd saved for shopping from her pocket. But he backed away. He was looking not at her but at Max's old poster of Rosa Luxemburg. His expression changed from self-effacement to contempt. Hearing his boots descending the steps, she shut the door and opened the package.

Frau Bernstein's gold-rimmed wine glasses. They'd drunk Riesling from them last week.

At first, Max was pleased with the new chancellor because he handled the Communists gently. But in February, Hitler passed the Law for the Protection of the German People, empowering the police to raid Communist headquarters at the Karl Liebknecht House.

"I know what they want," Max said.

Charlotte was sick of his politics. Wasn't it enough to face the Nazis? Did he also have to mark off an area between the Nazis and the Social Democrats for his party and hate both sides equally? Didn't they have enough trouble?

"They want us to lose our tempers and attack the police and the Social Democrats, so they can eliminate us as a threat to the Reich," Max said.

"And will you?"

She mustn't get angry now. But it was all gibberish, Stalin wanting friendly relations with the Nazis, not allowing the German Communists to rebel against the Nazis. Max's altruistic belief in equality was being manipulated by a dictator in another country.

"I don't like lying low when I'm angry and ready to strike."

Used to lying low, she hadn't spoken above a whisper since the stormtroopers took posts in their stairwell. Late one night, he moved restlessly in the bed.

"My mother wants to leave Germany," he said.

"She's right."

"They can't chase us out of our own country."

She only hummed the tune, but he knew the words.

When Jewish blood spurts from the knife.

"They'll go after Bielski, not me," he said.

Later she heard him get up and go into his studio. In the gray dawn, she eased herself off the bed and stepped onto the rag rug—they'd bought it last week from the second hand dealer in Kreuzberg—and pushed open the little window, breathed in the smell of coal smoke and damp streets, heard a tram bell clang and tires slurp over wet streets.

Despite his two old sweaters, she shivered as she dumped two heaping spoonfuls of coffee into the cloth bag, then poured the boiling water. The bed creaked, and she heard him padding towards his studio. He shut the door behind him. Hugging her arms, she paced the floor. At last, she knocked on his door.

No answer. She turned the knob.

He stood in the middle of the floor in his underwear, a paintbrush in his hand. Behind him was a sprawling, colorful canvas, full of figures clad in robes, hunched over carts stacked high with necklaces, socks, fish. The Hacke'sche Markte. He'd filled a canvas with peddlers. In the foreground, a white-clad figure bolted from the scene.

"I thought—"

But he turned from her toward the painting and placed a bright red dot on one of the carts. She picked up a pencil stub and wrote him a note—bread, onions, potatoes, sausage—and left it on the kitchen table.

21. I Won't Abandon My Country

Max spent the day pacing the floor barefoot. But next morning he put on his shoes and soaped his face to shave.

"If the SS sees you talking to somebody—" she said. The Nazis were arresting Communists for the Reichstag fire.

He put on his gray suit, the one he'd worn for their wedding. Once he was gone, she caught herself staring at the door, willing his return. By evening she was certain that he wouldn't come back. She'd heard the gossip in the bakery. The Nazis had arrested thousands of Communists for the Reichstag fire.

But finally, the key clicked in the lock. He slipped in, closed the door behind him, and stood in front of her like a little boy. His voice trembled.

"I went to the house where we used to meet. The Nazis had sealed it up—doors, windows, everything."

"You shouldn't have gone out."

"I could hear them inside, banging on the walls."

Anger came up in her, oddly directed more at him than at the Nazis.

"I wanted to do something, went to where the window was, but I ducked back into the shadows when I saw the stormtrooper—I'm such a coward."

He put his hands to his face. She led him to a chair and quickly made strong coffee. When she held it to his lips, he gulped it down, then coughed hard, like a man intent on turning inside out.

"On the way back, I heard screams from cellar windows. They got a guy I knew from the picket line—fifty lashes for being a Communist, fifty for being a Jew."

Max stayed indoors for three days after that, and Charlotte's spirits rose. Perhaps she could keep him after all.

She went to the bakery to hear the other women whisper. In their search for enemies of the state, the Nazis cleared out whole workers districts, broke down doors of tenements, and confiscated weapons, leaflets, books. If they didn't kill you on the spot, they sent you to Gestapo headquarters in Prinz Albrecht Strasse.

Then he went out again. While he was gone, she ran around town doing nervous errands. She brought food from Bernstein's for her parents—braised pork knuckles and sauerkraut—left her father with a large white linen napkin tied around his neck. From there she went to Unter den Linden. Frau Bernstein kissed her on both cheeks. Charlotte breathed in her French perfume, then sat demurely on the edge of the sofa.

"They'll come for Max. He's everything they hate," Frau Bernstein said.

Feet shuffled over the marble floor in the hall. Charlotte glimpsed Herr Esch waving a feather duster over a highboy. When she embraced Frau Bernstein, her mother-in-law felt frail as an undernourished pet.

The Nazis held leftist prisoners in deserted factories and cellars all over the city. But nobody protested, not even the academics. On March 3, 1933, some three hundred university professors declared their support for Hitler. At the end of the month, the Nazis forced all Jewish judges to retire.

Hitler made Charlotte sick—as if she had the flu. She couldn't sleep until the last tram passed over the track below.

Even in the silence, with the window closed, she stared at the wall and wondered when things would stop getting worse.

"Get sleeping pills from Dr. Goldstein," her mother suggested. When the state-run health insurance system denied claims to Jewish doctors, dentists, opticians, pharmacies and clinics, Charlotte decided she'd pay Dr. Goldstein from her earnings.

But when she approached his building, two stormtroopers stood on the steps, hands behind their backs. Inside the building, a third stormtrooper emerged from under the stairwell.

"Can I help you, Miss?"

Behind him, on Dr. Goldstein's mailbox, hung a scrawled sign.

Jewish Doctor—No Aryans.

"I must be in the wrong building," she mumbled, backing away.

The stormtrooper stepped forward and politely held the door for her. She hurried away. Her mother greeted her, holding a furniture rag. Mondays she polished. Tuesdays she baked. They didn't need a calendar.

"I can't see Dr. Goldstein," Charlotte said.

"When they're done with the Communists, they'll go after the Jews. What will we do about Max?" her mother asked in a thin voice.

Charlotte went into the kitchen and poured herself coffee. Her mother followed her, scribbled a name and address on the back of a receipt, and handed it to her.

"Dr. Wagner's a good German," she said.

"Max is also a good German."

Her mother lowered her voice.

"He helped overthrow the republic—"

"No, you did that—constantly whining about bringing the Kaiser back."

Mouthing the word *Bolshevik,* her mother folded the rag and placed it on the kitchen table.

"My school friend, Irmtraud, just divorced her Jewish husband," she said, pushing down on the rag as if to fasten it to the wood.

"We've only been married two months."

"You may change your mind after the boycott of the Jewish stores. The papers are full of it—*Don't buy from Jews*—what will happen to Bernstein's? Inconvenient. Just before Easter."

Charlotte slammed the door behind her. But going down the stairs, she held the railing to steady herself.

Back home, she turned the key carefully, listened for the sound of his voice. Silence. When Max rose from the sofa, wiping his eyes sleepily, she threw her arms around him and hugged him so tightly that they both rolled onto the floor laughing.

"They turned the old brewery into a concentration camp, Oranienburg—for District 28. I found out what they do," he whispered into her ear.

She turned away from him.

"They knock out your teeth, break your bones, inject acid in your penis so it burns like hell to pee."

He held her in his arms now, forcing her to listen to his hoarse whispers. She shook her head, trying not to hear.

"Those guys—my friends—the ones they sealed up in the building—Neighbors said the sounds stopped."

He released her, and they both got silently to their feet. He sat down at the kitchen table and studied the grain of the wood, running his fingers over the uneven places. For a long time, she was afraid to talk.

"You have to leave," she said at last.

He stared at her, his eyes hot.

"I'll go with you."

"I won't abandon my country."

"Did Stalin help the working classes? No. He chased out the

Social Democrats and fed the little people to the Nazis."

He rose, rubbing his stomach like an old man with dry skin.

22. Raising Flowered Skirts

Charlotte stood on the Schloss Bridge, breathing in the smell of sewage that rose from the water. She climbed the steps to the art museum. The statues of Greek warriors at the entrance provided stony witness to her two resolves. She'd stay with Max. They'd never have a baby. Caspar David Friedrich's moonlit gnarled trees confirmed her view. Life would continue, perhaps without her. Three shadowy figures perched on rocks looked out to sea, waiting for the sucking mouth of the ocean to swallow them.

Van Gogh's orange and gold brush strokes stunned her. She wanted to take them home. From her pocket, she took colored pencils and a tiny notebook, moved her arm back and forth until her elbow gave off heat. Gradually, the distance between herself and the artist fell away. Eyes closed, she kept on drawing. She lay in a field of poppies and marsh marigolds. Above her hung a hot, yellow sun.

"Miss—"

The guard's large face loomed above hers. Her pencils rolled across the wooden floor. The guard bent to pick them up, his knees creaking. Thanking him, she moved on to the German impressionists. But something was missing. The paintings by Max Liebermann and Lesser Ury were gone. She called out—made some sort of sound. The guard suddenly stood before her, the silver buttons on his jacket almost brushing her nose.

"Some paintings are missing," she said.

He looked alarmed. But when she pointed to the discolored rectangles on the wall, relief crossed his face.

"Jews. Gone since last week."

He said it in the tone of a grocer explaining that he was out of turnips.

Won't rutabagas do for your recipe?

"We've got some tree and lake scenes by some real German painters. You'll like them, miss." His voice followed her down the hall.

Walking home, she passed a boarded-up office equipment store. A groan rose from below street level, from the center of a dyspeptic earth. As a child, she'd read a story about a typewriter that screamed. Did filing cabinets groan?

They turn everything into torture chambers.

Afterwards, they would put the bodies on the loading dock for pick-up with the rest of the trash. She quickened her pace, but the sound echoed in her ears.

The door of a nightclub opened, and a boy with brightly rouged cheeks stepped out. Would he look at the audience and giggle while a pot-bellied banker labored over his buttocks? He sauntered along the sidewalk, swinging narrow hips.

The last play she'd seen here had featured a weepy male protagonist. Dead trees and yellowed grass reflected his mood. A breast hung out of the dress of the female lead. He'd scurried upstage.

The Nazis' taste ran to nude dancing at the Haller Review. Photos from the show depicted women with boys' bodies and apricot-sized breasts. They were plastered on the columns next to election posters. Charlotte averted her eyes from the side street, where men in tuxedoes raised flowered skirts with their silver-topped canes.

Her hand around the key in her pocket, she climbed the steps two at a time.

Max was in the kitchen, clipping the newspaper. A small

pile of articles lay next to his hand. She glimpsed a headline.

Germans—honor the boycott of Jewish businesses.

"Working hard?" she asked, hearing her own sarcastic tone.

His scissors squeaked as he cut out an editorial from the *Berliner Tageblatt.*

He was clearly obsessed, a professor in a burning building, analyzing the situation instead of running for the exit. In the studio, she propped up her sketch of Van Gogh's painting and transferred the landscape to the canvas in shades of tangerine. Angling her brush, she slid a thin red stripe of human pain into the sunny countryside.

Breathing calmly now, she glanced at Max's work. The woman's thighs were discolored. From the distance, over her bare shoulder, something black—perhaps a train—was bearing down on her.

Then she saw the other painting, half hidden by the chest of drawers. A wizened man sat on a chair in the middle of a stage, his legs spread wide revealing a swollen limb. A bosomy, red-haired woman pushed two small girls with blond pigtails towards him. The purple of his penis matched the little girls' hair ribbons.

23. I Won't Be a Coward

On the day of the boycott, Charlotte set out for Bernstein's. Signs in shop windows of non-Jews boasted—*Recognized German-Christian Enterprise.* Posters all over the city urged—*Germans Defend Yourselves. Don't Buy From Jews.*

Kohn, the jeweler in the Leipzigerstrasse, stood in front of his shop wearing his iron cross high on his chest. Behind him white paint dripped from letters scrawled on the window—*Germans Don't Buy From Jews.* At the bookstore, a stormtrooper paced, bearing a placard—*World Jewry Wants to Destroy Germany.* The shops along the Ku-damm bore the label *JUDE.*

Charlotte went home to fetch Max. Walking the two blocks to Bernstein's, they heard chanting. *Hang Them. Hang Them.* Nicely dressed people—smartened up for a boycott of Jewish business—gave the Hitler salute.

Max approached the door. Stormtroopers, linked like paperdolls, came toward him. The man in the center looked familiar.

"My mother's in there," he said.

In spite of the full uniform, down to the black boots, Charlotte recognized his smirk. Herr Esch. He said something into Max's ear, turned on his heel, and entered the store. But wasn't Max the heir to the business?

It dawned on her. The Nazis—not the Communists—had grabbed the world and presented it to the little man. Max took her arm, hurried her along. The fragrance of the mimosa

119

bushes at the Pleasure Garden almost gave her a headache.

"The dirty bastard—."

"What did he say?"

"Said he let her out the back door, told her she couldn't come back."

A shrill voice punctured the air. The little man with the slicked-back hair stood at the podium, shouting.

The Jews have ruined the economy. They're behind every evil –ism in the world—Communism, Liberalism, Socialism.

The audience seemed intoxicated by its own chanting.

Hang them. Hang them.

Every day, the Nazis "aryanized" more Jewish shops. They eliminated Jews from banks, the stock exchange, newspapers, law and medicine. Just as Goebbels had promised, the Jews were out of the German economy. Frau Bernstein's friends had no businesses and no jobs. She wrote to her relatives in London, sold her jewelry.

When the Nazis accused her of tax evasion, she sold Bernstein's at a low price.

"I'm leaving," Frau Bernstein told them at dinner on Unter den Linden.

"Sorry," Max said, as if he alone had ruined Germany.

Herr Esch refilled their wine glasses. Frau Bernstein said, "I think we're past the last frost. Time to put down some bulbs."

She gulped down her wine and set the glass on the mahogany table.

"I saw them make an old lady salute. I won't. They'll have to shoot me."

"You'll come back?" Max asked.

"Of course, darling."

"After all, this is your country," he said.

"Not true. Max Liebermann would still be head of the academy if—"

He laid a hand on her shoulder, but she shrugged it away.

Her eyes were little black coals.

"Get out now, both of you."

But Max shook his head, and Charlotte hated him for it.

On the way home, they passed Jewish shops with freshly smashed windows.

"Your mother was right about leaving," Charlotte said.

"I won't be a coward."

"I should divorce you."

"Good idea."

Something exploded inside her. She whirled around and slapped his cheek. The smack echoed off the buildings in the square. A man in uniform approached them. She slipped her arm into Max's and laughed giddily. Weren't lovers allowed to hit one another? The man ambled away.

24. Artemesia

A work crew chopped down the tall linden trees that had lined Frau Bernstein's street. The Fuhrer wanted more room for political marches. Now checker-board waist taxis claimed the space where trees had once stood. A taxi with its motor running waited directly in front of Frau Bernstein's house. Charlotte and Max entered the hall. Frau Bernstein stood beneath the chandelier, her purse under her arm.

"The Jews made Berlin into a great city. Now there's nothing for us here."

She snapped open her purse and fingered identity papers and cash. Max carried the two leather suitcases to the taxi.

When Max embraced his mother, she whispered something. He shook his head. She leaned against his upper arm as he led her down the steps. From inside the taxi window, she waved.

"What did she say?" Charlotte asked.

His eyes met hers briefly. Then he looked away. "'I've paid Herr Esch off.' That's what she said."

She sensed a turning point. Until now he'd never lied to her.

Most nights Charlotte lay awake waiting to hear footsteps in the hall, his key in the lock. Sometimes she woke up in the morning with the weight of his head on her arm.

One night Charlotte paced the kitchen, waiting for him. But when she heard his steps in the hall, she hurried to the sofa and began underlining passages in an old Heinrich Heine poetry book. *Not a drop of blood that's Moorish, neither of foul Jewish current.* Had Heine known? His lips brushed the crown of her head. He disappeared into the kitchen. She followed him. He spread the butter thickly on the roll, took it to the table, didn't bother with a plate.

She wouldn't ask him who was in the group. If she knew, they would come after her too, torture her until she cried out the names.

But he couldn't keep a secret.

"A countess joined our group," he said, chewing his roll.

"Don't tell me her name," Charlotte whispered.

"That means contacts in high circles—a real resistance."

The small sum they'd gotten for Bernstein's was almost gone. And where was Frau Bernstein? Living in Covent Garden? Walking down Bond Street, balancing shopping bags?

Max and Hitler were both born in April. On the Fuhrer's birthday, the Horst Wessel song blared from the radio. The papers featured photos of charcoal and brown dogs, creeping along like wolves—animals honoring Hitler.

The Pleasure Garden—dedicated to the memory of Sophie Charlotte—smelled of cut grass and trumpet vine. The image of sweeping skirts and monumental seventeenth century hairdos crowded out the recent mob's chanting *Hang them. Hang them.*

Christian Gottlieb Cantian's gray granite bowl, shoulderhigh to Charlotte, stood in the center of the garden. She took out her sketchpad and flipped past some bird drawings until she came to a blank page. Closing her eyes, she saw purple reptiles with bloodshot eyes chewing their own tails, apricotcolored monkeys picking bugs from under their arms, fish with emerald eyes laying eggs on the ocean floor. She drew quickly, then took out her gray pencil to create the granite bowl to contain them.

At home, she transferred the drawing to a canvas. In her old flower book, she found the tiny forget-me-not on its muscular hairy white stalk, the drooping bluebells, the cheerful pink with its yellow center. She painted them all growing up from the granite bowl. Finally, she added purple and yellow passion flowers.

When Max came home, the painting was ready. "How's the countess?" she asked.

"Can't talk—just know that something big's going to happen soon."

"Like every day."

"Another march."

"Shut the window, so we don't hear the drums."

"This one's about university students."

That evening they followed the crowd to Unter den Linden and walked past Frau Bernstein's house, occupied by a Nazi official and his family now. Herr Ulrich Esch had brokered the sale and stayed on to work for the new residents. Charlotte and Max followed the torchbearers to Opera Square. Young people ran along the street, their arms full of books. Up ahead, the sky glowed red.

At the bonfire, students were feeding books to the flames.

"Heine's books sold out," Max said. The words rang in Charlotte's head. *Heed not Moors nor Jews, spake the knight with fond endearments.*

A young man stood apart from the others. He had no books, and he was not singing. A stormtrooper nudged him.

"Let's see you salute."

The student put his hands into his pockets.

"Bolshevik, huh?" the brownshirt said and brought brass knuckles down on the student's head. Another stormtrooper joined in. The boy sank soundlessly to the ground.

Charlotte pulled on Max's arm when the kicking began.

Back home, Charlotte threw up in the toilet. She came out of the bathroom, feeling sour and empty as if somebody had pulled the plug on her feelings until they'd drained out. She drank water while Max ate a piece of herring on black bread—his birthday dinner.

She remembered the gift.

"A fantasy from another world," she said, handing him the picture wrapped in newspaper.

He ran his fingers over the monkeys and reptiles, studying the detail.

"Artemesia," he said, reaching for her. For the first time since his mother left, he looked relaxed. Desire—a feeling that Hitler had practically stifled—overwhelmed her. He unbuttoned her dress, and she watched his hands—rough as a worker's now—stroke her breasts. His hair smelled of smoke and dirt. On the couch, they caressed one another. She held herself back, watched herself make love to him, then succumbed at last, letting all her senses explode into pleasure.

25. The Bear Dance

During Kopenick Blood Week, the Nazis arrested and tortured over five hundred people. Charlotte wished Max would stop saving the world and stay home. She couldn't understand why he didn't share her desire to leave Germany. Jews had no jobs. They were banned from public sports fields, gymnasiums, and youth centers. Signs appeared on public park benches and in restaurants.

No Jews Allowed

Max could no longer attend the academy after the Nazis introduced quotas on Jewish entry to schools and universities. He appeared to absorb each indignity. How could his slender body contain it all? One morning in late summer Charlotte found him at the kitchen table staring at the newspaper—not reading just staring. She caught the headline over his shoulder.

Jews are no longer allowed to swim at the Wannsee Lake public beach.

She placed her hands on his shoulders, less from affection than from a need to anchor him and herself. How many years since they'd kissed in the bushes near the lake? He jumped up so quickly that she staggered backwards. He balled up the newspaper, threw it across the room, and strode to the door.

"Careful—" But the door closed on the rest of her warning.

That night he didn't come home. At dawn, exhausted with listening for his footsteps, she set out to look for him. Downstairs she stepped into a drizzly fog. A pair of coal wagon horses shifted their legs and snorted. A man staggered under bags of coal.

At Alexanderplatz, the smell of old beer came from an open door. A young woman, her apron flapping at her ankles, swept cigarette butts into the gutter. Charlotte hurried along.

At the police station, a heavy-lidded officer peered at her.

"My husband—" she began.

He raised an eyebrow.

"Disappeared."

"That's what they do. Every day. Bolshevik?"

She moved her hands as if to hide her face. He came at her from another angle. "A Jew?"

Her lip quivered. She covered her mouth. His breath smelled of yesterday.

"Bolshevik-Jew?" he chirped.

She nodded.

"Probably at the old brewery—Oranienburg. They'll inject acid into—"

She closed her ears. His eyes lit up.

"You his woman?"

She turned and walked away, heard him chanting behind her. *Peck. Peck.* Back home, she curled up on the sofa, shivering, her legs drawn up to her knees. Fear bit into her skin as if her body were pinned up by clothespins. Every night that week she kept the same stiff posture of vigilance.

One night, she lay curled under a blanket on the sofa. Between sleeping and waking, she heard a muffled sound at the door, like a cloth sack of potatoes against wood. *Thud. Thud.* She stumbled to the door. "Who's there?" she whispered. No answer. Slowly she opened the door. A punched-in, bloody-faced creature covered in rags stood in the hall. His mouth was a purple mass, his eyes sunk in puffy bruised flesh. Then she saw the leather patch on the elbow of his sweater.

Max.

She placed his arm over her shoulder and half carried him to the sofa, then rolled him carefully onto his stomach. He whimpered into the sofa cushions when she cut the sweater shreds from the sores on his back. Deep cuts puckered his back in a criss-cross pattern. She soaked towels in cold water, wrung them out, and laid them on his back. He stretched arms forward, and his fingers gripped the arm of the sofa.

Stupid Max. They could be sitting in Hyde Park with Frau Bernstein, painting ducks and trees.

"What did they do?" she asked.

A sound came from his throat, not words. For several days he slept fitfully, often crying in his sleep. One morning, when she was changing his bandages, he spoke. She brought her ear to his mouth. "Whipped us with hippo hide. Guards— they peed in my mouth."

She said nothing.

"Smashed in our noses and teeth. Made us do the bear dance. Big boots. No laces. They laughed. Made us jump. More. More. Made us sing nursery rhymes."

He seemed to have difficulty breathing. "Shhh," she said, touching his head. His hair felt unfamiliar, like fur pasted on his head. "Shhh."

His voice had a croak in it, as if it were coming from a narrow place. "There's more."

Studying the new bald spot on his head, she waited. His back and shoulders trembled. She covered him with the blanket, but she couldn't stop his crying. At last he said it.

"We beat one another."

His whole body shook. Choking sounds came from his chest. He went on like this for a long time until finally, like a broken engine grinding slowly to a halt, he stopped and lay quietly and slept.

One morning, he lay on his stomach while she changed the compresses. He raised his head from the pillow.

"One day I refused to punch my cellmate. Guard threw me

down. Kicked me. Alright I'll do it. They stood me up. And I punched my friend. He punched me. They kept standing us up. *Hit him. Hit him.* Laughing. When I stopped, the guard punched me. I went crazy. I kept hitting my friend and hitting him. Finally, he fell. They held him up, but his legs were like jelly. And then—"

She placed a fresh compress on his back. He winced.

"And then—he died. I killed him."

A groan came from somewhere deep inside him. More from the center of his soul than his lungs.

"It wasn't you—" she said.

"It was—it was."

Each day, she rubbed salve into his sores. Gradually, he got better. One day he stopped talking about life in prison. Later that day, he asked her to help him put on his shoes.

Standing at the door, he hesitated over the door handle as if he'd forgotten how to go out. A scar had formed next to his mouth. He walked with a limp, and he clutched his collar by the lapels.

"I'm going for a newspaper," he said apologetically.

"If you don't come back, I'll never forgive you."

In 1935, the Nazis crossed the threshold of Charlotte's bedroom with the Nuremberg Laws, the Reich Citizenship Law and the Law for the Protection of German Blood and German Honor. Jews could no longer vote and were forbidden to marry or have sexual relations with Gentiles. The child of a marriage between a Jew and a gentile was a *Mischling*.

She mustn't become pregnant.

The sign appeared in restaurant windows and at the cinema box office.

Jews not desired.

The new laws quickened old embers that smoldered in Charlotte's parents. That Sunday when Charlotte visited her parents, she discovered a Nazi publication, lying next to her father's elbow. Her father had encircled the update on racial incidents: *Jew arrested for raping Aryan neighbor.*

Her mother looked up from her baking. "All the Jewish accountants in your father's office are gone."

"Don't tell me about it," Charlotte begged.

"You know the Jewish spinster on the first floor?"

Charlotte walked away, but her mother raised her voice. "Yesterday the baker refused to wait on her."

"Does it concern me?" Charlotte asked.

"It's a bad time for Jews—" and without stopping for a breath, "The Cohen woman divorced her Jewish husband—didn't want to be defiled by a Jew in the marriage bed."

Her father's compressed lips underlined his wife's words. Mornings for thirty years, he'd packed a lunch in his briefcase and strapped it to his bike. Evenings, the briefcase had contained a banana peel and an old newspaper. He didn't break patterns.

"Max can't blend in now," her mother said, as if he were an odd-colored jungle animal.

She kneaded the dough with quick, vigorous movements. "After Frau Cohen divorced her husband, her brother got his job back with the government."

A happy ending. Charlotte hated her mother for thinking that.

Back in the days when she was bringing food from Bernstein's, her mother hadn't talked to her like that. She'd heated up the fillets of zander with radish-filled pancakes and poured the Charlottenburger Pilsener beer for her husband. They'd especially liked the berry compote with vanilla sauce, Bernstein's best dessert.

26. A Dolphin-like Creature

Charlotte woke up with a metallic taste in her mouth. Her throat felt furry when she swallowed. The thought of bread and butter made her stomach form a fist—still she was hungry. Wine puckered her lips, and coffee tasted nutshell bitter. No sign of blood yet. She was often late. But as she marked the days on her calendar with an x, a chill crept up the back of her neck. Her calendar picture, Grock the clown, mocked her. "A mistake," her mother said, pinching Charlotte's pale cheeks. A mistake, even before Charlotte told her.

Max's eyes widened at the news. For weeks, he ate only crackers, went to bed early, waited for her to cross the imaginary line on their mattress, and reach for him. He would carry the baby in his belly if only she'd let him, he told her.

She lived each day by the hour, chewing a bread crust and sipping malt beer—just enough to take the edge off her hunger without awakening the slumbering throw-up serpent. She shut the studio door against the greasy paint odor that made her stomach heave. Even the empty canvas had a smell.

On the way to the butcher's she sucked on a bit of chocolate to keep down the nausea. But the smell of blood overwhelmed her, and she raised a hand to her mouth while the butcher packaged her sausages. She ducked down a side street to vomit. After that Max bought their meat. He'd have to cook it too, she told him.

To regain her balance, she tried knitting. But forcing the needles through holes in the pastel-colored wool only tightened her stomach. She couldn't paint, and without the painting, her mood sank. One night, she lay trembling in Max's arms.

"I don't want a baby," she sobbed.

He dried her eyes with his fingers, told her to cry quietly. The neighbors.

Actions crowded her mind—the stormtroopers kicking the student, men beating one another with rods, Frau Bernstein leaving for London. Suddenly, she remembered.

"What did your mother say when she left?"

In the darkness, his breathing seemed loud.

"What?" she pressed.

He spoke in a ragged whisper.

"'Don't have a baby'—that's what she said."

The world no longer existed outside on the noisy street, nowhere but beneath her navel. When she could, she worked at the café—setting down the coffee pot and running to heave the contents of her stomach into the tiny toilet—furtively wiping perspiration off her forehead with her sleeve when she returned.

But after the first three months, when the dried crust on a closed paint tube no longer brought the bile into her throat, Charlotte started painting again. She sat at the kitchen table daubing the plover's orange beak on a miniature canvas from a photo in a bird book. The stocky little bird waded into the surf on legs like orange elbows bent backwards. In the corner of the page, she drew white speckled eggs. Her world shrank to a nest for Max, herself, and the baby.

At the museum, she moved quickly past the mutilated Greek torsos and the noseless head of Pericles towards the fleshy legs of the Christ Child and the rosy bosom of the Virgin Mary.

She and Max no longer made love in the usual hungry way.

Max lit a candle on the nightstand and, in the flickering light, stroked her swelling breasts and full hips. Then he lay back and talked about Georg Grosz—" that painting, the Agitator, that's how I feel."

Next day, at the gallery, she studied Grosz' sprawling paintings full of people doing hateful things to one another. The creature growing inside her kicked her.

One evening when she was in her eighth month, Max prepared dinner for her, washed the dishes afterwards, called over his shoulder that she should lie down, carried her to bed, made love to her with gentle strokes, circumventing their treasured centerpiece. Afterwards, he untangled his arms and legs from hers, taking care not to touch the belly that protruded into their future.

At night she lay awake while the baby pushed against the small of her back. Towards morning, Max caressed her belly, first along the sides, then over the top. She put her hands on his, and together they traveled over her skin, stopping when they felt the baby kick.

"Cramps in your legs?" he asked.

"Yes," she lied.

He rubbed her shins until the rhythmic movement made her drowsy. But the weight of the baby and the placenta pulled her into the mattress until Max placed one hand under the baby, the other under her shoulder, and rolled her over. Then he snuggled up behind her, his fingers exploring her belly, seeking the outline of tiny feet and fists. At last they slept, all three of them.

Soon her belly began brushing against café customers, and the manager asked her to stay home. Charlotte spent mornings lying in a bath fragrant with gardenia from Frau Bernstein's bath powders. When her strained muscles relaxed, the baby tried the usual jailbreak, this time kicking so hard at the wall of its marine world that the outline of a tiny heel appeared on her belly. A dolphin-like creature would swim out from between her legs into the warm water, slither along her hip, then splash to the surface. Charlotte closed her eyes. That's how it would be.

27. The Bear's Foot

The Nazis cleaned up for the 1936 Olympic games. Overnight the signs—*No Jews or Animals* and *Jews, the Road to Palestine Does Not Go Through Here*—disappeared.

Elderly Jews reappeared on park benches, their faces raised to the sun. Hitler was trying to convince visitors that he was not a hate-filled fanatic. Swastika banners and flags from all the German towns hung on the government buildings on Unter den Linden. The Brandenburg Gate was covered with flags and garlands.

Max wanted to visit a restaurant, an old favorite. The *Jewish Customers Not Desired* sign was gone. Bowing low, the waiter took their order for beetroot soup and spicy meatballs and veal with German noodles and herb dumplings.

"It won't last," she said, tipping her soup spoon sideways like he'd taught her.

But he wasn't in the mood for that kind of reality.

"The lower class—" he said, sipping his wine.

If only she could get him out of Germany, but his roots ran deeper than hers.

"—never gets what it needs. Krupp and Thyssen get rich off the poor devils' backs."

He talked of his dead heroine, Rosa Luxemburg. Her father called her "Bolshevik fish food" because her body had been dumped into the canal where it rotted all winter.

"People gobble down roast duck while the unemployed warm their hands over tin cans fires in tent cities," he said, slicing the tender veal.

Next day at the procession of the Olympic flame one hundred thousand spectators cheered when the airship Hindenburg floated over the stadium. Twenty thousand white pigeons flying up into the blue sky gave Charlotte a sense of hope. Another world must lie beyond this choked society.

It was a hot, humid morning, and Charlotte lumbered up the stairs, carrying canned goods and bread. Sweat formed under her sleeves. She blew like a bellows at every landing. Her skin felt like it would rip away from her sides, and the baby would drop to the floor. Inside the apartment, she turned on the radio. Stadium crowds cheered.

Jesse Owens the black American runner has won the race.

When Charlotte laughed, something inside her gave way, and warm liquid trickled down her leg. She reached between her legs. The water flowed over her hand into a puddle on the floor. No. She wasn't ready. Groaning, she went down on all fours and wiped the floor with a dishcloth. Digging her fingers into the kitchen counter, she raised herself from the floor. Water ran down both her legs.

When Max walked in the door, she lay on the sofa breathing hard.

"I'll call a taxi," he said, stroking her damp hair.

Shuddering under a contraction, she pushed him away. No money for that. They'd wasted it on dinner. He helped her to her feet, peeled off her wet clothes until she stood naked, like a huge leaking animal. Her body bore down on her like a runaway train. She could barely push her arms into the sleeves of the big cotton dress he held out for her.

A few minutes later, she sat next to Max in the front seat of the tram, a small suitcase between her feet, digging her fingers into his arm with each contraction. Stop it, she barked when Max stroked her knee. The flowing water formed a secret stream between her legs. The wetness of her seat humiliated her. Another contraction. The baby ripped at her muscles.

In the hospital bed, she writhed and sweated.

A woman in a stiff, white dress came towards her carrying a Great War gas mask like her father had worn. Was this a military hospital? The nurse placed a dead frog over her nose. She tried to push her away but she drifted on the smells of pond and rubber.

The world beyond the window was dark when she woke up. Charlotte glanced at the calendar on the wall. Still August. The frogwoman was at her side, stroking some creature. It had a flat nose and puffy cheeks in a red face.

The woman's voice rolled like something from inside a cave. Charlotte touched her belly. Gone. The frogwoman held a dead thing. She understood. It was a doll to comfort her. Her eyes brimmed over, not for herself but for Max. He would be disappointed.

"Go away."

But the pushy tart inched up to Charlotte's arm, placed the old, wrinkled doll on her chest. It was still warm from the tart's body. Then Charlotte saw the tiny movement. Its rosebud mouth quivered. She grasped its body with both hands, brought it to her nose and sniffed. Then she inhaled deeply. New human life had its own smell.

The first night back home, Max didn't miss a feeding. In fact, he was the first to hear the mewling cries before they became piercing screams. Charlotte sensed his fingers on the buttons of her nightgown, the baby's codlike mouth clamping her sore nipple, the sharp pull in her groin. Coming awake, she nosed the soft spot on Lena's head where the skull had not yet knit together. Her eyes met Max's over the infant's downy hair. Gently, he eased Lena over to the other breast.

• • •

Through the network of brave individuals ready to give their lives for a better world, Max met a botanist who was not afraid to hire a Jew. Wildflowers. Could Max draw and paint them? Of course. Anything. A whole book? A whole library. Whatever the botanist wanted.

At first Max got blurred vision from studying tiny hairs on stalks and leaves. He rode the tram into the countryside beyond Potsdam and took photographs of lady's slipper, hibiscus, and chickweed. Sometimes he cut wisteria, honeysuckle, and yarrow in the fields on the outskirts of the city, brought them home to paint. The smell of flowers in the apartment promised survival.

Accustomed to painting big shapes, Max squinted at roots, tubers, nodes, lines in the petals, details he had to capture on canvas before the plant withered. He studied botanical drawings from the Renaissance, done for the Medici family in Florence, tracing the swollen and desiccated nodes on the tuber of a spotted orchid by Bartolomeo Bimbi. When Charlotte paced the floor, burping Lena, he held up Bimbi's drawing of a cauliflower and a horseradish.

"Look at the legs and belly on that."

She developed an attachment to each of Max's nature paintings and missed them when they went to the botanist. At night men cut other men's throats on the streets below, but the little family cuddled together in its warm cocoon.

Sometimes after a feeding, Charlotte got out of bed and looked at the flower painting that would be gone the next day. The deep blue, fringed gentian with its flared petals was named after King Gentius of Illyria. Its roots could cure all things, including listlessness in love, but the flower was so delicate that it opened its petals only in sunshine.

The next day, with Lena sucking contentedly at her breast, Charlotte remembered the gentian and wondered if she could paint what lay hidden within flowers, something beyond the botanist's truth.

Max spent hours on the nectar tubes of the bell-like columbine, the sticky leaves of the carnivorous common butterwort, the white hairs on the stalk of the forget-me-not. But he also did sketches of Lena. By the time she was a year old, his drawings recorded every stage of her development—rolling over, pulling herself up, taking her first steps.

When she began to walk, she held onto the arms of the sofa, then dropped back to a crawl, later pulling herself up by a table leg. He followed her, sometimes crawling too, all the time making circles on paper, rendering her head, her trunk, her bottom from every angle. In his "mood" series, he depicted Lena sucking her thumb, laughing, brooding, then pinned a sketch to his easel and transferred Lena to a canvas.

After covering Jesse Owens' victory over the stocky Aryan runners, the foreign journalists left Berlin. The signs reappeared. A poster on the information column at the Ku-damm made Charlotte's skin prickle.

Without a solution to the Jewish question, no solution for the German nation.

Like before Jesse Owens, Jews only shopped at designated times against the backdrop of words scrawled on the wall of an abandoned building—Martin Luther's words.

The father of the Jews is the devil.

Swimming pools were off limits. Jews had to carry identity papers at all times. The worst ban for Max was the one forbidding Jews to ride the tram. For a few weeks he ignored it, rode into the country to collect flowers, then traveled across town with flower drawings under his arm for the botanist. But one day, he was sitting on the tram when two Gestapo agents entered at the Zoo station. One stood in the front and glared at the passengers.

"I smell garlic," he said.

Max fixed his eyes on the conductor's pay box.

The other agent approached the man seated next to Max and demanded his papers. Fumbling through his pockets, the man jabbed Max's side. His elbow felt warm, like an extension of his own skin. No papers. Through the window, Max glimpsed the man lying on the sidewalk, arms raised to protect his face. The tram pulled away, and Max faced forward. That night he whispered to Charlotte under the blanket. *His face was bloody. I couldn't help him. Just sat there.*

Next day she sat on the edge of the bed, sewing the hem on Lena's dress, waiting for him to return. Fool, going out at night. She wished she could lock him in the closet. And working with that resistance group, pinning his hopes on some countess. The hem grew crooked. She ripped out the stitches, then pricked her finger. Squealing, she barely heard him at the door. When he was finally inside with the door closed behind him, she blurted out the question, the one she didn't want answered because knowing wasn't safe.

"Who's this countess?"

He leaned forward and whispered into her ear. "Russian, a Romanov."

"How can a Romanov be working with a bunch of Communists?"

"Not just with the Communists—" he said, placing a hand on her knee. Normally, this gesture signaled intimacy. And before long she'd be in his lap. But now it meant only one thing. *Quiet. Or we're both dead.*

With his other hand he moved her chin so that their eyes met.

"They've arrested her," he said.

Charlotte searched his face for fear, came up empty-handed.

"Go underground," she said.

He shook his head.

"Our friends will hide you."

"I won't live like that, hiding in a closet, waiting for food, handing out a tin can of excrement to the people who risk their lives for me."

When she woke up next morning, he was still at his easel,

left over from the night before. His eyes were bloodshot, but his gestures were calm and his expression peaceful, as if he'd come to terms with something. On the easel was a painting of Lena, surrounded by flowers. She was laughing. Her eyes radiated hope.

Later, after he'd gone out, she went to the portrait and gazed at it. Gradually she began to see what she'd missed before. Within Lena's vitality lay its opposite—a sad lethargy. Max had placed something sinister behind the happy moment he had captured. Or had she uncovered something hidden, hidden even from him?

Christmas diverted Charlotte from the Gestapo, the Communists, the countess, and the humiliation of the Jews. She needed a teddy bear for Lena. That meant going to Bernstein's under the Aryan owners who'd bought it for a low price.

Nothing had changed in the store—the bright lights, the ornate columns, and the glittering display cases. She bought a bear with an intelligent face and brown glassy eyes.

It'll last for years, the clerk told her. The arms wouldn't come off when Lena dragged it around. Back home, Charlotte found a scrap of cloth and threaded the embroidery needle. She plunged her needle into the fabric, pulled it out again, formed knots, undid them, stitched words into the distorted little rag.

Lena Bernstein, born 1936.

She removed the felt pad on the bear's right foot and pulled out some stuffing. With a knitting needle, she pushed the cloth into the bear's foot and sewed the pad back on.

28. A Yellow and Blue Dress

When Germany attacked the Soviet Union in 1941, Charlotte ran the water in the sink so she could listen to the short wave radio. They drank the last of Frau Bernstein's Riesling wine to celebrate the poor performance of the *Reichswehr*.

But the Nazis decided to blame the Jews for the German defeat at Stalingrad. In September of that year, Charlotte had to stitch a yellow star on Max's jacket. If she didn't, the neighbors downstairs would turn them in. And if she did, sooner or later the Gestapo would pick him up.

At first Max wore his other jacket, the one without the star. But when the Gestapo beat up the Jews down the street for not complying with the badge law, he stayed indoors sketching the gray hairy stems of the chamomile.

Evenings, Charlotte turned hems and darned holes in socks until the original fabric formed a slender bridge between darnings. Days, she swept the floor, washed windows again and again, scraping an imaginary spot with her fingernail. For dinner, she chopped onions and cooked potatoes with a thumb length of sausage for flavor.

Lena, age five now, sang along with her—"Monday's baking day, Tuesday's washday. Every day's shopping day." At night Charlotte lay in bed tightening and releasing the muscles in her legs, feet, and hands. When that didn't bring sleep, she recited one of her mother's recipes—apple cake, one cup of flour, four tablespoons butter, a half teaspoon of cinnamon.

Slice the apples very, very, very thin.

One night, Max pressed against her back. His lips touched her ear.

"Keep Lena safe."

His heart pounded against her shoulder blade.

"Of course."

He fell back to his side of the bed.

When Charlotte cooked, Lena sat under the kitchen table drawing eggs in a bird's nest, speckling each egg with her pencil point. Sometimes she sat behind Max, talking to her bear, while he painted at the easel. The botanist had requested marsh marigolds and wild geraniums. After drawing the scientific version of each flower, Max blended the flowers together in a sprawling painting of yellow and blue blossoms.

At supper, Lena ignored the steaming potatoes on her plate. She stroked Charlotte's arm.

"Can you make me a yellow and blue dress?"

She sighed. No more sewing. Lena watched her over the rim of her glass.

If only she hadn't gotten pregnant, Charlotte thought. She'd been so careful. "I'll see if grandma has some material," she said at last.

Lena banged her feet happily against the legs of her chair.

Clutching her ration card, Charlotte set out early to shop. On the sidewalk stood a group of people. Each one held a small suitcase. Stars yellow as canaries brightened their dark coats. A truck pulled up. Without a word, they climbed into the back. Bielski came into Charlotte's mind. Rivka.

The next day the letter arrived. Charlotte opened it while Max slept. He was to report to the collection point in the Grosse Hamburgerstrasse. At breakfast she handed it to him. He read it and slipped it back into the envelope as if it were redeemable at his convenience.

Charlotte mouthed the words over Lena's head. "Somebody can hide you."

"It's nothing. Just means going to the East."

"East? What is it?" Lena chirped.

"A place for uppity Berlin Jews, so they can meet the little people in skullcaps and black cloaks, their fellow Jews," Max said as if Lena were not a child.

Charlotte placed a finger on her lips. But the letter had unleashed something in him.

"It's a resettlement scheme," he said. "—to knock the pomp out of the 'good German' Jews, the ones like me—the ones who look down on the pickled herring peddlers, the ones who think Bielski is of a different race from the rest of us Jews."

His cheeks were flushed from some inner fire she couldn't understand. Her own skin was cold with dread.

"Can you pack me a suitcase? Just enough paints for the trip to the East?" he asked in a polite voice, as if they barely knew one another.

Charlotte took the suitcase from the closet—the same one she'd brought to the hospital. Max was in bed before her. Lena lay asleep curled up in the middle of their bed, like a spoiled pet. Charlotte picked her up and carried her to her own bed. In the bathroom, she washed carefully. Finally, she applied the last drops of fragrance from one of Frau Bernstein's bottles. Then she undressed very slowly. Max lay on his back, waiting, his eyes open.

He lifted the sheet, and she crept under the covers. He drew her hungrily to him, wrapped his legs tightly around hers. They climbed upwards with a hard, painful pleasure towards the climax. At the top, came relief, not well being. But even as he was deep inside her, she sensed the cold beyond the magic circle of their locked bodies. When he withdrew, she placed a hand over her mouth. He must not hear her sob.

Next morning he stood facing her in the hall, the suitcase in his hand. He looked apologetic, not frightened. His cheek touched hers for a second—long enough for her to sense the otherness of his skin.

"Don't go."

But he left, and she cursed him for being gone.

The next morning before dawn, Charlotte left Lena sleeping, ran down the side streets, avoiding the streetlights. As she approached the collection point, she heard the shouts of officers and the growling of their dogs. Ordinary looking people climbed into the back of the trucks. But Max was not among them.

Every day she went. Finally, at the end of the second week, she saw him. He sat in the back of the truck, wedged between two men in threadbare jackets. His eyes looked into hers for a second, then down at the toes of his scuffed boots. By dismissing her, he was making it easier for her—she knew that. For a long time she'd wanted him to fear the Nazis, fear them enough to run away. But now she prayed he was still unafraid.

When the truck pulled out and lumbered over the curb, she stared until it was gone. Then she stood in the spot where Max once had been. On the pile of suitcases, she saw the label in red letters. Would the Gestapo send it to him? A dog growled next to her thigh. She drew back.

At home, she crawled into bed, curled up around Lena to warm herself. But Lena stretched and began the little movements that preceded her waking. Charlotte studied her curls, the vibrations of her eyelids. Perhaps it was the light, but she thought she saw a worry line between the eyebrows.

Suddenly the child's eyes opened.

"Is Papa back yet?"

"Still with the relatives," she said airily.

Lena got up and crept under the table where she kept her colored pencils and paper. Charlotte studied the hairs on Max' pillowcase. She drew the pillow to her chest and breathed in the smell of his scalp. She imagined a thick-fingered Nazi opening the little brown suitcase, squeezing the expensive paints onto a palette, then painting pornography. She ran her lips over the Bernstein monogram on the pillowcase, swore never to change it.

The next day, she and Lena moved back to her parents' home.

Charlotte and her mother were wiping out cupboards. Standing at the sink, rinsing out her rag, her mother narrowed her eyes, and gestured towards the bedroom where Lena slept.

"You've got to hide her."

Charlotte shook her head. "I'm going to make her a dress. Do you have any yellow and blue scraps?"

Her mother glared at her, but Charlotte didn't drop her gaze. Finally her mother brought a chair to the hall closet and began to search. Lena came out of the bedroom carrying a book about tigers.

"Read it," the child pleaded.

It had been hours since Charlotte had held Lena. She reached for her and hugged her until the child struggled for release. Then she read the book three times. Her mother was unfolding cloth on the dining room table, comparing blues. She eyed Charlotte curiously when she started to read for the fourth time.

Once upon a time there was a bear who wanted to be a human.

This time Lena shook her head, and Charlotte let her go. Her mother was placing the long strips of yellow cotton next to swatches of blue. "I know a nun," she said. Charlotte moved away, but her mother went on. "She's an old classmate—runs a convent school." She waved a hand to indicate somewhere outside of Berlin. "Boards non-Catholic children," she whispered.

Charlotte frowned. "She's only five years old."

"Who's only five years old?" a child's voice said. Lena picked up several strips of cloth and skipped around the room.

"Stop it. The neighbors."

Lena dropped the fabric and ran to her grandmother. Charlotte took the sewing box from under the bed. Long after her mother and Lena had gone to bed, she was still sewing. Next morning she woke up late. The sun's rays slanted across the bed, catching the half-stitched yellow and blue dress that lay at the foot of the bed. A stray sense of happiness came over Charlotte followed by guilt. She hadn't thought of Max since sometime yesterday.

"Grandma needs bread," a small voice said. Lena stood in the door holding a shopping net. On the way back from the bakery, Lena swung the loaf of bread in the shopping net and sang to herself. *All my little ducklings swim on the lake.*

As they approached their building, Charlotte glanced at the window of the first floor apartment. A little girl with a thin face peered at them. Charlotte had seen the girl's mother earlier that day, walking with hunched shoulders. Some people did that to hide the yellow star.

Now Lena saw the girl and waved. Between the lace curtains a hand moved back and forth. Lena ran towards the building, but another face appeared in the window, and the girl withdrew into darkness. Lena stopped and stared at the window.

A few days later, Charlotte watched as Lena rolled a hoop in the courtyard below. The sound of argument came from the first floor apartment. Two women emerged. One held a clock above her head. "Mine," said the other. The first woman raised her arms higher and ran across the courtyard. Lena disappeared into the apartment. "No," Charlotte called to herself and ran downstairs. Two men were carrying out a sofa. Charlotte found Lena inside the apartment, staring at the empty walls.

"Where's the girl?" she asked.

"Must've moved," Charlotte said, taking Lena's hand.

"I wanted to play with her," the child pouted.

Max had sat in the back of the truck, looking down at his boots. Too many people went East. The women in the bakery whispered about how people who went East never wrote letters. Later that day, Charlotte left Lena with her grandmother baking pancakes with dark flour and watered-down milk. At the Alexanderplatz station she asked about Max. An officer with full lips and glassy eyes shrugged in her direction. At the collection point, she presented another question. *How do I write to somebody who's gone East?* The uniformed men didn't answer.

That evening, her mother was frying onions.

"You heard about the family downstairs?" Charlotte asked, studying a spot on the wall, the one her mother scrubbed every week. It always came back.

Her mother nodded, adding potatoes and meat shavings.

Lena sat on the sofa drawing with a red pencil on a stenographer's pad. Under the lamp, her hair glowed softly. "Half Jews will go next," her mother whispered. "The nun will give her a new identity." Like a game, Charlotte thought. Loss surrounded her memories of Max. Fear clouded her love for Lena. Perhaps a temporary loss of the child could cancel the fear.

She turned to her mother. "Give me the name of the nun and the convent." Her mother's face brightened. Charlotte hated her mother for smiling.

29. Smell of the Hawthorn Bush

The women in the factory wore men's jackets over their dresses, kept the collars turned up, tied scarves around their necks. Some had married Jews, known as "privileged Jews," who lived a tenuous existence

Magda's nose dripped constantly with a head cold. She complained about her husband's meager ration card.

"My husband's gone," Charlotte said.

"But he was a political," Magda reminded her. "They went early," as if Max had been more efficient than the other Jews.

She'd have to hide Lena's fate. *You'll have to kill her and mourn her.* Those were her mother's words. So when the time came for Lena to disappear, Charlotte told Magda about the child's high fever, how no doctor would see a *Mischling*, how Lena had finally died in the night.

The day after Lena "died," Magda slipped an envelope of coffee into Charlotte's pocket, enough for a full cup, along with a piece of hard red candy from before the war.

At the convent, the nun reached for Lena's hand, but the child withheld it and clung to her mother. A little girl appeared in the doorway behind the nun.

"Look," Charlotte said, waving at the girl.

When the child waved back and smiled, Lena released Charlotte's hand and went with the nun. In the doorway, Lena turned around and smiled. Charlotte recalled she hadn't kissed Lena goodbye. She stepped forward. But the door closed. She turned and picked her way down the pebbled walk.

The Sunday after she'd brought Lena to the nuns, Charlotte brewed Magda's coffee and shared it with her mother. Then she wrapped a cloth around the candy and crushed it with a hammer. She and her mother sucked silently on the splinters of berry-flavored sugar.

"How do you know we'll get her back?" Charlotte asked.

Her mother tossed back the coffee. Her eyes brimmed over with the pleasure of the caffeine. "We will. I know it." But the thickness in her mother's voice put Charlotte on edge.

She liked the women at the factory. When Magda complained about feeding a "privileged Jew" on a ration card, Charlotte told her to stop whining. Some days she forgot to think about Max, but Lena was constantly in her thoughts.

In February 1943, the Nazis arrested Magda's husband in a "factory action." Magda went with a bunch of other women to the Rosenstrasse prison, stood in the street silently begging for the release of their Jewish husbands. On the last day, Charlotte joined them. She was happy and surprised when the Gestapo and the SS suddenly released the men. But the rejoicing also deepened her longing for Lena.

It was raining. Charlotte and her mother had just finished soup with bread, and Charlotte was still hungry. She knew she'd fantasize about Bernstein's fresh trout and the steak in oxtail sauce once she got into bed. After dinner, she tried to concentrate on the newspaper. The German army had made another successful attack.

"I have to see Lena," she said suddenly.

Her mother's face tightened in an uneven way, like ice after a thaw.

"Don't be a sentimental goose."

Charlotte went to the window, looked out into the darkness. She didn't understand the war. Were the Nazis fighting the Allies or the Jews? When the war went badly, the Nazis blamed the Jews. She moved her lips in prayer. *Let the Allies defeat us.*

Next day after work Charlotte joined her mother at the sink peeling potatoes.

"I want to see her."

Her mother's face softened for a moment. Then she tightened her jaw and threw the peels into the trash. Charlotte turned away from her mother, but she heard her words. "Lena's been there two years. She has a new name. By now she thinks she's somebody else."

She thinks she's somebody else. Charlotte fried the potatoes, flipping them with a spatula, sending some to the floor. Her mother picked up the potatoes with a spoon. Charlotte couldn't eat. She'd married a Jew and given birth to a doomed child. Worst of all, it was her fault they hadn't escaped to England. Now she just wanted to place her own cheek against the peach skin of the child she wished she'd never had. To smell her hair. To hear her high-pitched singing.

All my little ducklings swim on the lake.

The next morning, Charlotte tiptoed past her mother's bedroom, buttoned her sweater as she ran down the steps. The only other passenger in the train compartment was a slender young woman with a protruding belly. People would open doors for her. Charlotte remembered how considerate some people had been before Lena was born. A member of Martin Luther's devil race had resided under her belt. But they hadn't known that.

The girl would visit a farm, thrust ration cards into the farmer's hand, replace the pillow under her dress with a haunch of beef. Charlotte took a window seat across the aisle from her.

At the village, they both got out. Charlotte sat down on the bench facing the tracks and opened her purse. Watching the girl from the corner of her eye, she took out the note she'd written for Lena on an old bill from the electric company.

Lena, I love you always. Mamma.

Red ink hearts surrounded the words.

The air smelled of primrose and sweetpea. But as she walked through the freshly cut grass, the rotten smell of the hawthorn blossom crept into her nostrils. She mustn't let Lena see her. From behind the hedge, she'd watch the children play. After they'd gone inside, she'd creep up to the door and slip her note into the mailbox.

Her blood thrummed as she approached the door. She was surprised to find it open. On the steps lay composition books, a doll without a leg, pencils, and slates. She opened her mouth. *Hallo.* But an echo mocked her voice. Her knees crumpled, and the earth reached for her.

Her body hurt around the bones. A rough fabric brushed her cheek and a metal cup touched her mouth. The rim was cold on her lips. A man who smelled of animals stood next to her. A screwdriver and pencil poked up from his pocket.

"Looking for somebody?"

Her neck hurt when she nodded.

"I just live over there." He gestured to a small farmhouse, smoke curling thinly from its chimney.

She moved her hand in a way that took in the entire garden. "How did this happen?"

"Stormtroopers pulled up in a truck. Jumped out. Two ran around the back. One banged on the door with his gun."

She held up her hand. Enough. But he seemed to overflow with the need to tell.

"I grabbed my fork, went out, like I was pitching peat. One of the nuns opened the door. Stupid kids stuck their heads out the window."

She winced.

He spoke more gently. "I mean—should've gone under the beds."

Had Lena seen them banging on the door? How many horrors had she known? Now the farmer spoke louder.

"Pushed their way in. Nuns screamed—"

With difficulty she got to her feet and walked slowly towards the end of the garden. The farmer followed.

"Kids're screaming. Gestapo comes out with 'em in a head-lock, two at a time. Throws 'em into the truck. Jewish kids. They do 'em that way when they're Jewish."

Another sound. Charlotte turned her head. A small, round-shouldered woman had entered the garden. Her habit was gray in the white places. She gestured towards the stone bench. Next to it stood a statue of St. Francis of Assisi, feeding pigeons, his other hand resting on the head of a wolf—peaceful as if the Nazis had never stolen her child. Charlotte sank down onto the cold stone next to the woman. She realized she couldn't remember the name of her mother's classmate.

The nun licked her lips. "I was praying in the chapel, heard them banging on the door. 'Quiet. You'll wake the children,' I said. They laughed. 'Bring us the Jewish brats,' they said. 'I have no Jews here. These are Catholic children whose fathers are fighting the Red Army.'

"One of them was polite, almost as if he'd grown up in the church. 'They've misled you, Sister,' he said. 'We've got a quota to fill.'"

Why was this woman still here?

"By the time I got to the kids' beds, most of them were awake."

Charlotte's voice came out in a squeak. "When my daughter came here, her name was Lena."

The nun appeared puzzled. Then her face brightened. "I remember her." Charlotte sensed less happiness than the affirmation that her memory still worked.

"I saw her—your Lena—in the back of the truck holding Sister Maria Luise's hand."

At least the child had been with somebody. With her eyes,

Charlotte tried to convey her need to the nun, her need to conjure up a happy image. For a moment they sat in silence. At last the nun spoke. "Sister Marie Luise told the children it was a field trip," she said cheerfully.

Charlotte felt relief at the delusion. Games. A picnic among woodland violets and lush ferns. And why had this woman deprived herself of the fun?

"You escaped, Sister?"

"Didn't have room. They pushed me off the truck."

Charlotte almost clucked with sympathy. Then she felt contempt for this useless survivor, less valuable than her charges. Nevertheless she rose to her feet and shook the nun's hand. At the gate of the convent, Charlotte knelt among the discarded toys and picked up a small suitcase. Inside was a doll wrapped in a dishrag. Like the round-shouldered nun, the doll had been bumped from the field trip.

The train's wheels on the track shook the bones in Charlotte's back. Sister Marie Luise had lied to the children, and Lena had believed them. She'd sat quietly, her hands folded in her lap, and looked out the window at the rolling countryside, smiling in anticipation. But Lena hated long trips. She'd probably whined.

When will we be there?

The older children would have shrugged off her question, understanding that the field trip was something horrible. They'd told her the truth.

Silly, little fool. We'll never see our parents again.

Charlotte bit the inside of her mouth until she tasted blood.

30. The Tundra Painter

On the photo tacked to the wall at the Red Cross, Lena at age five had a round, baby-like face. The photo of another person lost in the war partially hid the Bernstein name. Charlotte adjusted the information sheet beneath it, stepped back and eyed it with satisfaction. At least people could read it now—just in case somebody knew about her. But Lena's photo bothered her. How did the child look at age eleven? A tall and lean adolescent? It chilled her to think that she might not recognize her own child.

On the way home, she eyed the single remaining wall of a bombed-out baroque church, complete with stained glass windows. She tried to remember how it had looked before the war. But she couldn't get the statues right. Nothing was the same anymore. Certainly not her child.

Just beyond the pockmarked copper dome, her mother's building came into view, and Charlotte slowed her pace, preparing the ritualistic answer she'd give for the last time.

Her mother stood in the gloomy stairwell. She'd been waiting for her. Her appearance was entirely gray, as if her hair color had seeped into her cheeks.

"Any news?"

Charlotte shook her head. Her mother leaned forward with the look that always added another layer to Charlotte's sadness. *We've lost everything but one another.*

If her mother were a different person, she'd tell her how Max's ghost visited the factory today. She'd been gluing labels on bottles. The women talked of shops that sold flour and peas. And of the men they'd lost. His hand had brushed her breasts, and she'd turned to him. But he was gone again. The moistness between her legs had born testimony to his visit.

Upstairs, seated across from her mother, Charlotte broke the news. "There's nothing for me in Berlin." She handed her mother the newspaper, pointing to the advertisement about farm jobs in Iceland. She'd disembark in another world. The ocean would block out her mother, nullifying her sweet sad sense of Lena.

"What do they eat up there? Grass? Fish?"

Charlotte admired her mother's ability to obscure all dramatic moments with practical concerns. But she also read the message in her eyes. *Don't leave me alone to deal with Lena.*

The message had become a needle stuck in the groove of a record. Not that she didn't love Lena anymore. But her memory was a weight heavier than she could bear.

"There's still a chance for Lena," her mother said.

"You read the convent report—no survivors."

They'd hidden Lena, rubbed out every connection to her Jewish father. Afterwards, they'd worn one another out with blame. And now she was as lost as if they'd sent her to England.

"We should have kept her at home," her mother said in a tired voice.

Charlotte twisted the knife.

"'Nuns'll save her.' That's what you said."

Her mother rose suddenly to her feet. She stood and gazed at the wall as if she'd lost her way in her own kitchen. Then she grasped a chair back, the kitchen counter, and moved along the wall towards her bedroom. Whipped dog came to mind. But Charlotte didn't care. She heard the door click behind her, then placed her hands over her ears to shut out the muffled crying that would come next.

She took out paper and pen and began a letter to Frau Bernstein.

We have posted Lena's picture and information with the Red Cross. We have heard nothing. This week I sail for Iceland.

She addressed it to the house in Covent Garden, the address her mother-in-law had given her when she stepped into the taxi so many years ago.

The next day, Charlotte booked passage from Hamburg to Reykjavik. Holding her ticket in both hands, she distanced herself from her surroundings, as if she were stepping out of a group portrait, and the other figures shifted to fill the gap. She visited the art gallery one last time to study portraits, memorize noses, measure the distance between eyes, note how the light raised a cheekbone, hoarding details like a farmer preparing for a famine.

Two days before she left, she searched the used bookstalls on the Potsdamer Platz until she found a German-Icelandic dictionary.

"Came in a box from a student flat," the bookseller said.

She took it gratefully.

"I have something else," he said.

He thumbed through books about early film stars until he came to a large one with a cover depicting rocks with lichens and a boxy man, shoulders to his ears. The title read, "The Tundra Painter." He'd studied art in Paris and Rome. But in his Montmartre studio, he painted from memory—wildflowers, lichens, rocks. Turning the pages, she saw the faces hiding in the flowers, orange and gold lichens that resembled humans embracing. Max had hidden Lena's face among the flowers.

She reached for her purse.

31. Rooted in Strange Soil

Henrik had always been a dreamer, forever losing his place, forgetting now to finish undressing. At last, he flapped his arms into his night shirt until his thin wrists emerged through the sleeves. A finger at the small of his back, Charlotte prodded him towards the bed.

She kissed him goodnight, but he held her arm. "I took all my bones out to the hillocks in my corner of the homefield."

What would her mother say if she knew Henrik played with bones? Lena had had dolls from Bernstein's and the expensive teddy bear. For Henrik the sheep bones were people, the cow's jawbone a horse and its rider. Siena and Jon Skafti, he called them.

In the late summer light, his sober face resembled that of a dwarf born before his own mother. Suddenly, he spun around the room dancing to music that lived in his head.

"Yesterday, my bones found wood. They built a fire and hopped around it. *Clack*. They killed each other."

She knew his armies of sheep bones advanced over daisy fields, shot the enemy until it bled onto the chickweed.

His eyes glistened.

"Tell me about the war," he said.

Her playmates had waged miniature wars, mostly in Berlin courtyards, boys digging like moles to recreate the trenches of the Great War, ruining the landlord's chances to grow bushes.

"They screamed when they went over the top and killed the British," she said.

He climbed into her lap, placed his hand over her mouth.
"The other war—your war," he said.

She pinched her thigh, a reminder.

Careful now. Don't ever tell the boy about the day Max came back with his shirt stuck in the bloody furrows on his back.

Henrik was right. It was *her* war, her own personal problem—Hitler's plan to ruin her life. All those people killed. But only one mattered. Henrik's arms were warm on her neck. Without the war, she and Ragnar wouldn't have come together in the night to make this boy. She wouldn't have needed to replace Lena. Taking his arm from her neck, she nudged him towards the bed.

"Slowpoke," a hard young voice said.

Tryggvi stood in the door, his lip curled, like Ragnar's when he talked of clumsy farmers who ruined a sheep's ear at the branding. She envisioned Tryggvi wearing that look at the sheep sorting. He would swagger among the tents, sipping from a bottle, bragging how the hillside farmers dug their own outhouses.

"Tell *me* the story, not *him*," Henrik said, cuddling against her, cupping his hands over his mouth. She could tell by the tiny movement of the muscles in his cheeks that he was sucking his thumb. His hair smelled like moss campion.

"Baby," Tryggvi hissed.

"I *am* the baby," Henrik said.

"Tryggvi picks the story tonight," she said.

He'd choose a scene from the *Iliad*, the kind that would put Henrik right to sleep, leaving her to discuss military strategy with him long after the story was done. But he surprised her.

"The frogs and the three princes," he said.

His eye lacked its customary coolness. She'd told Tryggvi that story before Henrik was born, during the days when she was still struggling to make sentences. Back then, Tryggvi had been hers alone. When he cried at night, Ragnar had asked her to pick him up. And when Tryggvi grew older, she'd walked with him among the rocks, naming birds.

Later she sent him to school in the village. She'd left baby Henrik with the old woman and walked Tryggvi to the main road each morning. Nonni from Butterdale had picked him up and driven him with his own boy to school. Returning to the farmhouse, her heart beating fast, Charlotte had often found the old woman rocking the baby, singing songs of flashing swords and bloody battles. At the beginning of Tryggvi's first school year, Charlotte had come to a crossroads. She tried to express the feeling in a letter to her mother.

It's been nine years since the war ended. And still no word of Lena. Don't you think perhaps you should give up the search? You could visit here. Tryggvi's a big boy now.

In the afternoon, she'd met the boys at the foot of the hillside, she walking briskly, they dawdling to trade worms and stones. On days when the wind nearly blew Nonni's car off the road, Tryggvi had stayed home. Secretly, Charlotte rejoiced over his company, letting him trail behind her while she did her chores.

But these days Tryggvi talked about horses, saddles, and mutton prices. He could end Ragnar's sentences. The distance grew between her and this big-toothed youth the summer he learned to use the scythe. He stayed just beyond the tip of Ragnar's blade. She'd watched from the steps, shading her eyes, wincing when he caught the blade in the tussock and saw how Ragnar eased it out for him. Evenings, father and son sat at the kitchen table, chewing dog sour leaves and studying advertisements for hay-drying machines.

It wasn't that she didn't want him to become a farmer. The cost of not succeeding on the hillside was high. Hadn't they locked Magga of Butterdale in the shed overnight because she couldn't hold a rake? But she missed her talkative older son, now a shorter version of Ragnar, nodding his head, muttering *yup-yup it'll rain for sure.*

Henrik was different. He was all hers. She tucked him into bed and sat on the three-legged stool between the beds. He reached out and rubbed her thigh.

"Start the story."

She focused on Maizie, the frog who smoked Camels and wore a red garter.

"There was a king who had three sons. Two were smart, but the third was a simpleton. When it was time for the king to appoint an heir, he told his sons, 'The one who brings me the finest ring, the best carpet, the prettiest daughter in law, will inherit my kingdom.'

"Each of the brothers had a feather. The first one's feather blew east. The second one's blew west. But poor Simpleton's feather went straight down. Simpleton scratched the ground until the toe of his boot knocked against wood. A door. He opened it. Steps led down into the earth."

From Tryggvi's bed came a croaking sound. Henrik jumped out of bed and punched his brother's arm, then slipped back under his own covers.

"At the bottom of the steps, he saw the gleaming eyes of a big frog and the sparkling eyes of a little one. Her name was Maizie. 'Dear frogs, I need a ring, a carpet, and a beautiful girl,' Simpleton said.

"'Take Maizie,' the big frog said."

Henrik turned his lips inside out. "A frog. Ahhg. Tell how he kisses her."

Tryggvi was out of bed now. He placed his lips against Henrik's cheek and made a sucking sound. Henrik cried.

Her voice thinning out, she resumed the story.

"Maizie was transformed into a beautiful girl. The big, old frog gave Simpleton a fine ring and a beautiful carpet. And Simpleton inherited his father's kingdom."

At the end of the story neither boy spoke. Henrik stared up at the ceiling.

"If we had a brother or a sister, would it be Simpleton?" he asked.

"No, she'd be smarter than both of you."

"She?"

Charlotte wondered why she'd said "she," then sensed Henrik's shaping the idea to fit his own fantasy.

"I could pull her around in my cart."

She smoothed the sheets, first on Henrik's bed, then on Tryggvi's, in a rhythmic, purposeless way. Henrik's eyes were closed, but Tryggvi was watching her. She stood up quickly, feeling a moment's dizziness and his eyes on her when she left the room.

In the kitchen, she sat on the bench and hung her head between her knees. The old woman would soon be brewing petals and roots. After several cups, Charlotte would be running to the outhouse.

Staring at the worn spot in the linoleum between her knees, she strove for a sense of being in a particular place on the earth. Dizziness wasn't the real problem. It was more that she'd come loose from what held her. It had happened in Berlin too—her mother's badgering her with secretarial school, then refusing to accept Max.

A Jew in the family won't help your father's career.

Sometimes the dizziness went away for years. Now she sat down hard on the kitchen chair. The window framed the green heath. She took out her colored pencils, sketched the carpet of moss that softened the lava rocks into a landscape that resembled a billowing green sea.

A small hand that smelled of fresh earth touched the back of her neck. The old woman massaged her neck and shoulders, until the blood rushed through her veins.

32. The Juice of an Orange

The chilly air stung Charlotte's hands as she staggered up the hill from the outhouse, carrying a bucket of urine. Behind her, Ragnar balanced a bucket in each hand.

"Pray we don't have a spring blizzard. It'll freeze the sheep," he said.

It had happened more than once. They'd found the sheep frozen, standing in their tracks like statues, heads erect, facing forward, proudly heading for richer pastures. Up ahead, she saw the old woman wearing a canvas fisherman's jacket and feeding manure wedges into the glowing fire. The wind off the ocean billowed her skirt. Below, shorn lambs frisked in the meadow. The sheep had spent all winter shifting their weight in a small dark shed, chewing and defecating, dreaming of spring while their woolly coats grew. Now the fleeces lay in a pile next to the iron pot, partially obscured by the smoke from the fire.

"Water's boiling," the old woman shouted, waving her paddle.

Charlotte's fingers ached under the bucket handle. She tipped the bucket and emptied it into the boiling pot of water.

The old woman held up two fingers, then one, to signify two buckets of water–one of pee.

"If the count's off, the wool won't clean."

She placed a hand on Tryggvi's arm before he emptied his whole bucket.

"Take the rest to the shed."

He staggered down the hill in an exaggerated fashion.

The old woman stirred the mixture, singing *A horse without its rider walked along the sand.* She lowered her face to the boiling mixture. When the steam curled around her chin, she rubbed her cheeks with her fingertips.

"Makes your skin young," she said, raising her skirt hem to wipe her face.

Charlotte leaned over the pot, drew in the ammoniac smell, and stepped back quickly. Liquid hissed on the hot manure wedges. She didn't want to be young again. Reliving her youth was chore enough. She fed the fleece, sticky with lanolin, into the bubbling mixture. The old woman prodded the fleece until it lay submerged like a drowned animal.

Standing high on the hill, overlooking the ocean, Charlotte felt her place in time, right behind the medieval women who had stood here, breathing in the muttony steam, seeking the longship that carried their men on the ocean. The wind shifted again, and the sharp sea smell—full of the past—cut the air. The old woman looked at Charlotte.

"My man didn't have the Viking blood. He was seasick, chewed kelp to keep down the bile. Still, he vomited green over the side of the boat."

Charlotte lifted the first fleece out of the pot and laid it on a wooden rack in the grass next to the glowing fire. The old woman dipped her tongs into the murky stew and raised a second sopping black and gray fleece. A pile of steaming fleeces lay dripping on the rack.

The wind had died down, and the smoke rose straight up into the air. The old woman leaned her head back and stared at the sky, then looked at Charlotte. Her gaze contained something wild.

"It can make you crazy," she said.

Anything could make you crazy, Charlotte thought—the sheep, the poop, the fleeces—the lack of strangers to break the monotony of constant family. Besides that, beyond the hillside lay nothing but ocean. Last time she'd embraced the ocean, her lover had been nearly lethal.

"Soldiers went crazy just looking at the sky."

Charlotte found it hard to believe that these legendary creatures—English and American soldiers—had ever come near the hillside. But one morning in May 1940, three British ships had risen like rocks out of the sea and sailed into the Reykjavik harbor. A year later, Americans arrived. They'd stayed the entire war to defend Iceland against people like her—the Germans. But hillside people were polite to her. They didn't call her a Nazi.

"They had a radar station right over there," the old woman said, tipping her chin to indicate a place beyond the hillside. "All day they sat around those disks."

"Looking for Germans?"

"Yes, but all they ever saw was thrushes, fulmars, guillemots."

"Our life's exciting by comparison."

The old woman glanced at her the way she might look at a cow who no longer milked.

"Three of them took turns staring up at the sky. I could see them from the meadow at the edge of our land. One day, I heard a scream, thought it was a fulmar chasing an intruder from her nest. But the scream went wobbly, like a human's. I ran to the overlook and saw him over on the ridge, standing next to the disk, staring up into the sky, screaming his lungs out, like a woman in childbirth. The other two grabbed him and threw him to the ground. He couldn't stop screaming."

"What did he see?" Charlotte asked.

"Nothing but his own mind cracking apart. That sky was full of boredom. Soldiers like to kill people, not stand in a pasture waiting for something to happen."

Hands on her hips, the old woman straightened her back. Charlotte caught a glimpse of how she must have looked in those days. They would have noticed her—even if she wern't the youngest woman in the county.

"My man was long gone then."

Charlotte recalled the Russian soldiers after the war in Berlin. The age of the woman hadn't mattered.

"'Stay away from soldiers,' they said. But I'd never been inside a car, not a real one. I'd ridden the bus. We had two cars in the village then. Doctor had one. Manager of the cooperative had the other. Crossroads at the village looked like a postcard from a foreign city. Vehicles went in both directions."

The cars took turns stopping, Charlotte thought.

"Soldier comes riding around the corner in a jeep, calls to me, *Hallo girl*, stops the jeep, opens the door. I jump in. He drives and drives. I loved sitting up by the window with the windshield wipers going. Click. Click. After a while, I started waving at the other soldiers along the road. My soldier began singing. *It's a long way to Tipperary. It's a long way to go.*

Finally, I got the words, and we both sang at the top of our lungs."

Charlotte closed her eyes, but couldn't quite picture it.

"Know what he gave me?"

Russian soldiers. Screams. Splayed legs. Uniformed men thrusting into women on the street in broad daylight. Others smoking and laughing, waiting their turn.

"An orange," the old woman said gleefully. "I'd never had one, saved it to share with Ragnar, but I really wanted it for myself."

The old woman and Ragnar must have closed the door to the sick woman's room—lichen milk for her—the woman who'd never caused trouble except for dying. Then they'd sat down with two plates and solemnly peeled the orange, pulling it apart slowly, placing each section ceremoniously on a plate, eating it over the course of a whole evening, talking about it next day, recalling how juicy it had been.

She and her mother had shared an orange after the war. The

bond it created between them lasted for days.

"Did you see the soldier again?"

The old woman shook her head.

"The girls in the village had read magazines, knew some English words. Went dancing in the half-moon huts. Fisherman's widow going out with a soldier—ridiculous."

"What happened to him?"

The old woman frowned, stirred the liquid, probed for a fleece, came up with nothing.

"He'd been kind to me, so I kept up with him, asked the other women, the ones who went to the dances. Turned out he was stupid. Eleven of them hiked to the glacier—to test their endurance. Didn't know about chasms and crevices—or storms, how it snows so hard you can't see, how you slip, fall so deep into the earth that nobody knows where you went. Five of them came back. My soldier didn't."

The words *my soldier* hung suspended like a thread between them, over which traveled the memory of the other ten. Glaciers rumbled over rocks, left them intact but scarred. Soldiers could leave marks on a population. Charlotte knew that from the Russians. The French shaved girls' heads after the soldiers were gone. Not here, though. Soldiers hadn't been the enemy. One had given the old woman an orange, then turned to stone inside the earth.

33. A Bird's Breath on her Skin

Across the rubble of a bombed-out church, she'd seen their broad shoulders in big coats. Two Russian soldiers climbed over the rocks towards her. One dangled a pair of sausages at her. He grasped her hand, placed it on the sausages—a promise. As he pressed against her, her mouth filled with water. Whatever she had, they could take, just so they fed her.

She made it easy for him, lifted her skirt, pushed aside her underwear, leaned against the broken wall. He grunted as he rammed into her. Over his shoulder, she saw the other soldier leering at her, unbuttoning his pants. When the first one was finished with her, she pocketed one sausage and braced herself to earn the second one.

Afterwards, as she climbed the steps in the dark stairwell, a hand between her legs, the sausages in her pocket, her shame gave way to pride. She'd been working for a living.

Her mother sliced half of one of the sausages, fried it with potatoes, kept her eyes on her plate. Throughout the meal Charlotte and her mother barely spoke to one another.

"They left a lot here," the old woman was saying. "Chocolates, stockings, oranges, babies, their bodies—oh yes and their cars."

But the old woman couldn't forgive the soldiers for one thing. They'd ripped the sphagnum moss off the rocks to bandage their cuts. And they stuffed it into their sleeping bags for warmth.

Charlotte picked up the other side of the fleece rack, and they walked to the creek. Its bank was yellow with marsh marigolds. It was the same every year. The day the marigolds shed their petals, the haymaking would begin.

Ragnar had anchored a crate to the bed of the creek so that water flowed through its slats. Groaning, the old woman almost dropped the rack onto the ground. Rubbing her back, she helped Charlotte drop each fleece into the crate, singing to herself:

Sing loud and dance
For the night it is so long.

This vision of the darkest days of winter chilled Charlotte—days just folded into memory—days of pulling, combing, carding, and spinning the wool. Fussy about each sheepskin, the old woman scraped it clean with a knife, stretched it for drying, tight as a drum skin, on the door of the shed. Later, she rolled it up, placed it on the top shelf in the pantry.

Sometimes Charlotte thought the old woman lived outside the passage of time. Even though the boys preferred rubber shoes from the cooperative store, the old woman unrolled the skin during the darkest part of December, cut it into parts, and stitched shoes for them. She dyed them black with bearberries, knitted woolen pads with their initials as shoes fillers, and made Tryggvi take his indoor shoes to school in his pocket.

Take off your boots. Wear the sheepskin in the classroom.

Of course, the old woman could have bought blue dye at the cooperative store, but she believed in self-sufficiency. So for Henrik she'd scraped the copper layer out of a discarded kettle, dissolved it in water, and soaked his shoes until they turned blue.

"Once our cat drank the dye. We found him dead," she'd whispered. Charlotte heard the pride in her tone—only the strongest dye for her boy's shoes.

Now the sheep cycle was beginning over again.

They spread the fleeces over the tussocks until the ground looked alive with hump-backed sheep. The wind would fluff the wooly skins into a curly dryness, and Ragnar and the boys would load them onto a handcart and bring them to the shed for storage.

At the end of the day, the old woman was stooped. She walked back to the shed rubbing the place between her neck and shoulders. From the shelf she took a packet of nettles. Out fell the gray green flowers and leaves covered with tiny spikes. She wrapped a dishcloth around the base of the prickly stalks and handed the bouquet to Charlotte. She slipped off her blouse and undershirt, then undid her skirt and pushed it below her hips. Her papery white skin glowed in the flickering light of the oil lamp. She turned her back to Charlotte, placed her hands on the wall.

"Don't stop until you see blood," she commanded.

Charlotte swung the bundle of plants, tapping the pale back and shoulders gently at first, then harder. Soon, the fuzzy hairs on the leaves of the stinging nettle would break the thin, dry skin and drive the phyto-medicine, a natural antihistamine, into the muscles. Tiny dots of blood formed on the thin skin.

Urtication, the old woman called it. Developing a rhythm to the flagellation, Charlotte thought of the golden paintings of Franciscan martyrs, carrying palm leaves and smiling radiantly. The blood on the axe blade lodged in the martyr's neck contrasted with the iconic gold.

The blood pinpricks joined into droplets on the old woman's back. Charlotte's eyes blurred at the emerging red landscape. A familiar disorientation came over her. Another younger and stronger back lay beneath her hands now. The torn flesh was a mass of red and purple wounds oozing into dirty bandages. Max had writhed when she washed his wounds.

"Harder," the old woman commanded.

Again, she slapped the bony shoulders with the prickly plant, hating the red streaks that formed on the skin. She began to talk to herself, saying things she could not herself hear, anything to stop the pain of her thoughts. *If only he'd stayed in the kitchen painting flowers.*

"Enough," the old woman said suddenly.

Breathing hard, Charlotte dried the old woman's back and rubbed it with salve.

Dressed now, the old woman waggled her finger at Charlotte.

"I heard you. I know you're hiding something."

Charlotte stepped back. "Me? What?" Then guilt washed over her. She'd promised Max not to tell. *They'll arrest me again.* She'd never told until now—maybe. Still he'd been arrested.

Over the old woman's head, through the window, Charlotte glimpsed the ridge of the hill. She lived between that hill and the dirt beneath her feet. She drew a circle in the dirt floor with her toe, felt the rough ground through her thin shoes. It came down to two things. She was *here.* The rest of the world was *there.*

Her back to the old woman, Charlotte undressed. Like a bird's breath on her skin, the old woman came close, whispered in her ear. "You know those pictures of goblins jumping out of a person's mouth?"

Yes, she knew about goblins from medieval woodcuts, how evil people harbored them, how the priest helped sinners spit them out.

"You have a goblin that sits in your throat. You need to get it out."

"How?" Charlotte asked, wincing with pain under the slap of the nettles.

"Tell it—the whole thing," the voice whispered at her shoulder.

Gradually the stinging feeling transformed itself into relief. First her skin, then her whole body relaxed. Finally the old woman stopped, and Charlotte sensed the blood cooling on her back and with it the memory of Max's ordeal faded.

Small hands traveled her back, and the smell of yarrow salve rose in her nostrils. Feeling faint, Charlotte grasped the timber beam in the wall to keep from sliding to the floor.

The voice at her shoulder again. "Just say 'I have something to tell you.'"

"Yes," Charlotte promised.

The old cowardly blood was gone. Her new blood would give her courage. The timber beam was her witness.

34. An Odd Desire

After a long day of raking and binding hay, Charlotte usually slept well, but in the middle of haying season, she began to awake to nightmares.

The dreams often started with a garish review of Max's paintings, the ones he did after he was banished from the art academy—the prostitutes with orange nipples, one legged beggars, erect penises poking from among rags. Pot-bellied gentlemen dandled rouged boys. The dancer, elbows on her knees, opened her legs, revealing a red-lipped cave.

She'd waited all night for him to return from a cell meeting. When he walked in the door, his face a bloody pulp, his eye hanging down to his cheek, she screamed at him.

We've got to get out of here.

His words made her blood boil.

I'm a German just like everyone else. Why should I go?

She picked him up and threw him down the stairs, ran after him, boiling with anger. At the bottom of the stairs, she kicked him again and again. A stormtrooper came. Together, they kicked Max's head until it resembled an overripe tomato.

Her own sobbing woke her. She lay back on her pillow, ashamed.

I loved Max. Why am I doing these things to him?

He'd taught her the difference in brushes, rabbit's hair, buffalo tail, pig's bristle. He'd taught her to paint what wasn't really there—the empty spaces, the made-up things. And now he kept coming back. How many times did she have to kill him?

Her toes stood out from under the sheet. She addressed them directly.

Go away. I have a new life now.

But she knew he'd be back. She swung her legs over the side of the bed and put on her work pants. In the kitchen, the old woman and Ragnar were talking. She could tell by the relaxed lines in their faces that they'd finished the milking and had fed all the animals. She'd overslept that badly. It was raining hard.

Ragnar reached for his sweater.

"Time to cut that grass along the barbed wire."

She nodded without looking up, didn't expect more talk from him that day.

Tryggvi came out of the bedroom, pulling on his clothes.

"I want to go too," he said.

"The weather—" she protested.

But Tryggvi took his overalls from the hook, stood on the steps and climbed into them. He buckled her old dress belt around his waist and looked expectantly at Ragnar. Stirring the bubbling rhubarb pudding, she ignored the gritty sound of men putting on rubber boots in the hall. Weather was everything here, but it also meant nothing. In Berlin, if it rained, they canceled the picnic. Here you rode it out, waited for the rain to pull back before you unwrapped the sandwiches, ate fast, huddled against a rock cavity.

Through the window, she saw them, the crescent moon of the scythe blades curved over their backs, the points aimed at their buttocks, until the fog enveloped them.

Again, the front door closed. Henrik was outside, running after them. She rapped on the window pane, but he didn't turn around. She flew out the door, chased him over the tussocks. Quick as an elf, he disappeared into the mist. Panting, she stopped and turned around.

The old woman met her at the door with a dry pair of
socks.

"Don't chase your boys like that. They'll see your fear."

Charlotte glared. She didn't want to hear the story again,
but the old woman was already gesturing with her hands.

"I used to spend a lot of time on the shore, like you. February mornings, we were on the sand. My boys too. We'd watch
for the lull between the waves.

"'NOW, Papa,' Ragnar would yell, but he was usually
wrong.

"Beyond the waves, the ocean was mild as a puppy. But it
crashed on the shore."

An odd desire rippled through Charlotte's body. She'd like
to go down to the shore now, but she mustn't, not with both
boys swinging metal in the field. The old woman took her
elbow and led her to the bench.

"In the split second before the next wave crashed, my man
and six others pushed the skiff into the sea, rowed like crazy
men. They got out of the soapy part of the surf before the
next wave crashed. I held my breath until I could see them
out beyond the waves. Then the boys and I walked back up
the hillside. I fed the animals, cleaned the shed, dug up potatoes until the sweat poured off me.

"Most days he came back. I'd be sitting at the spinning
wheel—after the boys were asleep. He'd peel off his clothes
in the hall, then he'd climb into bed smelling of cod and
ocean."

She closed her eyes, and Charlotte knew she was recalling
the exact moment when the tide changed, the moment of
greatest pleasure. And the old woman had known it in the
bed that she and Ragnar now shared.

"He loved me hard, helped me forget the work," the old
woman said.

She walked to the opposite wall and peered into the small
mirror on the shelf as if she'd lost something in the crack

that ran down its middle. She rubbed her fingers through her scalp.

"Thinning," she said. "My man liked thick hair."

She undid her plaits, stripped down to her woolen undershirt, reached for the salve of *Rhodiola Rosea,* and rubbed it into her scalp. A rose-like fragrance filled the room. While the rhodiola dried, the old woman washed her face in a fusion from the sundew flower. Its red basal leaves, sticky insect traps, made freckles fade. Charlotte had used it on the boys' bottoms against ringworms.

Rubbing the sundew over her shoulders, the old woman turned to her.

"Have you tried telling them stories from *Egilssaga?* I mean for courage."

"They don't need more courage," Charlotte said sourly, picking a carding brush out of the basket, cleaning out the wisps of wool and feeding them to the fire in the stove.

The burning wool crackled and gave off an oily muttony smell. Years ago, the aroma had repelled her, but now it made her think of her children. They smelled of sheep.

The old woman dried her hair.

"If we don't have courage, we just memorize something and do it over and over again, always working on making it easier and safer, drawing a smaller and smaller circle around ourselves."

Charlotte knew about circles, smaller even than the one she'd fended off when her parents had hoped she'd learn to type and file. Their lives on the farm were tied off at each end by the sigh and the smile of a sheep. The only break in the pattern was violent weather, the equivalent of dropping your typewriter if you were a secretary. The weather cleared up, and you raked the last patch of hay. In the office, you got a new typewriter.

She cleaned the noses of her new children while her mother searched Europe for her old child. Her last letter troubled Charlotte.

I went to the Red Cross today to give them a new picture of Lena. The old one was yellowed and curled up.

But Lena would be twenty-two now. How could her mother provide a new picture? Another picture of a five-year old? The old woman was eyeing her.

"I wanted to make Lena safe," Charlotte said.

"It took courage to give her away."

"I didn't give her away."

Yet she liked hearing "courage." It soothed her pain, like moss covering lava rock. But the hardness would remain underneath.

Behind the statue of St. Francis in the convent garden had been a cluster of pink and purple fairy foxglove. Lena had run to the flowers, touched them with the tips of her fingers. *Pretty.* Then they had both sat down on the stone bench. Charlotte had buried her nose in the child's hair, enjoyed the softness, breathed in its pine fragrance.

A nun—"the nice nun"—approached the child, her hand outstretched.

I am Sister Marie Luise.

Charlotte stood to make it easier, but the child clutched her thigh.

It's only for a little while. Mamma will come and get you soon.

It would have been easy to pick Lena up and walk out. But instead she'd nudged Lena towards the nun.

Mamma will come back and get you.

Her eye on the door, she'd walked backwards out of the garden. Now her broken promise formed a noose around her happiness.

The old woman was watching her.

"I wasn't brave. I was just a fool. I should have kept Lena with me."

"Are you sure she hasn't survived?"

"My mother checks with the Red Cross."

The old woman's voice went deep now, the way it did when

she imitated ducks or geese. Her favorite poet was Egil, the Viking warrior. She sang of his mother's dreams for him:

I'll scour for plunder, the stout steersman of this shining vessel:
Then home to harbor, after hewing down a man or two.

"Egil's mother was a bitch—she'd have gotten the job done at Auschwitz," Charlotte said, putting up potatoes for lunch.

The old woman raised her eyebrows.

She shouldn't have brought it up. She'd hated the Nazis more than Max ever could. On the hillside, she apologized for the Third Reich, as the hillside residents read about how the Germans had wanted the island during the war. Dog-eared newspaper articles got passed from farm to farm.

But those articles didn't explain the war, the time afterwards when the city lay in ruins, and ghosts stalked you. You took a dead friend to the movies. But when you laughed, she remained silent and reproachful. And she never walked home with you. Your vanished child sat in your lap, her cheek soft against yours, but when you talked to her, she didn't answer. Your dead husband lay next to you in bed. No matter how much you caressed him, he could not—

Charlotte missed her mother, somebody who shared her memories. Sometimes the old woman worked next to Charlotte for hours in silence. Today she was garrulous.

"It was night, and I was out looking for the northern lights. Suddenly a ball of fire lit up the sky. I thought it was the volcano erupting."

Once when Nonni came to fix the fence he'd told her the same story, a hint of accusation in his tone.

Germans had fired at the fishing boats for target practice, sometimes even wasted torpedoes on them. She knew the rationale. The Grimsby fishing boats had been converted to convoy boats. It was up to the Icelanders to provide the British with cod. The old woman said it often.

The soldiers kept us safe from the Germans.

And added—*I didn't mean you, dear.*

35. Giving Birth to Life All Over Again

The sound of the potatoes rattling in the saucepan reverberated on Charlotte's temples. She took the feverfew from her pocket, bit off some leaves, chewed rapidly, anticipating the rush of *sesquiterpane lactones* entering her bloodstream. She opened the window to let out the steam. Then she heard the cry and saw the boy running towards the house. She pulled open the front door, and her elf child fell into her arms gasping his brother's name.

"Tryggvi. Tryggvi. He fell on the scythe. Blood."

The old woman began plucking things from her cupboard and placing them in her shawl.

"How?"

"He jumped down from the wall. Didn't see it. The blade—"

She began to run. Henrik was somewhere at her side, reaching for her hand. She clambered over the tussocks, cursing Ragnar for not flattening them. Running and tripping, she had to keep picking up Henrik. At last, she saw them. Ragnar was naked to the waist, his blue-white skin prickled with goose bumps, bending over Tryggvi.

"Breathe easy, boy," he was saying.

Tryggvi's overalls lay between two tussocks in a bloody heap. His mouth was a grimace. Bunched up below the boy's waist was Ragnar's blood-soaked undershirt. Under his head was his work shirt.

She took off her blouse, handed it to Ragnar, and shivered

in her undershirt. He kneaded it into a small tight package. When he eased the undershirt off the wound, Tryggvi's flesh contracted in the cold air, and the blood oozed upwards, spilling over the edges of the cut. He laid the folded blouse over the wound, and the boy groaned. Blood seeped quickly into the white cotton.

She looked towards the farmhouse. Where was the old woman?

Ragnar pointed to the blood-soaked undershirt.

"Wash it in the creek."

Charlotte walked quickly to the narrow run of water that divided the field. Henrik clasped her skirt. When she dipped the makeshift bandage into the water, the stream ran red. She tried to remember the thin biology textbook she'd studied in high school. The ragged drawing of the liver, the stomach, and the intestines. How deep could a scythe go without killing you? The cold water hurt her hands when she wrung out the shirt.

At last the old woman appeared in the distance, hobbling along, holding her skirt at her knees. Panting when she joined them, she placed a hand on Ragnar's shoulder, eased herself to the ground, to Tryggvi.

He glanced at her, and his breathing seemed to grow easier.

"How often has the compress filled with blood?" she asked.

Ragnar couldn't remember.

The old woman took a handful of leaves from her pocket, lifted the compress, and dropped the leaves on the wound. Charlotte recognized the dark green lady's mantle, covered with tiny hairs, and the slender leaves of the lion's foot. She placed the compress back on the boy's belly, pressing gently and murmuring, "Mary, holy mother of God. Frigg and Freyja, gods of the earth. Heal this boy."

Charlotte closed her eyes and prayed to the tiny hairs on the leaves. *Stop the bleeding.*

When she opened her eyes, she saw that the wadded up blouse on his belly was still white around the edges. She moved next to the boy's head and stroked his hair. Ragnar sat back in the grass, took Henrik between his legs. The little boy held his father's knees.

The old woman recited Tryggvi's favorite poem into his ear—*a horse without his rider ran along the beach*. Repeating the verse, she lifted the blood-soaked blouse, dropped more leaves on the wound, and replaced the compress. From her bodice, she took a flask, put it to Tryggvi's lips.

"Round-up drink," she said.

Tryggvi raised his head and drank, giggling at the forbidden taste. Ragnar took his mother's shawl and wrapped it around the boy's shoulders. The tightness at the boy's mouth had loosened. At last the old woman touched the boy's forehead and his cheeks, examined the wound again. Blood oozed slowly.

"Bring him home now," she said, pulling herself to her feet.

Ragnar slid his arms under the boy and lifted him easily. Charlotte held his legs. The old woman and Henrik led the way. At the house, the old woman went into Tryggvi's bedroom first to fill his pillowcase with sweet-smelling herbs.

They laid him on the bed. Charlotte sat at the foot of the boy's bed and watched him sleep. She mustn't leave him for a moment. Then he would die. She sat up with a start when the old woman entered the room. Their eyes met. For a long moment, neither looked away. Love grew in their gazing, a look rich with their shared feeling for the boy.

The old woman sat down at the foot of the bed.

"We were talking about fear."

"I remember."

"It came on me—the fear. Did you see it?"

"No."

"Just like when my man was coming in through the surf, off

the sea. That's how afraid I was, watching that wound. The blood kept coming and coming. I didn't know if it would stop."

Hadn't she cured dozens of humans, calves, lambs?

Her words were more important than a red wedding dress or a yarrow cure for a fever, this admission of self-doubt, the old woman's gift of herself.

"One more thing," the old woman said.

Charlotte stroked the sheet next to the boy's shoulder. "About life."

A long silence but for the boy's steady breathing.

The old woman cleared her throat. "When you almost lose it, but not quite, it's like giving birth to life all over again."

Alone again with the boy, Charlotte thought of her own mother sitting alone in her kitchen, obsessed with waiting for a child that no longer existed. She willed her message of life across the Atlantic Ocean.

My real child lives, Mamma. You should see him. A big-toothed boy, half a man now.

Bearing a cup of tea that smelled of flowers and herbs, the old woman entered the room. The cup clicked against the saucer as she set it down on the nightstand.

"If he wakes up—"

But the boy was sleeping comfortably. Entirely relaxed now, free of all his manly posturing, he looked very young. Something rippled up the back of Charlotte's neck. By the time it stung her eyes, she recognized it as gratitude.

36. He Was My Man

Lichen holiday, the old woman called the camping trip. She would need the ugly, sticky lichens that grew on the distant moor to mend their respiratory and digestive systems all winter long. The best time to pick them was in the early morning when they were soft and wet from the dew.

You'll never catch cold, not even when you've been searching for sheep for three days in drenching rain. Keeps your bones from aching in the middle of January

Charlotte lay on her back, staring at the point where the two sides of the tent met above her head and listened to the rain drumming the canvas. Henrik was wedged between her and the old woman.

Even after twelve years on the island, Charlotte found it difficult to sleep when daylight lasted all night. This was especially true when she was worrying about her children's safety.

"I don't want Tryggvi to go with Ragnar to the sheep round-up in the fall," she said.

The old woman put her finger to her lips and whispered. "Don't let Henrik hear you. He's already afraid of everything."

"His fear will keep him safe."

The old woman had the covers up to her nose, and her voice sounded as if she were praying in a cave.

My teeth solved my troubles

And tore out his throat

She pulled back the covers.

"No such thing as safe."

The old woman's eyes gleamed with story.

"My son Gunnar wanted to go out with his father. Swan was the boat's name. Thank God Ragnar didn't like boats. He just puttered around the farm. But Gunnar begged and begged. At last his father agreed. I didn't like the way the sea looked that day—almost no gaps between the waves. They could barely launch the boat. But Gunnar was eighteen, a man really. What could I do?"

Charlotte understood. She owed life a certain stance. No more cringing. She touched her eyelids, felt her eyeballs vibrating, enjoyed the sensation of being alive. At Christmas, when they ate sheeps' heads, she'd studied the dead eye surrounded by fat. Ragnar plucked the eyes out with his fork, ate them first. She nibbled on the singed skin from around the ears. But she never ate an eye.

Listening now, she could distinguish the old woman's breathing from Henrik's. They all lay here breathing, eyes vibrating. The definitely dead—Gunnar—couldn't do that. Somewhere Lena lay in bed right now, breathing, counting the seconds until her alarm clock rang.

The old woman sat up suddenly.

"It was Gunnar's first time out. I waited for them all night and the next. Bits of their boat washed ashore farther down the coast. Bodies came back, finally—"

The ocean borrowed bodies, then gave them back. During the loan, death marked them.

"You were lucky that his body came back," Charlotte said.

"Lucky?"

"A person isn't completely dead, I mean forever and ever, until you see the body."

Still, when General Eisenhower went into the camps and reported what he saw there, Charlotte knew that he was telling her that Max was dead. She didn't need to see his body. Lena's case was different.

The old woman peered at her. "Don't think about it."

"I want to."

"Why?"

"To keep her alive."

The old woman shook her head, pointed to the sleeping boy. Charlotte read her look.

This is the one who is alive. Forget everything else.

The other truth rose up in her.

"I didn't want a baby."

Henrik was staring at her. Had he only pretended to be asleep? The old woman said nothing as if Charlotte hadn't said what she'd said. Tired of being a terrible mother, she rolled away from him. But he reached for her shoulders.

"Let's start the picking."

"Go outside and pee, boy, " the old woman said.

He crawled quickly out of the tent.

"Does Ragnar know?" the old woman asked.

"He doesn't like me to talk about Lena—or Max."

"Use these words on him, 'I have something to tell you.'"

He'd changed the subject to mixing cement for the dung channel in the cowshed.

Don't tell me.

Charlotte eased herself up out of the sleeping bag and found her boots. She pulled on the thick gloves, still warm from cradling her head all night. They hiked through wet moss and dewy heather until their boots were shiny above the ankle line. Henrik ran ahead, and the old woman placed each foot higher and higher on the slope. At last they reached the picking place on the moor. The mountain lichens glistened with slime. The old woman dropped to her knees and pulled the lichens out of the ground and pitched them into her basket, singing:

My teeth solved my troubles

And tore out his throat.

Henrik skipped about. "Don't step on them, boy," she said.

For years, the old woman had fetched lichens here, brewed them to cure Ragnar's first wife's consumption, spoon-fed her lichen milk, thumped her back to bring up the phlegm, watched her die. For a few years after that, she put her faith in other edibles.

Finally, hauling baskets and bags of lichens on her back, the old woman led the way back to the tent.

37. Troll Games

Tryggvi's wound appeared to have healed. But even if he could run, he didn't. That was for little kids like Henrik, who ran across the field, hay rakes in his arms, the heads banging together. Tryggvi sauntered along, hands in his pockets, chewing a wad of sheep sorrel, sucking in his cheeks at its sourness.

Ragnar had cut the grass that morning and separated it into rows. The family fell into line behind him. The sun was hot on one side of Charlotte's face. Each time they changed rows, the sun switched cheeks to the sound of their rakes scratching the earth's scalp.

By mid-afternoon, they were turning hay on the incline, one foot higher than the other. Panting, the old woman had dropped two rows behind. Charlotte tied her sweater around her waist and wiped the pearls of sweat from her forehead.

"Coffee, Mamma," Ragnar called over his shoulder.

The old woman finished her row and toed the ground to make an indentation. She raised her rake high into the air and plunged the wooden handle into the ground so that it vibrated against the blue of the sky. Henrik threw down his rake and ran ahead to the farmhouse. Ragnar and Charlotte turned the remaining rows without talking.

They drank their coffee in a place sheltered by rocks. The warm sun drew out the sweet, spicy fragrance of thyme. A tiny pink alpine azalea nestled at Charlotte's feet. She imagined invisible creatures hiding at its roots and wondered how she would paint them. Her inner eye would discover the secret, secret even from herself until she painted it.

The old woman stripped to her woolen undershirt and lay on her back in the sunshine. The thin skin of her arms hung from her bones and rested on the earth. Henrik's hard little knees gripped Charlotte's arm, and his gritty hands cupped her ear.

"Come to my killing place," he whispered.

A goblin pair appeared to dance in his eyes. One of the dancers made her think of herself on a good day. She rose to her feet, and followed him to his favorite place, the gray ring of rocks, where he garrisoned his quarrelsome bleached sheep bones.

He wasn't a killer. When her mother wanted to send him toy Prussian soldiers, he'd said no. Instead he collected sheep skeletons in chasms and made them live rich lives. Last year's May blizzard had frozen a family group where it stood in the field. And on a bright July day Henrik found a live sheep lying on its back, its feet up in the air. Crows were pecking at its eyes. He couldn't help the sheep to its feet, so he screamed until the crows flew away.

Give me a gun, Papa. I need to kill all the crows in the world.

But Ragnar had said no, so his hatred of crows and trolls came out in other ways.

One of the rocks was covered with a glossy paste of buttercups. He showed her his executioner's instrument, a small sharp quartz stone, with buttercup petal scraps clinging to the stone. He dragged a finger through the paste, and she saw the blisters the buttercup oil had raised on his hand. The old woman always wore gloves when she mixed crushed petals with butter for her joint salve.

Henrik picked up the rock, crushed the remaining buttercup heads, and added them to the yellow carnage. Charlotte thought his hatred of trolls went back to the day he found her tundra painter book—One of his drawings showed a troll's penis ramming into a tiny farmer's wife. Another depicted a thumb-sized fisherman lost in the forest of a troll woman's pubic hair.

He'd thrown the book on the floor, called it "troll games."

Later that same day, fetching the cows, they'd heard the concert of whinnying and snorting, had seen the stallion biting the mare's back. The stallion reared up, splayed its forelegs over the mare's back, and mounted her.

Henrik called that troll games too. In his mind—and she knew his mind—the only way to fight the trolls was by making an alliance with the hidden people, good creatures who wanted to join the human race. The hidden people lived among the flowers, in the fog, behind rocks, in caves.

In a gravelly spot next to the buttercup carnage a gentian stretched its open face of bright blue petals towards the sun. Charlotte dared not look away. As soon as the sun withdrew, the flower would close its petals. She lay down next to the flower and touched the white-tinged blue of its petals with the tip of her nose.

Henrik pulled on her sleeve. "Don't."

"I won't damage it, darling."

He balled both fists. "You'll scare away the hidden people."

She recalled his stories of how the hidden people had suddenly appeared in the mist, talked to him when he was lonely, helped him find the cows in the fog, led him home.

They let me stroke their tails.

"I want to marry one of the hidden people," he said.

Marry? He was only five years old.

His eyes twinkled. "So I can see her tail fall off in church."

Henrik knew the songs of the hidden people. Last Christmas Eve he'd refused to sing *To us a child is born*, had chanted instead from behind the sofa:

There's joy in every hillock
A song in every rock

"I saw her again," he said suddenly.

"Who?" But she knew.

"She wanted you. Said you're a—" He searched for the word. "—a midwife."

A cloud passed over the sun. The gentian withdrew its petals, hugged them to itself.

He wiped his buttercup fingers on a pad of moss, then climbed into her lap and took her chin in his hand. "She had a little girl with her," he said.

Charlotte tried to smile, the way people did with certain kinds of children.

"I recognized the girl," he said.

She held his thin body against hers for comfort—her own. His lips moved against her chest, as if he were speaking not for her ears but directly into her heart.

"I chased her, but she got away."

The child was still invisible. Even the best painter could not see her.

"Her eyes were the same as—"

She studied the top of his head, the place where the hair swirled around the cowlick.

"Same as?"

"Same as the eyes of the girl in Max's painting," he said.

"Market place painting?"

"No. The one with the man—he's got a knife. The girl's looking up."

Not a girl, she started to say. Isaac. Or was it?

"There was another time—" he said.

Many other times, she thought.

"It was foggy. A woman came towards me—calling me 'little boy,' and asking, 'Where's your Mamma?' I said, 'Home, asleep.' She didn't like that."

Charlotte touched her finger to his cowlick, traced a circle. How precious he was, and how little he got from her. Had the memory of Lena sucked the love out of her? The love that was his by right?

"The lady turned ugly," he said. "I started to run away, but she followed me. I ran as fast as I could until I tripped over a tussock and fell and hurt myself. I closed my eyes. When I opened them, she was gone."

The chasm between real and unreal widened underneath them.

"They had a cow," he said.

She thought of Skjalda.

"They called her Io."

Charlotte had told him the story of Io, how Zeus had loved her. His wife, jealous Hera, had transformed Io into a cow. Argos, with his one thousand eyes, became the cow's jailer.

"When the fog got thicker, I ran away."

His body trembled, perhaps exhausted from containing his imagination.

"I saw the eyes in the fog."

Footsteps crunched the gravel beyond the rocks. A shadow passed over them. It was Ragnar, rubbing a tuft of hay between his hands.

"Just a couple of more turns," he said.

They followed him. As they approached the pasture, she took Ragnar's arm.

"I have something to tell you."

"Later," he said, pointing to the sun.

The sun was low in the sky when the hay was finally dry enough to pack into bales. Charlotte and Tryggvi pulled the ropes between them until the hay bale was tight. The horses waited patiently while Henrik and Tryggvi placed layers of peat on their backs. Then Tryggvi and Ragnar heaved the bales of hay onto the trusses. Charlotte stood in front of the horse, measuring the hay parcel with her eyes and hands until the hay hung down evenly on each side.

Tryggvi took the rein of the lead horse. He wore his father's overalls, rolled up at the ankles. As the horses swayed toward the barn, Charlotte took Ragnar's arm. "Let's go for a walk."

He looked at her in surprise. They never walked together except for the times they'd midwifed the sheep.

"I know a hollow," she said.

He nodded, walking slowly, waiting to be led. If she wasn't careful, he'd spend his talk on cow stalls. Or he'd hang his words on his planned treat for her—the toilet. He'd already ordered the pipes. She walked quickly towards her secret place, the hollow. His large rubber shoes and broad hands looked odd in this sacred place. "Climb in," she said, offering him her hand as if to help him into a pitching boat. Seating himself, he crushed a cluster of violets. Then he lay back and rested his head on a tuft of moss. Charlotte placed her hands on the earth and felt its warmth.

She touched his ankle, moved her fingers under his pants leg, and rested her hand on the skin just above the sock. He seemed to be waiting for her to talk, but her words didn't come. Far away, the sea splashed on the shore. She felt the familiar tug in her chest.

"My mother didn't want me to marry Max."

It sounded wrong.

"It wasn't that she didn't like Jews. She was afraid. We were all afraid then. We thought if we kept saying YES, nothing terrible would happen. Some people divorced their Jewish spouses."

Ragnar squeezed her ankle.

"Did *you* ever think of divorcing him?"

She'd hated him for being Jewish, for giving her a baby, for refusing to leave Germany, for being a jackass, for making love to her so exquisitely that her body ached for him long after he was gone. But divorce him? Never. If only because her mother wanted her to.

The old anger flared up inside her.

"Even when the Nazis wouldn't let him attend the academy any more, he stayed. He said stupid things like 'I can't abandon my country. This will pass.'"

She placed her hands on her chest, pushed down to bring herself under control.

His voice was tentative.

"You fight with him at night—"

"Why didn't you tell me?

Silence.

"I didn't want to embarrass you."

Embarrass her!

He must have slept like a dead man the time she'd risen up from a dream, dressed herself, and run as fast as she could around the farmhouse, dodging haying tools in the dark— running, along the fence that marked the home field. Three times she'd passed the gable outlined against the winter moon before the dream had finally released her. At last, she'd lain in the frozen grass, her head burning.

Another night, she'd woken up sweating. She'd made her way outside, into the sheep shed, to the fields, into the cow ditch, to the ocean. He'd carried her back like a sick ewe, saying soothing words, then placing her in the bed. But when she tried to tell him what she'd seen, he hadn't wanted to hear it. Now she had him. She tightened her grip on his ankle and began.

"Lena looked like a frog at first. I wished she hadn't been born."

Silence from his end of the hollow.

"Two years after I brought her to the convent, I wanted her back. But I was too late. The curtains were blowing out of the open windows. Toys all over the garden. One good thing about that visit—"

She stopped, couldn't go on.

"What?" he asked.

"I didn't see her bear in the convent garden among all those toys. Perhaps she took it with her to—"

Unable to go on, she sat up and hugged her knees. He extended his hand, pulled her to her feet. On the way back, the fog insinuated its way between them, yet he held onto her hand.

In the kitchen, Ragnar sat on the bench, his head bowed, shoulders sloped. She went to him, took his hands and rubbed udder cream into the hard places. That night, when he held her, she assigned Max to the back of her consciousness. Obediently, he stayed there.

38. A Weak Light across the Snow

After the milking, the old woman stayed in the shed to mix her *angelica archangelica* digestive, and Charlotte found herself alone in the kitchen. She pulled out the letter from her mother.

I went to the Red Cross today. They told me about a couple of young women who'd come to Berlin from Poland, looking for their families. I became very excited, thought one of them could have been Lena. But it led to nothing. I was so disappointed, I didn't go out for two days. Still, these incidents raised my hopes. Every morning I tell myself, perhaps today. So you see, my dear, my trip to see you and your family will have to wait.

Her mood dropped. The faces. The dreams. They'd meant nothing. The old woman bustled into the kitchen, cradling herbs in her apron and singing to herself about cutting a warrior's throat. She scraped the scales off the salted cod and cut the fins. The boiling water steamed the room with the odor of fish. Finally the old woman skimmed the foam off the water.

When they sat down to eat, Charlotte stole glances at her sons. Ragnar wanted her to paint them with the old oils from Berlin. But she noticed something odd about the boys. They looked like sheep, especially around the nose and mouth. They smelled like sheep. And why not? Didn't they live in a wooly mutton world, cutting and drying hay for the sheep, then shearing and slaughtering them? Hadn't she spent one hundred winters on this farm untangling sheep's wool and knitting from it?

"How did the calving go at Nonni's?" the old woman asked.

"Lost it—breech birth," Ragnar said.

She helped herself to some more suet. "Should've called me. I've got something for that."

Ragnar turned to Charlotte, as if to include her in the conversation. "What about Skjalda's sore?"

The cow had cut her udder on barbed wire. They'd applied a poultice of chopped lady's mantle and dog sour leaves, but the cow had worried it with her hoof. Charlotte hadn't looked this morning.

"The sore?" he repeated.

She took a guess. "Better."

Ragnar started to say something, but Tryggvi interrupted in an excited voice. "Next fall Papa's taking me to the sheep round-up."

"You're being rude," Charlotte said.

They all looked startled at her tone.

She glared at Ragnar. "He's too young to ride through the mountains—all that drinking and rough talk with the men," she said.

"I'll ride Red—he's sure-footed," Tryggvi said.

Ragnar slumped in his chair. "I told him he could hold the sheep's horns, help pull them from the pen."

The bond between father and son filled the room, leaving her no space to breathe. Her head hurt. She pushed back her chair. In the outhouse, she stood over the hole, tore her mother's letter into tiny pieces, and watched them flutter down where the waste covered the paper's whiteness. She thought of her mother's words. *I have a feeling she's alive. It's just a matter of time.* Lies. Her muttony boys, Henrik and Tryggvi, were her new life. Her baby with the curls that smelled of pine was gone forever. Even if she weren't, she'd be a grown woman now with swinging breasts and crow's feet on her grown-up skin. The loss stung her eyes.

The short, dark days arrived, the period when the sun barely rose above the mountain before it set again. When the electric light machine ran out of fuel, the Aladdin lamp flickered unsteadily over the table. Each day Charlotte rose reluctantly from her bed and often spent all day trying to shake her desire to crawl back into bed.

Every winter since she arrived, the hillside winter seemed darker than the year before. Traveling between farms on a starless, moonless night was like being blind. You tripped over tussocks and fell over rocks. Last year, the cow had bellowed in pain. The old woman couldn't shift the calf's position, and Ragnar was at Butterdale. Charlotte had set out in the darkness and had walked into the barbed wire fence and ripped her clothes. By the end of November, a sliver of light separated the black morning from the gray afternoon. Life was a cave so deep it hardly seemed worth it to get out of bed. Daylight was a dream too soon over.

It was three in the afternoon. A snowstorm had canceled today's daylight. Charlotte had had enough. She climbed the stairs to the loft and came back, holding a red candle. She lit it and set it on the window sill. Its tiny glow raised her spirits.

"Keep that up, and the Christmas witch will get us," the old woman said from the sofa, where she sat knitting.

"Just one," Charlotte said, moving as close as she could to the yellow glow without singeing her hair.

"You said that yesterday," she said cheerfully.

Charlotte admired the old woman's good disposition, how she always seemed happy. And Ragnar was at peace with his existence in a way she could never be. At night she cuddled up to Ragnar, welcomed his large hands, his hungry stroking, his abrupt thrusting. Afterwards, she often felt despondent for hours while he lay sleeping beside her.

She treasured every word he said, knowing that he was drawing on a small collection.

"So soft," Ragnar said one night, stroking her hair.

Max had played endlessly with her hair, buried his face in it, talked to it, wrapped it around his cheeks. On canvas, he'd transformed her brown hair to a blend of auburn, chestnut, and apricot, showed it flying like an orange pinwheel around her head. Sunshine glinted off wild red curls that danced on her shoulders.

"Touch my hair again," she said.

Ragnar obeyed.

"Repeat the word."

"Soft," he said huskily.

He'd used the same tone when they bought Red with his thick flaxen mane and forelock.

Next day, she found herself talking to Skjalda, telling the cow that they wouldn't ever slaughter her, salt her meat, and eat it with turnips, the way some farmers did. They would eat the cow at Butterdale instead. She told Skjalda the story of Io.

"For a long time Io had horns—"

Tiny fingers walked her spine. Henrik. "Everyone laughs at me for talking to myself. But you do it," he said.

She gave him a serious look.

"Tell it again," he said.

This time she told it louder, assigning different voices to Io and Zeus, singing nonsense verses in between. By the time the milking was done, Charlotte felt a rosy glow, a promise that spring would one day return with its long, bright days.

But by early afternoon, when she sat alone in the dimly-lit living room, threading elastic into the waist of the boys' underwear, her mood sank. Snow covered the home field, and darkness lay thick on the window. The old woman was in the kitchen chopping and grinding. Ragnar and the boys were in the shed. Charlotte reached for Ragnar's new socks that the old woman had just slipped off her needles and pulled them on.

"I'm going for a walk along the fence," she called gaily into the kitchen.

Outside the snow blew into her face and refreshed her. Her

boots sank deep. Walking downhill, she soon wearied from pulling her feet up out of her own tracks. She heard the crash of the ocean. The blood pulsed in her veins. She ran down the hill, stumbled then stopped, remembering her promise. But she just wanted to look at the ocean. That couldn't hurt. Carefully she trod the path to the village.

The lights came into view. She passed them and kept on walking until she came to the coarse sand at the shore. The blood throbbed in her ears when the water came into view.

At last she stood at the water's edge. The cliffs, the sand, the ocean—black as coffee. The waves roared. They crashed at her feet echoing in the cliffs. She stretched out her hands and threw back her head. The snow had stopped, and the clouds parted. The moon lit up the crest of the waves.

Warm now, she took off her boots and the thick socks, held them in her hands, and stepped into the water. A hand touched her shoulder.

39. Christmas

After he brought her back, she heard him turning the handle on the telephone. Gisela arrived the next day. Heavy-set and sensible looking, her friend bore little resemblance to the wild woman she'd met on the boat. In fact, her disapproving look grated on Charlotte. Was it Gisela's business if she swam in the ocean? She cast about for a safe topic of conversation.

"Christmas? What will you do?" Charlotte asked.

The downward lines in Gisela's face disappeared. "Tobacco for my farmer. Cooperative store toys for the kids. You?"

"Shaving things. Socks." Actually Charlotte dreaded Christmas. The darkness. The cooking. But then she remembered, "maybe some artwork." She'd revised the golden saxifrage sketches she'd begun in the summer, doing them over and over again, never throwing anything away, searching her mind for the secret, the magical element that was missing. Now she took them from the back of the cupboard and spread them out on the table.

Gisela smiled politely.

Charlotte brought out the watercolors—the yellow and white camomile, purple scurvywort blossoms against rubbery leaves, bulbous yellow and green meadow sweet, the tall springcress with its delicate lilac color, and her favorite, the sea of wild geranium, purple against the yellow of the buttercup.

Watching Gisela, she saw it herself. Not a stamen was out

of place, not a line was wrong on the petals, like the detailed plant drawings Max had done for the botanist. Even the shadows on the rocks were perfect. But the essence was missing.

"You could've been a photographer," Gisela said, folding her arms and leaning back in the sofa, smiling at her discovery.

Quickly Charlotte put her artwork away.

"You wrote me once about how you wanted to see the moss and rocks in a new way, how you thought you could make people realize that lichen lived," Gisela said.

How stupid she'd been to talk about what she herself didn't understand.

"What did you mean?"

"I don't know," Charlotte said.

"Coffee," the old woman called from the kitchen. Charlotte cut the brown cake. The heat rose between the slices, and the smell of baking soda made her feel ill. The old woman traded recipes with Gisela while Charlotte stared at her cake. She and Gisela drank cup after cup of coffee.

"I'll brew more," the old woman said, getting to her feet.

Gisela leaned towards Charlotte. "You won't find what you're looking for in the sea," she whispered.

Charlotte locked eyes with Gisela. "You're wrong."

The old woman was back, filling their cups again. She turned to Gisela. "You look tired. Got any monk pepper in your garden?"

Gisela shook her head.

"Tea from monk pepper's good for the 'change.'" Glancing at Charlotte, "Cures the shaky feeling you get just before you bleed." A scraping of chair as Gisela reached for her purse and took out a tiny notebook to record the information.

The old woman set down her cup and placed a hand on Gisela's shoulder. "And if your man gets too wild, grind up some monk pepper seeds and throw them into his tea." Gisela wrote this down also. She only stayed one night, and Charlotte was glad when she left.

The day before Christmas, Charlotte took the leg of smoked lamb from the hook in the smokehouse. She'd been tending the fire with manure chips for several days, and now the meat was crisp and brown on the outside. Her hands smelled like smoke from holding it. She put it to boil on the stove.

Used paper bags, saved over the year, and colored pencils lay on the kitchen table.

"Wrapping paper," she called into the living room. "No paper, no gifts."

Like lengthening shadows, Henrik and Tryggvi glided into their places at the table. They picked up pencils and grunted and sighed as they drew. Blue lions with wings. Green and yellow dragons. Dancing cows with a thousand eyes. Singing seals. And Tryggvi drew a frog named Maizie, smoking a cigarette and wearing a garter belt.

"Go away now," she said, slipping into German. *Weg mit euch*. Alone she wrapped books and underwear in the decorated bags. She chose the green and yellow dragon paper for Ragnar's shaving brush.

That afternoon Ragnar cut branches from the bush that grew at the side of the house and put them in a vase and set it on the side table in the living room. Charlotte placed the gifts under the branches. Henrik came up behind her, his arms full of ungainly packages wrapped in old newspapers, decorated bones like last year she suspected.

Charlotte cut out paper dolls, like the ones she'd seen holding hands and dancing across Christmas trees among red and white flags in Danish magazines. Henrik pinned them on the tree with clothespins that he'd colored red. She whittled two tiny candles to clip on the tree.

"At least you left us some," the old woman said out of the side of her mouth.

That evening, she and Henrik sat on the sofa and gazed at the candles.

"I had a funny dream last night," he said.

She braced herself.

"I was out in the fog, looking for the cows. Io was there, you know the human one."

She nodded.

"Next to her was the ugly one, the one with a thousand eyes. You called him Argos in the story."

"Yes."

"In the fog, I saw only the eyes, not him. And the eyes were beautiful, millions of them bright and shimmering, just like in the picture of a peacock's tail."

"Must've been beautiful," she murmured.

He leaned against her.

"Tell me a story."

She told him about the bear who came to the young woman's bed as the unseen lover. The young woman welcomed him, felt his long, hard body. Every night she ran her fingers through his thick curly hair and smelled the warm musky fragrance of his skin. All night he caressed her, whispering poetry into her ear.

Charlotte raised a finger.

"He warned her, *Don't ever try to see me, or you will lose me.* But the young woman loved him so dearly that one night when he slept, she crept out of bed, lit a candle, and held it over the bed. She saw the curly hair of her handsome lover. A drop of tallow dripped onto his cheek. A large white bear climbed out of her bed and lumbered to the door. She never saw her lover again."

After the old woman had gone to bed, Charlotte lit a Christmas candle, set it next to her bed. She felt like Candle Stealer, one of the Christmas elves. It had taken her three Christmases to learn all their names, and now she'd become one of them. She lay in bed, watching the flicker of the candle, pondering Henrik's visions.

Soft as moss, the image of Henrik and Lena meeting wrapped itself around her old wound. She fell asleep envisioning Henrik and Lena in the mist, surrounded by eyes from the peacock's tail.

A whisper awakened her. A man, his face misshapen and bloody, stood beside the bed. She gripped the covers and pulled back. He mustn't stain the sheet. Ragnar wouldn't like that. He sat down on the bed. The look in his eyes frightened her.

"Why didn't you tell me about the East? The camps?" he asked.

"I didn't know," she said.

His features softened. Sadness overwhelmed her. They'd missed so many years together. She lifted the sheet, and he came into her arms. His blood smelled of sweetened meat. It soaked her nightgown. Very gently, she peeled away his clothes, and made love to him—holding herself back for fear of hurting him.

His moan told her he'd forgiven her for not saving him. Afterwards, she kissed his face, told him Ragnar wouldn't mind if he stayed in the bed. Grateful that he had come to her again just before Christmas, she fell asleep stroking his chest.

Much later, when Ragnar came to bed, she woke with a start. Max was gone. She pretended to be asleep, but Ragnar's hand enclosed her breast. Dutifully, she climbed upwards through the silent stages of lovemaking with him. Pleasure consoled her for her loss. But at the peak, she cried out the forbidden name. *Max.*

On Christmas Eve, the tiny candles flickered on the bush branches. Otherwise, the room was dark. Henrik kept glancing at the window. She knew why. It was the night when the troll came up out of the darkness and hung on the window.

If you look, you'll turn to stone.

The boys touched their knives and forks with their fingertips, the nice cutlery, a wedding gift from the hillside farmers to Ragnar and his first wife. Charlotte raised a finger.

"Not yet."

The old woman sat up and leaned her back against her chair. She expanded her chest as if to sing to the thrush. Her mouth looked small and young, and her eyes glistened when she sang:

There's a joy in every hillock

A song in every rock

Ragnar carved the smoked meat, cold from the pantry. The snowy white mashed potatoes, the canned green peas, and the pink meat formed a landscape on the unchipped holiday plates. Afterwards, he moved the side table so they could do the Christmas dance around the bush branches. Charlotte grasped the old woman's hand and Henrik's. Holding up their clasped hands, they walked sideways, singing.

Adam had seven sons. Seven sons had Adam.

They shook their hips and clapped their hands. When Charlotte glanced out the window into the darkness, Henrik pulled her elbow.

"You musn't."

And she remembered the warning about troll's faces at the window. But she sought a different face.

40. Dog Day King

Charlotte loved how the cows bolted from the shed in the spring. The memory of the long, dark, ill-smelling winter in the shed disappeared. A new life took over. Frequent rain squalls dismissed the winter snow and turned the grass bright green. The thrush pumped out his raucous song, and new lambs dotted the fields.

Herding the cows, she relished the many shades of green in the moss and heather. In Berlin, landscape had meant paintings in the gallery. Here it curled at her feet and carried her vision up the mountain on one side, down to the sea on the other. On dry days, after she'd finished the washing and baking, she slipped out past the knolls and flopped down on the grass, breathing in the life that came from the earth.

The long bright days of spring illuminated the dark corners she'd avoided in winter. Her burden of not knowing grew lighter in the sunshine.

But certain things never went away. Despite their talk in the hollow, Max lingered as a barrier between her and Ragnar. For weeks after her phantom lover had shared their bed, Ragnar had barely spoken to her. Silly man—jealous of a ghost. But she also knew another truth. The more Ragnar withheld words, the larger Max loomed for her.

She carried a pail of milk into the kitchen. The old woman was sorting berries, leaves, roots, and bark, humming to herself. In the pantry, Charlotte spooned curds into the boys' bowls. She strewed sugar and minced scurvywort over the mixture, so that it resembled a snowy scene with traces of grass. Over this she poured Skjalda's warm milk.

A clattering on the stairs. Henrik and Tryggvi sat down to breakfast.

Ragnar was in the outer field cutting hay. While he was gone, she would grind dried manure wedges for scattering on the field at the far end of the farm. But suddenly she remembered the letter from her mother that she'd carried in her pocket for a week, the one that ended with *I believe she's still alive.* It was time. She sat down by the window in the living room, looked out at the lime green grass blowing gently in the wind, and picked up a pen.

Dear Mamma, it's so lovely here. I've done dozens of flower sketches and watercolors. Come and visit us before the boys grow up. Please give up on Lena. I've had dreams, and I no longer believe that she is alive.

Relief came immediately. She'd finally made a decision. But after she'd sealed the envelope, she became uneasy. The letter wouldn't stop her mother from visiting the Red Cross and asking about Lena every day. She'd only try harder when she realized that her daughter, the child's mother, had given up. But most importantly, Charlotte wasn't sure she'd told the truth. She wasn't sure she believed what she wrote.

A sound of banging pots came from the kitchen. Charlotte dropped the letter. Over the kitchen door hung a banner. *Long Live the Dog Day King.* The old woman pointed to the day calendar. *June 26.* It was the day of the Dog Day King, and the old woman was baking dog day pancakes. In 1809 an English merchant had sent the Dane Jorundur Joergensen to Iceland. He rode around the island shouting *I am your king. Down with Danish monopoly. Down with Danish rule.*

The old woman set the pancakes on the table. Charlotte saw the wild look in her eye. "The Dog Day King was the first to get us independence," she said. It only lasted a month. And the Dog Day King was sent to prison in Tasmania.

The old woman disappeared into the pantry. Charlotte heard her splashing in the pickling barrel. On most farms, they fed the intestines to the dogs. But at slaughter time, the old woman scooped the intestines out of the carcass. The old woman washed the guts with water, followed by whey. Back in the fall she'd braided them before boiling them, called them blue gut for their off-white color. The boys groaned when she held up a dripping handful of what resembled knotted worms. The sight sent a shudder through Charlotte.

"Dog Day King's favorite," the old woman said.

Henrik picked up a piece of blue gut, sniffed it, dropped it back onto the plate. The old woman fixed her gaze on him. "Spoiled brat. Do you realize what we got for treats back in the days of the Dog Day King?"

He shook his head gloomily.

"We dipped a slice of sheep's hide into a saucer of cod liver oil and licked it."

Hah, Charlotte thought, picturing the old woman eating the soldier's orange, peeling it slowly, arranging the slices on a plate, sniffing them, taking one slice, popping it into her mouth, keeping her eyes closed, murmuring, savoring the flavor with her tongue.

Charlotte poked a slice of blue gut with her fork, felt the old woman's eyes on her.

The boys were arguing about how the Dog Day King had looked. Under the noise of their talk, the old woman turned to Charlotte. "Did you talk to him?"

"Yes."

The old woman climbed up on the bench next to Tryggvi and took the herbal guide from the shelf. She blew the dust off the top of the book, opened it to purple violets rimmed with yellow, and read aloud:

"Violet tea cures a flaming temper. Makes you regular. Grows by the side of the road." It'll help you handle Ragnar."

"He's quite regular, I think."

The door opened and Ragnar walked in. He took a pencil from the tin can by the sink and a bill from the stack on the table. He began making calculations on a pad. She peered over his shoulder, saw geometrical shapes next to the figures, recognized the outline of a toilet bowl. He covered his drawing.

She fixed her gaze on him. He moved his lips, and she knew he was about to say something. She decided not to fill the silence but to wait.

"Can you teach the boys how to draw?" he asked finally.

She recalled how he'd described leisure activities as courting the devil. "Isn't that a waste of time?" she asked, deliberately using his words.

He looked like an obedient animal who had accidentally piddled on the floor.

"I just meant during haying season."

"Teach me," Henrik said. He was already rummaging through the silverware drawer for a pencil stub.

"Like this," she said, starting a new portrait of Ragnar, sketching the back of his head, then adding his thick dark hair. Henrik pressed against her free arm. His breath smelled like the Danish peppermints Ragnar bought at the cooperative.

Tryggvi came in from the shed. She could smell his overalls at her shoulder.

"Change clothes," she ordered.

"No. I'm going out again." He jumped out in front of her, his fingers in his nostrils. "Do me," he said. The pleasure at his own body reminded her of Max. She blinked his memory away.

The old woman smiled when Ragnar joined her in the blue gut meal. While they ate, the sunny dog day weather changed to rain. But Ragnar pushed back his chair and signaled Tryggvi to join him. Charlotte heard them in the hall, blundering through the pile of boots. From the living room, she watched them walk down the road, their macintoshes and shovels already shiny in the rain. Filling holes with gravel, Tryggvi would become a man like Ragnar, the kind of man she couldn't understand.

She took out the salted gills, an ugly and gelatinous food, rinsed them and dropped them into a pan of water. In the pantry, she opened the burlap bag, took out a salted cod for tomorrow. Holding it by its tail, she admired its flat, triangular form. It had been the island symbol when the Dog Day King called for independence, prettier than a flag, she thought.

She washed the fish in cold water, cut it into pieces, and covered it with water. Tomorrow she'd remove the scales and cut off the fins, boil it, and serve it with melted sheep fat and potatoes. And on and on until she rolled over dead. Did secretaries in Berlin feel this way about ritual tasks? Or was something wrong with her? Did she have some kind of intolerance for daily life?

And those cows. No matter how often she emptied their udders, they always filled with milk again. Again and again, twice a day, forever and ever. She had no say in what happened at the farm. The seasons, the animals, and her boys' nature determined everything. The wind keened when it vibrated in the metal strip in the front door. The sound struck a chord at her temples. Soon they would throb.

Charlotte reached into the old woman's juniper canister and took out a handful of the needle-like leaves and dried berries. She ran to the smoke house, ducked to enter, and fastened the door from the inside with a block of wood at the top. She leaned against the wall, so that the piled sod cushioned her shoulders and the lava rock probed her vertebrae. A leg of smoked lamb hung above the fireplace, and the cold hard smell of moist earth rose from the packed floor.

Her head was an animal trying to break out of prison. She took her mother's letter from her pocket and placed it on the manure chips in the fireplace. Around it, she scattered the juniper leaves and berries, then reached for the box of wooden matches on the lava rock ledge. She struck the match and touched the flame to the corner of the paper, watched the fire curl around her mother's foolish words. *She's alive.* As the fire released the juniper aroma, she leaned forward and breathed deeply until the headache released her temples.

A canister of cream from the morning milking stood on the floor. The old woman must have brought it here. Charlotte peered into the churn, saw some leftover cream, grasped the handle, and sloshed it up and down, until it finally clotted into yellowish lumps. She scraped the butter off the sides of the churn.

41. Old People Talk to Cows

Charlotte and the old woman were sipping daisy tea from coffee-stained mugs. The hinge of the bedroom door squeaked, and Henrik stood in the doorway, his eyes puffy with sleep. His underpants hung by one button from his undershirt. In one arm he held his eyeless teddy bear. Bone King, he called it. Her mother had sent it.

He sat down at the table, and the old woman made him breakfast. He pushed the thick gray oatmeal cereal down with his spoon so that the milk rushed into the hollows like the lakes in a glacier. With his other hand, he scratched his head. The old woman came up behind him, pulled apart two handfuls of hair, and talked into his scalp.

"I see you in there, you devils."

From the shelf, she took her mixture of butterwort leaves and margarine. She made it from the sticky plant that grew alongside the road and trapped insects on its leaves. Holding Henrik's head firmly against her belly, she rubbed the salve into the boy's scalp. He jerked his head away.

"Still, boy."

From the cage of her embrace, he called. "Raisins."

"They'll give you lice," the old woman said.

Charlotte stirred a second bowl of oatmeal for Henrik. Then she fetched a handful of raisins from the pantry. Henrik set the raisins down on the table. He took one and dropped it onto a peak of oatmeal.

"This is the farm. Now I'm traveling to Reykjavik. Hop. Hop.

Hop. Then onto the ship," he sang.

He picked some raisins out of the milk. Charlotte knew he'd take them to the tussocks and feed them to his bones. The old woman needn't look so sour. She didn't know about the special meaning of raisins during war, how you could wake up in the middle of the night dreaming about touching their wrinkled little skins and mincing their sweetness between your front teeth.

For the old woman the war had meant some German Heinkels strafing the land, dropping an occasional bomb, taking a village boy's leg off. When the Hudsons flew out to sea, you knew a German torpedo had found its mark. Survivors hung onto the ship's wreckage, unlikely to be saved.

"We had so little to eat. That's why I spoil the boy with raisins," Charlotte said.

"We were lucky. Kids got goodies, learned how to chew gum and eat chocolate at the same time. And the smoking—" The old woman rolled her eyes, and dropped her voice to a whisper. "A tipsy girl could straddle a man in a Quonset hut without falling off—but it took practice."

Charlotte had seen some children in the village who looked a little different from the other villagers. "War's never easy," she said.

After Gisela's last visit, Charlotte stopped writing her friend for a while. Then gradually she started again, rarely mentioning how the wind had taken the roof off the shed or how they'd lost a cow, recording instead for Gisela every detail about Berlin from her mother's letters. Like nourishment she took in Gisela's news of stores on the Kurfurstendamm, rebuilt churches, and how the bombed-out front tower of the Kaiser Wilhelm church was left unrestored as a reminder of the war.

Charlotte carried Gisela's latest letter down the cow path to the meadow, leaned into the wind, held the paper with both hands and reread descriptions of Gisela's sister's picnic in a park in the American zone. It had been hot. Not a leaf moved on the trees. If Charlotte closed her eyes, she could see it and feel it. Touching Gisela's letter in her pocket, she walked quickly back to the farmhouse. She sat down at the desk and wrote.

My mother writes that a lot of the flowers are still in bloom in Berlin. The Pleasure Garden must be so beautiful. Hmmm, I can almost smell the lilacs and elder.

About Lena, my mother goes to the Red Cross every day, looking for her. I don't think she'll find her, but then what if she did? What would I say to her? "I'm sorry I gave you away to the nuns." If she's one of those smart types who does her fingernails and talks about hemlines, I wouldn't know how to talk to her.

Charlotte

The pen felt thick between her fingers. She rubbed her aching eyelids. Her mood spiraled downward into a new mystery. Would she discover a daughter and mourn a lost baby?

She addressed the envelope and sealed it, placed it next to the letter to her mother. Ragnar would make a trip to the village next week.

In the cowshed, Ragnar's and Tryggvi's pants lay soaking in the tub. She rubbed Tryggvi's pants over the washboard until her knuckles stood out cold and red.

It will be all right. Tryggvi will ride into the mountains on Red.

She fed the pants into the wringer, watched the thick gray water ooze out of them, talked to the water.

He'll live—I won't lose him like Lena.

Henrik stood in the doorway, holding a small bucket of potatoes. He was staring at her. He set his bucket down, and one of the potatoes rolled across the floor. He ran after it, picked it up and disappeared into one of the cow stalls. She heard him talking quietly to himself, raising his voice, then edging into shrillness.

Io. Io. I pray every night that God will make you human again.

Wiping her hands on her apron, she went to him. He had

both hands on the stall railing. Tears glistened on his cheeks. She put her arms around his shoulders, rested her chin on his hair. "Who are you talking to?" she asked.

He shrugged himself free.

"Nobody."

"Do you sometimes talk to Skjalda?"

He pulled his head forward then back, knocking against her chin.

"Only old people talk to cows!"

"I see," she said, rising to her feet.

He followed her to the washroom, approached the tub, and put his muddy fingers into the water.

"Stop it."

He jumped back. Together, they carried the basket of clothes to the clothesline. Solemnly, he held up Ragnar's pants for her. She clipped them to the line. Holding the empty basket, Henrik led the way to the house. When had she begun to follow her children?

42. The Tug of the Ocean

The fog pushed against the windows. In the hall, Tryggvi and Ragnar spoke in the quick, hard voices of people preparing to leave. Charlotte held her cup of coffee with both hands, felt its warmth against her chest, and followed them out to the steps.

She pictured the sheep skittering away at the sight of them. Tryggvi and Ragnar would surround them, so they had no place to go but down the mountain toward the sheep pens for sorting. Charlotte could foresee the horror the lambs faced once they arrived back at the farm where they'd been born back in April.

Henrik would begin crying at the sight of Nonni of Butterdale, striding across the tussocks cradling his gun. One shot to the head, and the skinny legs would buckle. The old woman would catch the blood in a pot. In slaughter season everything became guts, fat, and fleece. The old woman would take the intestines to a separate cutting board and press out the filth, then wash them. Ragnar would treat the heads with respect. He would cleave them down the middle to form two halves. Outside he'd singe off every scrap of wool. After he'd removed the brain, he'd wash and brush the heads, and place them in the old woman's pot, flat side down. They'd simmer in a frothy brew, steaming up the windows.

Thinking of Tryggvi's trip to the mountains and all its consequences, she wished he hadn't gone. It wasn't worth the risk. But even if he didn't go, the smell of hot sheep eyes and singed skin would still fill every corner of the house. When the old woman lifted the lid of the pot to skim off the froth, Charlotte would picture life inside a ewe's womb. At Sunday dinner, they'd eat the heads served cold with mashed carrots and turnips.

Charlotte stood on the steps shifting her weight, wishing they'd leave soon, so she could begin waiting for them to come back. Finally, father and son each raised a hand in a goodbye gesture. In the horses' quivering rumps, in the thickest part of their twitching tails, she foresaw a hard trip up the mountain, horse and rider slipping, hurtling faster and faster downhill. Her child's broken body would land on a cold ledge, next to the skeleton of the old woman's soldier.

The fog closed around the horses' tails, then seemed to wrap itself around the hillside.

"Hair of the hidden people," the old woman said.

The horses wouldn't see the earthquake rifts and chasms. The earth changed itself, so that it could trick creatures and trap them in its innards.

The old woman reached into her pocket and held up dried berries between thumb and forefinger. "Chew it."

Charlotte took some. The old woman popped the rest into her own mouth.

For a long time, they stood on the steps, moving their mouths over the bitter skins, grinding the hard little seeds that stuck in their teeth. The fog had thinned into wisps, streaking the green hillside with tufts like sheep's wool caught on barbed wire against a green pasture.

"May God bless the hidden people—our friends," the old woman said, crossing herself. But Charlotte knew how she meant it. If Tryggvi or Ragnar needed help, the hidden people would emerge from the mist, arms outstretched. She'd learned that from Henrik.

He clutched her skirt. "Next year I want to go with them."

She vowed to keep him close all day. That afternoon, he

helped her with the wool. He soon grew tired and sat in front of her, the skein of unspun wool looped over his sagging, outstretched arms.

"Almost done," she said, chasing the wool around his arms while he stared disconsolately at the living room wall. But suddenly he sat up straight and pointed at Max's small painting of the market place in Berlin. The skein of yarn fell to the floor.

"It's moving," he said, covering his eyes, then peering at the painting through his fingers. "It's me. I'm running away from that thing."

"Silly boy," she said, picking up the yarn.

Then she raised her eyes to the painting and tried to see what he saw. He was right. The green and white figure was chasing the small white one.

His eyes blazed. "You left me alone at the market."

"It's not you."

But she sensed that he didn't really mean *me*, but somebody so close to him that it hurt.

She placed an arm over his shoulders, drew him close. "I won't leave you."

He cuddled against her breast. "Tell me a story."

She took a deep breath.

"Tom was a lonely farmer who lived on a cliff by the sea."

"Like Papa?"

"Papa's not exactly lonely—doesn't talk much—but not lonely."

"But he's a farmer," Henrik said, putting his thumb into his mouth, leaning against her, sucking vigorously.

"One day, Tom was walking home across the moor. He'd been cutting grass in the outer fields. Down below, the ocean crashed on the rocks. The tide was coming in. Then he saw something he'd never seen in that place before. A figure sat on a rock. It appeared to be a woman wearing a hood and looking out to sea. The waves rose higher. He hurried down the hill. Soon the rock would be covered, and the woman would be washed away.

"He ran to her, caught her arm, but she moved away, tried to fling herself into the water.

"He grabbed the hood, but she got away and slid into the sea. Tom was left standing there, holding the hood.

"The next day he walked past the ocean. Again she sat on the rock. He climbed over the rocks towards her. When she saw him, she wailed, 'Give me back my hood.'

"Her red hair blew around her face. Her green eyes matched the color of the sea on a sunny day.

"'Only if you come home with me and marry me.'

"She wailed again. But he wouldn't give it back. Marry me, and I'll give you back your hood.'

"He extended his hand, and together they walked up the hill to his farm. He led her into his kitchen, brought her a chair, and made her some tea. When she raised the cup to her lips, he saw the webbed fingers for the first time. He was fascinated. He watched her drink the tea and decided she was beautiful. He even liked the small stiff hairs that grew at the corners of her mouth."

Henrik sat up straight, extended his arms, and spread his fingers.

"The next day he brought her to the church. But after the wedding ceremony, on the way back to the farm, she stopped, looked at him and said, 'Give me back my hood.'

"'No—later, after we've been married for a while.' She didn't ask again. She too was in love. Besides she knew where the hood was—she'd seen Tom lock it in the big chest at the top of the stairs. At first she thought about it, but gradually she forgot about it.

"Soon she was expecting their first child. The woman was so happy to have a little daughter that she almost forgot about the hood. Her next child was a fine boy. The time she spent with her two small children was the happiest time of her life.

"But one day, she was reading to the children. Suddenly a barking sound came from the sea. The woman ran to the window. For the first time in many years, she remembered the hood and ran up the steps to the chest. But, of course, it was locked. She cried and frightened the children. At last, their father came back from the fields.

"'Mamma isn't well,' the little girl whispered to him.

"That night there was a knock at the door. The little boy opened it. On the steps stood one of the men from the village.

"'We've just killed three seals. Can you help us skin them?' he asked the boy's father.

"But before Tom could speak, their mother made a hoarse barking sound in the back of her throat. The children began to cry. Their mother ran past the villager out the door. They called to her, but she ran towards the beach. They went after her. Finally they found her on the beach staring at the bodies of the three seals.

"She bent down and closed the seals' eyes and made a sign of the cross over them.

"Then she fainted. Tom picked her up and carried her home. He put her to bed and heated some milk for her. Her son and daughter rubbed her cold feet and prayed that she would get well and be their mother again.

"Finally she got well. She took care of her children, made food for them, played games with them, read to them. But then it happened again. A barking sound came from the ocean, and she ran upstairs to the chest, but this time it was unlocked. The children heard her rummaging through the things in the chest. At last, she appeared. She wore a tight-fitting gray hood on her head.

"'Mamma, you look funny,' the little girl said.

"'She looks like a seal,' the boy said.

"But when they saw her face, they stopped laughing. Her lip was quivering. The long hairs around her mouth twitched.

Without speaking, she went first to the girl—straightened her hair, then to the boy—stroked his cheek. They wrinkled their noses because suddenly she smelled of fish. Then she walked out the door.

"They missed her terribly. The father did his best to raise the children. When they were old enough, he taught them to fish from a little boat in the inlet. But they always longed for their mother. Then one day, they went out too far on their boat. The wind came up, and they couldn't get back to shore. They clung to the sides of the boat crying.

"A seal swam up to the boat and began circling it, never taking its round black eyes off the children. She sang these words, 'Pity me. For I have two children on the land and two in the sea.' They lost their fear and brought the boat back to shore. When they looked out to sea, they saw the seal's profile against the horizon.

Henrik sat still. "Who was she?" he asked.

"Their mother."

His eyes glistened. "I knew it." He pulled on her arm. "The painting—the one that came alive today—"

Even in the dim light she saw the red dot Max had made on the canvas so many years ago. A smell of the garden rose from his scalp as Henrik snuggled against her. "Where did you get it?" he asked.

She couldn't remember *not* telling him. He spoke before she could.

"I know—it's from Max, my first father."

He was an odd boy, always weaving a web that connected all of them. Looking into his eyes, she saw something new, a longing she hadn't seen before. "I wish we had a sister?" he said suddenly.

She stretched her mouth into a smile, but her cheeks felt rubbery. Ragnar had wanted a daughter. She'd thought it, but never said it. *No, it might be a girl.* Why had she resisted? Who was she saving a place for? Henrik leaned against her. His body felt fragile, too narrow to contain such a big wish.

43. The Plash of Oars

The rocks that studded the slope above the farmhouse were a favorite spot for the sheep. They nibbled on the sweet heather that nestled among the smaller stones. Charlotte followed them, climbed to the higher ledge, her sketchpad under her arm. She scanned the rocks, saw how the cracks divided the rocks into ragged sections. A lone dandelion struggled for survival between the rocks. In the dark line that separated the rocks she began to draw, laboring over the flower's many-petaled shadow where it fell on the rock. Finally she drew the bright yellow flower itself.

She climbed higher until she approached the ridge—the place that looked out over the ocean. Then she saw the yellow mountain saxifrage where it grew out of a cleft in the rock. The dandelion was a pauper by comparison, the drawing of it just a practice session.

Charlotte made a quick sketch. When she held the drawing at arms length, she sensed a falseness but could not determine the point at which it began. Eyes closed, she went over it again, the cleft in the rock, the emerging flower, its slender red-tinged yellow petals, the thick leaves.

Back at the farmhouse, she opened the sketchpad and recognized the same old problem. Gisela had put it into words. It was a photograph, botanically correct, like the ones Max had drawn for the textbook, but their essence was missing. How had they smelled and felt? What secret did they contain? Max had always introduced her as an artist. But she wasn't. Not yet.

In bed that night, Charlotte ran her hand over the space where Ragnar usually slept. Whole nights went by without her touching Ragnar, but she didn't like to lie alone in the bed. When she closed her eyes, the images began. She saw Caspar David Friedrich's painting of moonlit figures sitting on a rock looking out to sea at low tide, surrounded by seaweed-covered rocks. Words from one of the old woman's songs entered her mind.

A young woman waits by a seaweed-grown inlet
Listening for the plash of oars.

How long did she wait for him, Charlotte wondered. Longer than was safe, with the ocean gurgling under the seaweed, billowing it higher and higher.

Her mother's voice from long ago, thirteen years now, rose up from some dark memory pit.

Your father has done everything for his country. Even earned the Iron Cross. Now he's been working for all these years for the Republic, not advancing . If only we had the Kaiser back. And now you want to be a Bohemian! A painter! The Imperial School for Secretaries is the place for nice girls without means. Bernstein? A Jew! Give the child to the nuns.

It was a message. She had to put an end to the eternal waiting. In school they'd read about Theseus and how he slew the minotaur. His father King Aegeus thought the minotaur had killed Theseus. He went to the water's edge and leaned forward until he fell into the sea. But Theseus was still alive.

Splash. She was sinking down, down to the bottom of the sea. Something gripped her arm. She opened her eyes and saw Henrik. No, she wasn't Aegeus.

"Fire," the boy yelled.

He was fantasizing again. But she dragged herself from the bed and followed him to the doorstep. Up ahead the sky glowed red. A few years ago the volcano had broken through the ice cap on the glacier. Miles away, the blaze that lit up the sky seemed like something personal, like their own bonfire.

The cows lowed under the reek of rotten eggs.

Charlotte and the old woman climbed to the highest ridge of the hillside. Henrik ran after them. The glacier was surrounded by black smoke.

"We'll have a flood again," the old woman said.

Panic marked Henrik's face. "Like Noah's flood? My bones can't swim."

"Not up here," the old woman said. "Down there." She waved her arm over the countryside to the east, the long stretch of creek-riddled sand that ended in the sea.

Then she raised her head to the sky, deepened her voice, and spoke in the gloomy tones of a prophet. "The crater in the glacier will overflow, and the glacier's innards will rush over the sand, bust out the bridges, wash away the road, and end up in the ocean."

Fear crept up Charlotte's spine. The earth's violence always frightened her.

They walked back towards the farm. At the gate that separated the home field from the meadows beyond, the old woman waved them on. At the steps to the house Charlotte turned and saw her pacing the gravel, head back, nose to the wind. It was as if the sulphur had triggered something in her brain.

44. With a Man's Heart

Last year's eggs from the back of the refrigerator thundered up out the earth's bowels. Icebergs rolled out on glacier water. The band of gray filth poured into the ocean, separating the sea into two glassy green parts. For days, the water ran over the sand, sending streams into new channels, changing the flow of rivers from north to south. Charlotte felt the tug of the ocean. Just a little peek from up close couldn't hurt.

When she told the old woman, her mother-in-law looked startled. "You can see it better from here," she said. Charlotte was already pulling on her boots.

The old woman stood behind her. "I'll go with you—collect seaweed for rheumatism season."

She disappeared into the kitchen and returned with a bucket, knife, and gloves. Charlotte rarely drove the truck. Now she got in quickly, with Henrik squeezed in next to her and the old woman with her braids pressed against the window. Charlotte put the vehicle in gear while she eased it down the hillside, tapping the brake all the way. Henrik gripped her thigh with both hands as if to anchor her to the seat. She drove east for a while, beyond their usual place, then parked at the edge of the sand, now a swamp, studded with rocks and icebergs.

The old woman stepped into rubber boots and tucked her skirt into her underpants. The sea gargled languidly in the shelter of the inlet. Green seaweed and shiny brown kelp undulated on the surf between the rocks. Tiny snails dotted the plants.

"Brown one's for lungs. Green for rheumatism," she said wading into the slurping water. She cut seaweed and dropped it into her bucket. Later she would wash it, dry it on the field like hay, then pack it tightly into a wooden container until it formed a sweet-tasting, pearly coating.

Water dripped from the green kelp in the old woman's hands. "Perfect for arthritis compresses." Charlotte cut green and brown strips of seaweed and piled them onto the back of the flatbed.

Henrik scurried along the sand, calling "I need shells."

"I'll pick the snails off. You go find shells with the boy," the old woman said, climbing onto the back of the truck. Charlotte sensed she wanted to be alone.

She found Henrik crouched in the sand, dusting off a seashell. Seeing her, he stood and pointed to the murky strip of glacier water that invaded the ocean and colored it brown.

"How can the fish swim in that?"

"They can't," she said.

Up ahead, the rocks formed an arch. She longed to swim through it, out into the open sea. Henrik tugged on her skirt.

"Look. Look."

He splashed into the water up to his knees, pointing at something. She ran after him. Then she saw what he saw.

A child in a white dress was caught in the surf. It struggled towards the shore, but the waves kept pulling it out, farther and farther each time. She ran towards the small figure and plunged in. The icy black water gripped her body. Somewhere behind her Henrik screamed.

The waves crashed over her, but each time they receded she glimpsed the child. At last she grasped its arm, then held its small body under her arm and thrashed at the ocean with the other. But it slipped out of her grasp and disappeared below the surface. She'd seen its eyes, the embroidery on its dress, called its name.

"Lena Lena."

Water filled her mouth. She found the child again, gripped her this time with both arms. Together they sank into the black water. It no longer felt cold. She and Lena floated down dark hallways, seeking the exit. People talked in shrill tones. Faces floated. Their noses seemed flush with their cheeks.

Where were her hands?

At last she found them, palms down on the sand. Empty. Where was the baby?

Hands—not hers—went under her body.

Steady now.

And she was airborne, weightless, skimming the shore— a godwit, her red neck gleaming in the sun. She flew into a leather cave. Nonni sat in the driver's seat, his wife next to him, Henrik somewhere between them.

She felt the old woman's familiar dry hands on her legs. "The child?" she asked. But nobody answered.

The old woman's hand smelled of seaweed. It touched her cheek. The car stopped in front of the farmhouse. Charlotte was glad they hadn't brought her to the hospital like last time.

Hands helped her into the bed, pulled off her wet clothes. The lavender scent of her nightgown curled around the wild odor of the sea. A hot water bottle glugged under the blanket.

She was central to a death vigil, her own body lying in the coffin. But she wasn't dead. A dull knife was mincing her skin into tiny pieces. From somewhere came the aroma of valerian and grass of Parnassus. All hammer and nails now, the old woman brought her tea.

"For the nerves and liver."

But she still hadn't answered the question.

"The child?" Charlotte asked.

The old woman sat on the chair next to the bed and fixed her with icy blue eyes. "Henrik screamed. Then I saw you in the water." Skin against papery skin, she crossed her legs, folded her hands on a knee. "You were swimming after a baby," she said at last.

Charlotte stared up at the ceiling. The baby *had* been in the ocean, in her arms.

"You called it Lena."

The sound of the name in someone else's mouth felt good. The old woman did not avert her gaze when tears warmed Charlotte's cheeks.

She wasn't sure when Henrik had entered the room. She reached for his hand, but he pulled back, turned to his grandmother.

"It was my fault she went into the water."

"No, boy," the old woman said.

From the other side of some mysterious divide, Charlotte watched them, Henrik toeing the floor, the old woman talking to him in a soothing voice.

Henrik approached the bed. "Were you trying to save it?"

Charlotte nodded obediently, wondering at the word *it*.

He turned to the old woman. "Tell her about it."

The old woman placed her palms on her thighs and stroked her hands down her skirt. At last she opened her mouth.

"He's about a week old, still has his umbilical cord and his birth hair. Must've lost his mother in that mucky glacier water."

Charlotte glared at her. How cruel. This animal fantasy. Closing her eyes, she returned to the moment when she glimpsed the embroidery on the white dress. How she'd struggled to sew the tiny cherries onto the collar.

"You nearly drowned," the old woman said.

Charlotte smiled, reliving the moment when she'd held the child in her arms, just before she lost her. Half dozing, she heard the old woman's voice.

"Chew this. Calms your liver."

It seemed like weeks later when Charlotte discovered something special. It appeared behind the old woman, framed by the window. A new day. She sat up and accepted the warm boiled birch bark and began to chew.

The old woman, perched at the foot of her bed. "Were you really seeking a child?"

Charlotte nodded.

"I have something to tell you."

Charlotte held up her hand. She didn't want to hear it.

But the old woman took a piece of seaweed from her pocket, gave some to Charlotte and put some in her own mouth. For a long moment there was silence but for their chewing. At last the old woman spoke. "You know my favorite warrior is Egill Skallagrimsson?"

Charlotte turned her head to the wall.

"Egill lost his son, Böðvar, to the ocean. He went into his bed closet and shut the door. Why? Because he couldn't avenge his death against the sea. He wouldn't eat or drink, was trying to starve himself. His daughter, Þorgerður, went to him. He let her in but nobody else. She lay down on the other bed. Egill told her he wanted to die. The sorrow was too much. They just lay side by side. Þorgerður was chewing seaweed. Egill took some too. They both chewed. Didn't talk. Suddenly they were both very thirsty. Þorgerður offered her father a drink from her horn. He drank long and deep. But it was milk. Egill immediately felt better. He wouldn't die yet.

"'Now write a poem for Böðvar,' she said. He composed a long poem, begins like this.

My mouth strains to move the tongue
To weigh and wing the choice word

"When he'd finished the poem, he didn't want to die any more."

Henrik climbed onto the foot of the bed and crept under the blanket. Charlotte felt his small leg warm against her shin.

She turned to look at him, but his eyes were fixed on the old woman. He clutched her big toe and squeezed it. "Mamma, would you miss me if I drowned?" She nodded. He climbed down from the bed.

"Egill ended his poem like this," the old woman said. *Not in misery and mourning, but with a man's heart.*

When Charlotte opened her eyes, Ragnar was sitting next to the bed. Tryggvi was talking in the hall. Back from the round-up, he had not tumbled down the mountain and cracked his head on a rock. She struggled to rejoice over his safety. But her sense of loss was stronger.

Ragnar's eyes looked kind. He took her hand.

"You promised me."

"But I saw her in the water," she said and was immediately sorry for her words.

He looked sympathetic in the way of people who nod their heads over the strange customs of others without ever understanding. The baby in the water had been more real to her than the tiny nostril of a lamb or the soft lip of a cow—even more than putting your arm into a cow's birth canal up to the elbow and turning a calf.

"I'm sorry," she said at last.

"No, I am."

Had she heard right? But he was the only person in the room.

"You kept trying to tell me, but I didn't want to hear it. It reminded me of something from long ago."

She nodded, sensing he had more to say but knowing also that he wouldn't say it.

Last time, in the hospital, she'd heard screams. Her own. Running feet. The rustle of starched fabric. Large hands on her arm. *Steady now.* A needle plunging into her arm. Darkness. Peace. But she wouldn't need that now.

He stood up carefully, as if he was afraid to break something that had come loose. She watched him walk out the door. Her hair felt greasy, and she smelled her own sweat on the sheets. Turning towards the wall, she closed her eyes.

The next morning, she pulled herself up and tottered into the kitchen.

The old woman was boiling birch bark, steaming the windows. Both hands on the saucepan handle, the old woman carried the hot broth to Charlotte and placed it under her nose so that the woodsy fragrance rose in her nostrils.

"It'll clear your head," the old woman said.

But the briny smell that blew in off the ocean was stronger. It drew Charlotte to the open window. She breathed deeply, felt the power of the sea in her lungs.

A wailing sound came from far out on the ocean. Turning, Charlotte met the old woman's gaze and realized she'd heard it too.

45. Phantom Lover

They sat in the kitchen, listening to Ragnar tell the story.

"The seal wouldn't go back into the ocean. Poor thing, all covered with baby fur. Fishermen carried it along the shore, wriggled the whole time, tried to get back on land. They brought it to the place where they found it, put it in the water and pushed on it."

Henrik stood at her side, turning her hand over, weaving his fingers between hers.

"They're not webbed," he said quietly. She stretched out her hand, spread the fingers, so that he could see her perfectly separated fingers. Raising his eyes to hers, he asked the old question.

"Who's Lena?"

How many times had she told him?

"You were shouting her name. I heard you."

Now he had her. She wanted to hug him, but held back, for fear of breaking something between them. The old woman's words rang in her ears. *Just say 'I have something to tell you.'*

She took his hand and led him to the sofa in the living room. In the kitchen Ragnar kept babbling about the seal—everything was animals for him.

"But it was crazy for land and scrambled back on shore, trailing its umbilical cord. Finally, they gave up. One of them took it home—big family, kids, dogs, chickens. The seal was just one more."

They faced the painting of the little girl, surrounded by wildflowers.

"Max painted her many times. This is his best one," she said.

"What happened to Max?"

"He died in a concentration camp."

She'd never said those words out loud.

Henrik had the hungry look of one who'd just begun to eat. "And Lena?"

She pored over all the different versions of Lena's fate. The starkest one suited her mood.

"She also may have died in the concentration camp."

"*May have?*"

"Yes—yes, she did."

She envisioned her mother looking out the window in Berlin, then putting her keys into her purse, going once again to the Red Cross—just in case they'd found Lena. And now she'd killed Lena without even telling her mother. And what about herself with nothing but the space from the sofa to the wall in which to recover from Lena's death?

Henrik's face was screwed up tightly in the silent crying of adults. No tears—just distorted features. His sister? No sooner had he met her than she was dead. He got to his feet and stood in front of her, hands on hips, like Lena used to do.

"Liar," he shouted. "I saw her that night in the meadow. Liar. Liar. Liar."

Then the sobs came. But he wasn't the same boy she'd left on the beach that day. That boy would have fallen into her arms. Henrik ran from the room and out the front door. She knew he'd cry his eyes out among his bones.

The old woman dumped some chopped dandelion heads into Charlotte's coffee.

"Your liver needs an extra kick today."

Charlotte looked at the calendar and realized she'd missed most of September.

She plucked a floating dandelion head from the coffee and chewed on it while she watched the old woman chop the troll sour root and dump the pieces into a pan of water.

"All this excitement," the old woman said, patting her belly.

She'd save the cooked troll sour root in a jar and take it as a laxative, disappearing to the outhouse for hours with her herbal books. Knowing the outhouse was occupied, Charlotte often sent the boys to the ditch with a newspaper from the 1940s.

Nobody will see you.

"Best thing for diseases of the private parts," the old woman whispered, "the kind men get in foreign harbors."

Perhaps the soldiers had used it during the war, Charlotte thought.

The dandelion coffee got Charlotte's heart going. During all her time in bed, she'd only drunk tea. Closing her eyes, she shut it all out—Ragnar, the boys, the letters from her mother. An old one lay on the table at her elbow. She had already read it ten times.

I still check with the relocation authorities every day. So far they've got nothing on Lena.

When she looked up, the old woman's eyes were on her. A sailor's widow, she knew about the sea, slept in bed with the backboard from her husband's eight-oared boat. Now Charlotte understood the words carved on it.

God above me in all things that I do.

She picked up the piece of knitting that lay in a heap at the end of the bench, something she'd started ages ago. The old woman stood at the stove, making syrup from bearberry leaves and berries, medicine for the boys' winter colds. Long, dark days loomed ahead.

She pointed her wooden spoon at the knitting.

"You'll cut off the kid's circulation with that tightly knitted instep."

Charlotte unraveled the yarn, threw it down, and went back to bed.

But the old woman followed her into the bedroom. She sat on the chair while Charlotte undressed, then moved in closer.

"My man used to row out with seven others in the winter," the old woman began.

"I know."

"If I tell you again and again, maybe you'll understand."

"I already understand."

The old woman shook her head.

"The fear started the night before when I soaked his shoes, just to take the hardness out of them. He got up in the middle of the night, wouldn't take anything but codliver oil, half a cup. 'Anything more'll slow me down,' he said. I pushed oatmeal at him. 'If I drink cod liver oil, the fish won't notice me. I can sneak up on them,' he said.

"One time, the ocean was so rough, the boat tipped, and we had to haul the men in on ropes. Even after we thought we'd saved them, two died. They lay on the sand, like seals. I saw their chests moving up and down. But then they stopped. When my man saw they were dead, he closed their eyes, made the sign of the cross over them.

"Back home that night, I had to untie the ropes on him. Sheepskin outfit kept out the sea. Rope was tied around his waist and through the crotch. He couldn't even see the knots that night.

"After I finally got his sea clothes off, he sat there all soft and wooly drinking his coffee.

"I stood up to get him some blood pudding. He liked it with curds. Then I saw his shoulders shaking. I took the sheepskin off the sofa, wrapped it around him. But he kept shaking. I looked into his face, tight as a purse. He was crying. When he saw me looking at him, he tried to pull it back inside himself. He put his fists in his face and pushed on his eyes. But his shoulders kept shaking and shaking.

"I did what I did with the cows when they were calving. I stroked and stroked. *There. There.* Finally he stopped. I had my arms around him like around the head of a cow. I could hear him breathing, real deep each time. When I pulled away, his head fell forward. He was fast asleep. I was strong as an ox in those days, but I couldn't budge him. So he slept sitting on the bench."

"Where was Ragnar?" Charlotte asked.

"Asleep."

Still, he must have known about his father's near death. Shame flooded her face. She'd never asked him.

The old woman's eyes gleamed.

"Nights, he smelled like fish oil, but I always welcomed him back. The other men fought the ocean all day and came back in the evening limp and drained. But my man drank wild orchid tea, and his body was always full of blood in the right places, gave me what I needed in bed. Other women on the hillside envied me. Sometimes I couldn't sit at my spinning wheel the next day."

Smiling a little at the memory, she went on. "You lose things along the way. Enjoy what you have of life—even if it's only a memory."

They locked eyes for a second, the way they had several times over the years.

"Did I tell you about the trollwoman Brana?"

Charlotte rolled her eyes to the ceiling. Brana sounded like the name of one of those fisherwomen who rowed out faster than the men, pulled cod out of the ocean with their bare hands, always gave birth to twins.

"Her foster father was in love with the king's daughter. What princess could love an ugly hairy troll? But Brana was smart, had a garden like mine, grew wild orchids in it. She chopped up the roots—they look just like testicles—and slipped them into the princess' food."

"Did it work?" Charlotte asked.

"It worked for you—you've got two fine boys—that's what I mean about life."

Charlotte remembered the odd delicacies the old woman fed her during the first year of her marriage.

"And Brana's father?'

"The princess climbed up his leg and begged him to make love to her—right then, on the castle floor."

The old woman rose quickly and left the room. She returned with an envelope labeled *orchid*, took out two of the pink spotted flowers, and pointed to the root. It had two nodes, like testicles, one dry and shriveled, the other swollen.

She dropped the flower back into the envelope, patted it as if it contained cash, something to tide you over.

"I keep it on the second shelf behind the bread," she said, "just in case."

That night Charlotte dreamed that a stormtrooper pulled Lena out of bed, stuck a gun into her back, and made her walk in her underwear to a waiting truck. General Eisenhower began describing what he'd found in the concentration camps. *General, please stop*, she pleaded. But he kept talking.

Torture. Starvation. Gas chambers.

Max, skinny as wrapped twigs, walked past. When the guard wasn't looking, he whispered, *Save Lena from this.*

She woke up screaming. Ragnar touched her shoulder. "Your phantom lover again?"

But his tone was gentle.

"He's dead," she said, her voice breaking on the last word.

"Yes," he said.

How did he know? She'd never told him, barely told herself. In the darkness, his nearness, his breath on her shoulder comforted her. Her body responded to his big hands.

The next day was better. Charlotte milked Skjalda, and Tryggvi was happy to turn the job back over to her. Later she sewed buttons on their overalls. At lunch, the old woman chopped a swollen orchid node into tiny pieces and dropped it into Ragnar's bowl of rhubarb pudding.

That night, Charlotte lay in bed waiting for Ragnar, thinking of Brana. How would she paint this woman? She envisioned her square face, her orange hair, emerging from the rocks.

When Ragnar came to bed, she reached for him. He came into her arms, and she stroked his back, careful not to speak, lest she frighten him. He kissed her breasts. As her pleasure mounted, Max came to her and unleashed her deepest feelings. But she kept that to herself, wondering if she too were a phantom.

46. I Have Something to Tell You

When Charlotte poured the steaming milk into the canister, it gave off a rich smell. Skjalda was a healthy cow. Ragnar stood next to her.

"I have something to tell you," she said.

"You've already told me."

"You promised to show me the fields we're going to level next."

"This afternoon."

His bare arm touched hers as they put the milking things away. All day she looked forward to the afternoon. The sun was low in the sky when they set out, but it was still warm.

They walked the hillside, he higher and she lower. Still, he called down to her, explaining, just like he had years ago when she was first learning the language. They stopped on a level piece of ground. He extended his arm over the field of tussocks below, and she saw the pride in his gesture.

"When my father came to Dark Castle, all the land looked like that—hard little nubs of dirt that he cut and crushed day and night, sometimes by the light of an oil lamp."

"I thought he was a fisherman."

"He fished during the winter. She likes to brag about that. The rest of the time he fought to survive up here. They built the animal sheds with driftwood and other scraps. He and my mother combed the beach for floating trees uprooted on the Norwegian coast, brought them back up here by horseback, one piece at a time. When they had a little pile of wood, they borrowed a saw from one of the farmers."

He described how they transformed knolls into fields so that a horse could drag a mowing machine across. She'd dreamt of how they'd sell the farm and move to Reykjavik. The glow in his eye told her he'd rather be buried in his own field than in the town cemetery.

"I'll call in Nonni and a few others like last time—"

She touched his arm.

"I can help."

"You get a sharp tool and slice off the top of the tussock, like a small square carpet. Set it aside. Cut the next square. Pile up your squares in a neat pile. You'll need them later."

He was breathing heavily, as if exhausted by his own words.

"Chop what's left of the tussock into little pieces. Beat the devil out of its center. Make it as flat as you can. Use the little square carpets before the grass dries. Grind up some manure. Strew it over the chopped-up tussocks before you lay the grass squares."

Last year she and Henrik had ground manure for days, he chattering constantly about elves and hidden people. Ragnar wasn't done yet.

"Take each little grass carpet. Lay it on top of the manure, like new turf. Make the edges even."

His face, aglow with a vision of success, contradicted the old woman's words, whispered just last autumn during the hay binding.

We'll all be at the fish-packing plant next year.

But Ragnar preferred squeezing a living out of this hilly piece of land. Summer snowstorms and rain that stayed in your bones all year long didn't bother him.

She took his hand. "The hollow is near here. Let's get under the breeze."

The sun had warmed the heather that lined the hollow. The smell of sweet thyme rose in their nostrils as they lowered themselves to the ground.

"Ankle to ankle? Like last time?" he asked.

"No, I want to face you," she said.

Like twelve-year-olds who've just thrown off their backpacks to play hooky, they lay down, giggling a little.

She placed a hand on his chest. "It's about Max."

He started to say something, but she kept talking.

"Friends offered to hide him from the Gestapo, but he refused, said he wouldn't risk his friends' lives. He'd rather go East and see the 'real' Jews. He was sure it was just a temporary transport and that it would knock some of the elite Jews off their high horse."

She took some deep breaths, tried to relax.

"When they took Max, my mother said we had to hide Lena. I brought her to a convent. I never saw her again. She might be alive somewhere under a different name."

He moved his head in a sad gesture, and she realized that he knew all these things. And she remembered his wish for a daughter.

"I have—"

She waited.

"I have something to tell you," he said at last.

They lay there breathing in silence for several moments until he began.

"When we were kids, Gunnar and I pushed a rowboat into the surf. We each held an oar. The ocean started pitching. The waves came over us. Gunnar laughed, rowed into them. I was huddled on the floor of the boat. Finally a big wave washed over us and pushed the boat all the way back onto the sand. Gunnar wanted to go out again."

His eyes were on her, waiting for her reaction. But she said nothing.

"I jumped out of the boat, splashed through the surf, couldn't get away fast enough."

Poor man. And he'd had to pull his wife out of the ocean.

"There's more," he said. "About Gunnar—"

The one they never talked about.

"Gunnar—he didn't drown."

"But your mother told me—"

"It's been so long. By now, she believes he drowned."

"How then?"

"Bringing the boat in, he cut himself. Next day he had a high fever. Herbs. Lots of herbs. Then, the hospital—too late."

He lowered his eyes.

"Your father?"

"Disappeared. Went to sea one morning. Never came back. Years later, somebody saw him on a boat on the Western Fjords. He disappeared into the sea. We practiced telling people that."

She saw the relief in his face, a traveler who'd passed a heavy suitcase to somebody else. But she needn't carry it either. She placed her hands on his chest. He stroked her shoulders and her arms all the way down to her hands. His lips brushed across hers. She arched her back, and he moved his hands to her breasts.

Slowly, he unbuttoned her blouse. As if they didn't live on a farm where every minute of the day was accounted for, he moved his fingertips very, very slowly across the swell of her breasts. He slipped the front of her brassiere down, brought his mouth to the nipple.

She stroked his thick hair while images of a dozen madonnas, rosy-lipped babes nuzzling their breasts, filled her mind. Charity, suckling two babes, and Caravaggio's young woman offering her breast to the starving old man in the painting called *Misercordia*.

Breathing rapidly, she ran her hands over his back, drew him to her. Then with deliberate slowness she pulled away, took off her clothes and placed them next to a cluster of dandelions.

Shivering, she helped him undress.

Like synchronized swimmers, they moved legs and arms

gracefully against one another. She rolled onto her side and raised both arms above her head. He stroked the tender skin of her inner arms, ran his fingers over her sides and across her ribs. The sweet spicy smell of thyme blended with the musky warm fragrance of his body. His inner thigh rubbed against hers, and she glided over him, scissoring her legs, brushing his chest with her breasts, running her fingertips along the rim of his ears, down both sides of his neck.

Her hair brushing over his belly and chest, she placed both hands in the heather to either side of his body, and drew her body over his. She took one of his nipples into her mouth, tongued it, then moved to the other. Moaning, he stroked her hair. Throbbing with the need for him, she rolled onto her back and took him inside her.

Eyes closed, she danced slowly over a yellow hill of buttercups in a thin white dress. Moving quickly now, she stepped into an orange, gold and siena sunset. Her feet left the ground, and she floated over a field of blue gentians, edged with lilacs.

An aquamarine wave climbed higher and higher. She ascended its snowy white tops, rising, rising, moving now in rhythm with the entire universe. When the ocean pulled away, she glimpsed the jade green of its depths and shuddered with pleasure. At last, she lay exhausted on the shore listening to the music of a single violin while the warm surf caressed her whole body.

A golden plover sang in the nearby tussocks. *Dirrin-dirrin-di,* then pattered over the ground and flew off.

She dressed quickly in the cool breeze.

"I hope my mother fed the chickens," he said, adjusting his suspenders.

Afterwards, crossing the fields next to him, she felt tall and lean. A weight had lifted from her, and a promise of new strength nestled in her muscles.

"When can we begin leveling the tussocks?" she asked.

He turned towards her. "Soon."

She knew he'd never look at her the way he looked at a cow that gave rich milk, or at horse that could carry him to the interior without a slip. But she sensed that he considered her an asset to the farm.

The gable of the farmhouse emerged over the hill in the distance. The sun was low in the sky. They'd been gone a long time. The old woman would raise her eyebrows. But some things took a long time to tell.

They approached the trestles for drying fish, a wooden framework covered with turf. The posts were set in the ground and supported by large black basalt stones. Cod and shark, in brown, withered pairs, swung gently in the breeze. The old woman had prepared an ointment for rash—valerian, violets, red clover, and bedstraw—traded it for fish caught during the winter fishing season.

Charlotte decided to bring back a couple of hardened fish in her apron. She would cut them into pieces, crush the heads and feed them to Skjalda for calcium.

Ragnar gestured towards the trestles. She pictured him as a tour guide. *This, ladies and gentlemen, is the Parthenon, temple to the goddess, Athena.*

"My father collected driftwood for years before he could build this. Gunnar and I went down to the shore about once a week to see what we could find."

He approached one of the posts, placed an arm around it.

"We found this one rolling around in the seaweed. He got so excited that he climbed over the rocks and fell into the water trying to get it. The tide was coming in, and we had to move fast before the ocean covered the rocks. We thought it had been uprooted from the banks of the River Volga, then traveled the ocean to us. We used to make up stories about wolves scratching that tree in the dark forest. We carried it up the hillside on our shoulders."

She'd never brought back a single piece of driftwood.

"Can you do a painting for me?" he asked suddenly.

She'd expected to be buried in his field before he asked this question.

"Two boys carrying a log up the hillside. We could hang it next to the painting of Lena."

Nearing the farmhouse, they fell silent. The old woman met them on the steps.

47. Do Everything They Say

Lena sat up in bed and rubbed her eyes. Someone was at the big door downstairs. He didn't use the brass knocker. It wasn't the milkman. He was banging it with something, like she did when she had to go to the bathroom and mamma didn't hear her at the door. The yelling made her feel afraid. Now she heard Sister Marie Luise. Why was she speaking in that strange voice? Squeaky, like the women in the puppet shows. Boots climbed the stairs. Louder and louder. The door opened. He was in the room. Didn't he know only girls were allowed in this room?

He wore a brown uniform and black boots. The boots frightened Lena. She and mamma had been in the park. Those boots had been kicking a man. Mamma had pulled her away, but she'd looked back over her shoulder.

"Get the kids dressed and into the truck," he shouted.

Sister said something to him, but Lena couldn't hear him. The man in the boots looked angry.

"Children, we're going to a summer camp," Sister said. "You'll play games and have fun."

But Sister's face looked funny. She talked into the man's face. "I'll bring the children down."

The man in the boots backed out of the room. Now Sister stood at Lena's bed. She helped her with her dress. "Bring your bear. He'll enjoy the trip." Lena was holding Sister's warm hand, and the other children were following them. The door was open. That was funny. It led to the back of a truck.

One of the big girls was the last in line. Grete's red hair stood out stiff and uncombed. Usually Grete didn't talk to Lena, but now she let her stand beside her.

"Hurry up," the man yelled.

Something horrible happened. A girl fell. The man picked her up by an arm and a foot and tossed her into the truck. She cried when she landed on the floor of the truck.

Sister let go of her hand. "Take Grete's hand, and climb in," she said. "Quickly now."

Lena sat close to Grete on the hard bench. When the truck pulled out of the driveway, the children all knocked against one another. The ones who were standing fell on the dirty wooden floor. It was funny, but Grete didn't even smile. They drove for ever and ever. Lena heard trams on tracks. Milk bottles clanged. Somebody was baking bread. The smell made her think of mamma. She mustn't. The wheels made a big sound when the truck stopped. She saw an angry face. He wore a helmet.

"Out," the man shouted.

The children lying on the floor scrambled to their feet. Lena clasped the fold of Grete's dress. She recognized the train station. And the kiosk. That was where mamma bought a newspaper for herself and a caramel for her.

"Stand here," shouted one of the boot men.

And they stood. It's really hard to stand still for a long time. Lena moved a foot to wake it up. A man with a helmet shouted at her. When he bent to light a cigarette, Lena whispered to Grete, "Where's the train for the summer camp?"

But the man hissed. Grete didn't answer. Lena was tired. She didn't want to go to the summer camp.

"Move," a voice said.

Lena followed Grete. They walked and walked. At last they came to the end of the platform and stopped. She saw train cars with sliding doors, like her toy train at home. No windows. No seats. Her toy cows and pigs traveled in those cars.

The man pointed to the train car. "Get in."

But she couldn't climb into the car because it was too high off the ground. "Bring me a stepstool," the boot man yelled. "*Jawohl, heil Hitler,*" another man said. Somebody was always saying that.

The man disappeared into the train station. He came back with a small stepstool and hurried away.

"Get in."

Grete climbed in before Lena. Then Lena stood on the stepstool and reached for Grete's hands. But she wasn't fast enough. The boot man grasped her. The station twirled. She hit the inside wall of the train car and fell onto the straw in the car. She sat up and rubbed herself. Another child—a small boy—came flying in the same way she had. He cried.

A tall girl bent over him. "Shut-up."

Lena saw her pointy breasts under her nightgown. "She's not dressed," she whispered. But Grete pinched her. "Quiet." Grete lowered herself to the floor. So did Lena. Their backs were against the metal ridges of the car.

The big door rolled shut. It was dark in there. The other kids smelled of sweat. Nobody said anything. Klickety klack. The train was leaving the station. Lena fell asleep. Splash. Grunt. Splash. Somebody sat on the bucket. After that everything smelled. Lena's nose hurt from the bad air. She saw the boy who took pills at every meal. He sat with his nose at the tiny cracks in the side of the car. Somewhere a dog barked. That made Lena think of people who didn't go on trips, people who stayed home and petted the dog.

Grete sat stiff and silent next to her. The train was slowing down. Less klickety klack. Shouts. The door opened. The air smelled sweet.

A man reached in and took the slop bucket. He said a bad word. "*Scheisse*—what a smell." Had they been pooping for a couple of days into that bucket? The station looked like a cardboard toy house, the kind mamma had made for her toy train.

Hands pushed a can of water into the car. Lena was so thirsty. But they all reached for it at once. Some of it spilled on her dress. She sucked the cloth until her mouth was dry. The door was still open. The girl in the nightgown and a big boy pushed the boy who took pills to the door. His shirt tore and the skin of his chest caught on the rough edge of car door. They pushed him out. He landed somewhere below. "Why?" she whispered.

"Dead," Grete said.

The empty slop bucket was back. The door rolled shut. Grete slumped against the wall. A grinding sound. Lena's belly hurt with hunger. Grete's mouth was at her ear. "We lie near the door. Pretend to be dead. They'll throw us out."

Out. Lena said the word to herself, rolled it on her tongue. Grete didn't speak after that. Didn't move. Mamma. When would mamma come and save her? She leaned against Grete. *Mamma.* She hadn't meant to say it. Grete pulled away.

Lena pretended to be dead. Forever and forever passed. The train kept going. It was one of those days they put at the beginning of the week. Sunday or Monday? She didn't ask, just kept being dead. At last the wheels slowed. The big boy stood over them. His breath smelled like old food. With rough fingers he probed her eyelids. Finally, he said it. *Dead.* The train moved slower and slower. The door opened. Men talked funny. The man who took the slop bucket was clumsy and the waste spilled over the edge.

The big boy's hands felt warm on her shoulders. He dragged her to the door and pushed her out. She held her bear tightly as she fell. The ground was hard. She opened her eyes. She lay in a ditch next to the train tracks. *Play dead til they're gone,* Grete had said. She closed her eyes again. Mamma was holding her hand, and they were walking in a garden, smelling flowers, wearing clean clothes.

The door of the train above them shut, and the train rumbled to a start. Grete lay next to her, her arms and face bleeding. Above them was a dark sky. Grete began to crawl along the ditch. Lena followed. She scraped her knees on the rocks, but she didn't say anything. Birds flew low overhead.

"Bats," Grete said.

In the fading light, they looked like mice. Each time one swooped down, Lena looked into its bulging eyes. Grete picked up a tin can. She ran her finger along the inside. She gave Lena a can and showed her how to do it without cutting herself. They licked their fingers.

Grete saw the apple core first, but she shared it with Lena. Something tightened in Lena's stomach. She gagged, then retched into the grass. An empty flour bag lay on a rock. Grete reached for it. A flick of a tail, and something scurried over the rocks. It sat up. It wanted the flour bag, but Grete held onto it. She picked up a stone and hit the rat on the head, leaving a small splash of blood on the rock. The creature lay on its side. Grete dropped another rock on it. Her teeth looked very white. "Meat," she said.

Grete knew how to do things. She cut the rat down the middle with a sharp stone, pulled off its skin, and squeezed out its guts. With thumb and forefinger, she tore off the flesh, put it in her mouth. She offered a strip of meat to Lena.

They chewed the meat, making squishy sounds with their mouths open. Lena dug her fingers into the carcass for more. Her belly didn't hurt anymore. But Grete said they couldn't stay here. She pointed to the dark forest up ahead.

"Wolves?" Lena asked.

'We'll catch them with our bare hands and eat them," Grete said. But she smiled. Lena hadn't seen her smile since they left the convent for summer camp. They started walking. Twigs crackled. Lena thought she heard a wolf. She began to cry. Grete slapped her hand over her mouth. Tears came into her eyes. Every time Lena spoke, Grete squeezed her hand hard. Lena thought she might crush the bones.

A golden glow came up ahead between the trees. It looked

like the sun had fallen into the forest. Three men sat around a campfire. They had beards. Lena thought they looked like goblins. They drank from tin cups and smoked.

The biggest one raised his cup and said something Lena couldn't understand. But they made room for them on one of the logs. The big one offered them a drink from a tin can. It made Lena cough, but the burning liquid washed away the taste of the rat. A woman came out of the tent. Lena thought she was beautiful. She had black hair piled on top of her head.

The next morning, she woke up in the tent wrapped in a blanket. Grete lay close beside her. She saw the shoulder of one of the men and the dark hair of the woman.

Lena followed Grete out of the tent. They stepped over the logs from yesterday's campfire and pulled down their underpants. Softly, they peed on the pine needles. Grete looked straight into Lena's eyes.

"Do everything they say, or they'll send us back to the boxcar," she said.

Lena nodded.

"I mean everything."

Lena held her bear so he too could pee.

The big man came out of the tent, yawned noisily and stretched his arms. He smiled. He had big teeth. Lena's felt fuzzy. She hadn't brushed them since she got into the boxcar. He tweaked Lena's ear. Grete moved closer to Lena. He entered the woods. She saw him unhitch his pants.

Lena had barely talked to her bear since the beginning of their trip. She raised him to her face. "Yesterday I think I was a little drunk," she said.

The woman came out of the tent, buttoning her blouse. She made the fire and handed each of them a saucepan.

"Come," she said, gesturing to them.

They washed their faces and hands in the creek. She made each of them carry a pan of water back to the campsite. The woman was pouring the water into a big pot. The smiling man came up behind her and touched her in a rude place. She set a dented frying pan on the fire and sliced a chunk of fat into it. In a tin can, she mixed some grain and water. She dropped it onto the sizzling fat.

The big man went back into the tent. Lena heard him yelling at the sleepers. They must have been wrestling because she saw the sides of the tent moving. The other two came out of the tent. They rubbed their eyes like little kids. The woman served them something she called graincakes. Lena liked it better than rat, but she dropped her cake into the leaves. The woman was nice, like Sister. She placed a large, warm hand on her shoulder and gave her another cake.

The men cleaned their guns. The nice woman treated them like little boys. She told them to run into the woods and hunt squirrels and birds. She handed Lena two rocks and gave her a handful of walnuts. Lena crushed nuts, took the meat out, and gave most of it to the woman. But when the woman turned her back, she gave some to her bear.

"Mamma will get us soon," she whispered into his chest.

The woman gave Lena a knife and made a chopping movement with her hand. Holding the blade with both hands, Lena chopped the walnuts into little pieces.

The men came back with rabbits slung over their shoulder. The big one skinned them.

The rabbits looked funny when they were naked. The big man threaded them onto a long stick and held them over the fire. One of the other men poured the drink. It was different from last night. This time it tasted like freshly baked bread. They talked and talked, but Lena didn't understand a word.

"It's Polish," Grete whispered. But Lena didn't know what that meant either.

Grete asked the big man, "Where are we?"

He nodded, picked up a stick, drew a map in the dirt at their feet. He said a lot of strange names.

Krakau to one side. *Rybnik.* Just below it *Ostrava.* Between the two *Bielsko-Biala.* Moving the stick all the time, he made an x west of *Krakau* and northeast of *Bielsko-Biala. Osviecm,* he said, grinning now. Lena didn't know whether to like him or not. She would have to ask Grete.

That night Grete whispered in Lena's ear, "Partisans. They can save us from the Nazis."

Lena nodded. She didn't understand, but Grete's tone soothed her.

In the middle of the night, she woke up suddenly. She heard a noise outside the tent. She lifted the flap and peered out. In the light from the campfire she saw Grete's white leg, her small breast. Above her was the big smiling man. His bottom moved between her legs. His hand covered Grete's mouth.

"Grete," she screamed, but the man kept moving on her. He was panting and grunting. At last, he rolled off Grete and disappeared into the bushes. Grete lay on the ground like a wheelbarrow turned upside down. A tuft of hair between her legs sparkled wet in the firelight. "Go away," she said. Then she turned over and reached for her clothes.

They crept away from the campfire and slept in the woods the rest of that night, curled up together. The next morning, Lena felt something hard and cold against her skin. A knife lay between her and Grete, the same knife the big man had used to skin the rabbits.

"We've got to get out of here before he comes after us," Grete said.

"Where are we going?" Lena asked sleepily.

Grete said nothing.

All day they wandered through the forest, but they weren't alone. Ragged people with sunken faces skulked about the woods.

It was dark again when they came to a campfire. Grete took Lena's hand.

"We stop here."

Somebody stood up from the campfire. Lena recognized his big teeth. He walked towards them. They ran through the woods, crashing into branches, stumbling over roots. Lena heard his voice behind them.

At last they ducked into a hollow below a fallen tree trunk. They saw him stumble past them and disappear into the woods. Lena found Grete's hand in the darkness.

Lena woke up to the sound of a scuffle next to her. He had pinned Grete down. Lena picked up a stick and swung it at his head. When it hit, he arched up. Grete moved her hand to her waist. Lena knew she kept the knife there. The blade flashed. Grete pushed it into his belly. He groaned and fell forward. Grete rolled away quickly. Together they pulled and pushed him over on his back. Grete pulled the knife out of his belly and cleaned off the blood with oak leaves.

"We won't make that mistake again," she told Lena. What mistake, Lena wondered. But she was afraid to ask.

At last the woods opened up onto a meadow. It was a farmer's field. All the haystacks were covered with canvas. At the edge of the woods sat some men dressed in pajamas. They looked frightened. Lena couldn't understand why. Afraid herself, she hugged her bear. "Just kids," one of them said in German, and they seemed to relax.

Grete helped them start a fire. Lena looked for twigs. Suddenly shouts came from below the meadow.

Yid. Yid.

"Villagers—they hate Jews," one of the men in pajamas said.

"What are Jews?" Lena asked.

"Quiet," Grete hissed. The voices of the villagers grew louder. Grete and Lena followed the pajama people to the nearest haystack. They buried themselves under it. There was room for all five of them with Lena in the middle, farthest from the edge of stack. The villagers were shouting and laughing. Something hard thrust its way into the earth.

"Pitchforks," Grete whispered.

One of the pajama men screamed. The pitchfork people cheered. Lena heard them running around the haystack. They must be playing a game. More screams. A pitchfork prong stabbed the earth next to Lena. Grete groaned. Finally the pitchfork people stopped playing. Everything was quiet, but Lena was afraid to move.

She placed her cheek against Grete's, but it was cold. All day she lay under the haystack, holding her bear. Maybe if she lay there long enough Grete would come back to life—or even one of the pajama men. But they didn't. When she was sure it was night, she dug her way out from under the haystack. She went back into the woods and sat down against the trunk of a tree. She remembered the big man's map, but she still didn't know where she was.

48. A Dirty Old Thing

Lena looked up and saw a woman with a broad face. Her head was covered with a red kerchief.

"I am Piroschka." She spoke like the men Grete called partisans. "What's your name?"

Lena hesitated. She knew she had a different name, but now she couldn't remember it. So she said her convent name.

"My name is Monika," she said.

"Quick, before they come back," Piroschka said, picking Lena up in her large arms.

She carried her through the edge of the woods until they came out on the other side. She put Lena down, and they walked a dirt path. At its end, Lena could see a wooden house with chickens in the front yard.

"Hurry, hurry. Nobody must see you."

Inside, the house was so dark Lena could barely see Piroschka bending over the stove, heating water. The woman gave her a cup of tea.

"You can stay in my root cellar," she said.

A wooden ladder led to a storage area with a dirt floor.

"Later, when this is over, you'll come upstairs and stay in my boys' room. They're gone—"

All day, Lena felt like a prisoner in the root cellar. In the evening Piroschka let her out, took her onto her lap and stroked her hair. She told her the story of her brave boys who resisted the Germans back in 1939.

"They swung swords at them, didn't stand a chance."

The woman quivered silently for a moment. "But little Monika, you have come into my life. You will be mine."

Lena wanted to stand up, go outside, and breathe fresh air. But Piroschka said no. Finally Piroschka made her a bed from old blankets. She crawled between them with her bear and thought about Grete. Was she still under the haystack? Piroschka began to teach Lena Polish, read to her from books about bears who wore clothes and had office jobs.

"My boys loved these stories."

Lena imitated the way Piroschka said the words. Soon Lena began to forget the German words for things. But sometimes she thought in German, and then she remembered what she thought she'd forgotten. One day she asked Piroschka in Polish, "How can I find my mother?"

"Your parents are dead. You're the only one alive."

This made Lena cry. She had thought it might be true, and now Piroschka had made it real. She hated Piroschka for telling her.

Piroschka took her in her arms and rocked her until she stopped crying.

"Do you know the story of King Kasimiri the Great? He lived in a castle nearby, in Krakau."

Lena rubbed her eyes, held the bear to her chest.

"One day King Kasimir was out hunting near Opoczno. A bear came running towards him. King Kasimir called to the bear. It stood up on its hind legs. The king ran towards the bear and speared it. As the bear fell to its death, it swung its paw at the king, ripping his fur coat with his claws. The king went to Meilech, the Jewish furrier in Opoczno, and asked him to repair his fur so that it was seamless again.

"As King Kasimir sat on a bench waiting for Meilech to sew up his fur, the door to a back room opened, and in walked a beautiful young woman with pearls wound into her black hair, Esterka, Meilech's daughter.

"The king fell in love with her on the spot. But Esterka refused to go with him unless he promised to marry her and to let her raise their girl children as Jews. He loved her so much that he agreed. So they were married, and Esterka made the king very happy. King Kasimir was always good to the Jews because of Esterka's advice to him. Even though he never crowned her queen, she was really the queen of Poland."

"I like that story," Lena said.

"Tomorrow I will make you a dress of purple, and I will call you Esterka."

The next day, Lena lay on her mattress all day in the root cellar, hugging her bear, while Nazi soldiers clomped on the floors above.

"Slaughter the pig and the chickens," a German voice said.

And she heard Piroschka's familiar footsteps move across the floor to the door. Laughter. Shrieks. Soon she couldn't tell the difference.

Lena thought it must be morning—she'd been asleep. Somebody was descending the ladder into the cellar. Her heart beat fast.

"Esterka."

They hugged one another and lay together in the darkness for a long time.

For the rest of the war, Piroschka and Lena lived on fried flour and grain cakes. Sometimes they ate carrots and turnips from Piroschka's garden.

Lena begged Piroschka to let her go outside.

"Maybe at night."

Piroschka brought her into an enclosed garden where they sat on the steps. She whispered to her the names of flowers and vegetables that grew in rows.

"You must say them in perfect Polish, or you won't be safe here."

Sometimes Lena had a vision of her mother. She looked very pretty walking in a garden, cutting irises and daffodils. One night she asked about her mother.

"Where is she?"

Piroschka frowned. "Who?"

"My mother?"

The hugging began. Piroschka's body felt like bread dough just before you put it in the oven.

"Poor little Esterka. Your mother's dead. Everyone's dead in Germany."

Her voice had a trill at the end that made Lena uneasy. Piroschka led her back inside.

"The neighbors will be waking up."

Sometimes when Lena thought about her mother, she wondered about her real name. When she was alone, she lay on her mattress saying names to herself. If only somebody would tell her all the names in the world, then when she heard her name, she could say "That's it. That's my name."

Sometimes Piroschka sat on the mattress with Lena holding a flashlight over a Polish children's book, pointing to pictures and naming things. Piroschka often wore a purple silk robe. She made a blouse for Lena from the same fabric.

"Like mother and daughter," she said in a giggly voice, fluffing up the sleeves.

One day the Russian soldiers marched in. They were very noisy. Piroschka didn't come to the root cellar the first night after they came. Lena stayed awake, listening to the noises upstairs. Screams. Laughter. Singing. The boots on the floorboards made her think of horses' hooves. All next day, Piroschka didn't come to her, and Lena began to think she was dead. She cried, then laid her hot cheek against the cold dirt wall.

At last, she heard Piroschka's heavy step on the ladder. When she put her arms around Lena, she smelled different. And she wasn't wearing the same old housedress.

"You must stay hidden," she said. "They do terrible things to women, even to little girls, things you can't imagine, my little Esterka." Lena thought of Grete lying in the woods like an upside down wheelbarrow. Piroschka hugged her, and Lena felt the rough edge of a bandage against her cheek.

Suddenly, Piroschka was busy all day. In the evening she came to the root cellar wearing a dirty housedress and carrying a rag.

"Your room—it's ready."

Lena followed her up the step ladder into the kitchen, then up some broad steps. The closet was full of shirts and pants. Lena had nothing but the purple blouse and the ragged clothes she'd worn in the woods. The room had a nice chest of drawers, full of clean socks and underwear, and sweaters and long pants that Piroschka's boys had worn. Lena placed her bear on top of the chest of drawers.

"That old bear. Throw it away. I'll get you a new one," Piroschka said.

"No."

Lena reached for the bear and put it under the pillow and covered it with the blanket and sheet. Piroschka backed away, looking hurt. After that, Lena always slept with the bear. She decided she didn't like everything about Piroschka. One night, she woke up in the night. She needed to go to the bathroom, but the door was locked. She'd had a bathroom accident in the convent once, and everyone had laughed at her for weeks.

"Piroschka," she screamed, banging on the door.

At last the key turned in the lock. "I'm sorry, little Esterka," Piroschka said, but she looked strange. Lena rushed past her to the bathroom. After that, Piroschka did not lock the door again. But every evening before she went to bed, Lena checked the door.

In the summer, Lena helped Piroschka in the garden. She took a pair of pants and a shirt from the closet and rolled them up. Piroschka grew tomatoes, cucumbers, turnips, carrots and potatoes. And every Saturday Lena went with her to the market place in Krakau. They set up a stall next to St. Adalbert Church. The same group of children always played in front of the Marien Church. They climbed the steps at the foot of the Mickiewicz statue and hid from one another. Lena watched them. One day, when customers crowded around Piroschka asking for sweet, ripe tomatoes, Lena ran and joined the children. She met Hanne, a girl with short black hair and a thin pointed nose who lived in their village. Hanne sometimes sat with Lena at the foot of the statue and told her things.

"Some funny people came back the other day. Egg woman told my mother."

Funny? Clowns? Dancing dogs?

"Said the house belonged to them. They wanted it back. Egg woman's husband threw the funny people out."

"Who? Juggler? Fat lady?"

"Jews—kept saying egg woman took their house. We thought they were all dead in those fireplaces at Oswiecim."

Piroschka had told her about the Jews, the people who were mostly dead. Piroschka thought Lena might be one. Why else would she be on a train going through Poland? But Lena didn't tell Hanne about that.

There were so many things she wanted to know. One day she and Piroschka were picking bugs off the potato leaves. "What happened during the war?" Lena asked.

"They killed all the Jews—all but you Esterka because I saved you."

Piroschka didn't let Lena go to school that first year.

"I can teach you," she said.

So Lena learned letters and numbers from Piroschka, but she was lonely. She thought about the children who played at the foot of the statue in the Krakau market place. One day she walked with Piroschka to the big store. Hanne was there with some girls buying hard candies to suck on.

"I want to go to school," Lena said on the way home.

She hated it when Piroschka dabbed her eyes with her handkerchief. At last she looked at Lena with wet eyes.

"Yes, you'll go to school."

She enrolled Lena under the name of Esterka.

Piroschka brought her to the gate and picked her up at the end of each day. But sometimes Lena went home with Hanne. Then she always asked Hanne about the war.

49. A Choking Feeling

After Lena finished the basic school, Piroschka got her an apprenticeship with a furrier in town. Even then she walked with her and stood crying on the platform when Lena waved to her from the window of the moving tram.

Erik, the furrier's son, wanted to know everything about her.

"You aren't that woman's daughter."

He said it with a certainty that made Lena feel that she must look odd.

"How can you tell?" she asked, patting her head. Were horns growing out of it?

"The way you talk. And you don't look like her."

But did it make any difference? she wondered.

"You're one of the 'lost people'" he said triumphantly.

She'd known that for a long time. But now she wasn't sure that she wanted to be found.

"'Lost people' go to the Red Cross or something like that—some displaced person's organization. Just tell them 'I'm lost.'"

He found this funny and threw back his head and laughed. He was handsome as a Cossack in Piroschka's children's books.

"I think I'm one of the lost people," she told Piroschka that evening.

"They're all dead," Piroschka said, and Lena didn't dare mention it again.

Erik stayed late every evening to teach Lena how to stitch together the skins of tiny animals so the coat would appear seamless.

"The women of Warsaw will elbow their way to our store if you learn to stitch the skins," Erik said. She liked his friendly manner.

They sat close together on the bench, sewing skins for many nights before he dared kiss her. His last name was Kasmierski. It sounded nice when she said it out loud. She couldn't remember ever having a last name. Sometimes she stroked his back when he kissed her. Afterwards she chanted the beautiful name. *Kasmierski. Kasmierski.* When they married, Erik's father gave them the cottage behind the fur plant. She liked introducing herself to customers, extending a hand. *Hello, I am Monika Kasmierski.*

Once when Piroschka was visiting she saw the ragged old bear sitting on the chest of drawers in Erik and Lena's bedroom. "I'll get you a new one," she said.

"No," Lena said quickly.

When Lena gave birth to a daughter she named her after her foster mother. Little Piroschka was three years old when Erik made her a dolls house. Together Lena and the child made dolls from big Piroschka's empty spools. Lena glued together matchsticks and matchboxes for furniture. Erik brought home fur scraps, and Lena turned them into carpets, quilts, and fur coats for the dolls. Her foster mother crocheted tablecloths and dresses and found pretty pictures in magazines that Lena cut out and pasted on the walls—family portraits.

The doll family was awaiting the birth of another baby. Lena and little Piroschka talked endlessly about what to name it. But soon the name talk began to disturb Lena's sleep.

It was after midnight, and Lena lay wide-eyed in the darkness listening to Erik's snoring. At last she turned to Erik, stroked his back and ran her hands over his shoulders.

"What?"

He sounded so drowsy that she felt ashamed. But she couldn't stop now.

"Give me a new name," she said.

"Why?"

"Say one."

"Monika," he said languidly, waking up now, reaching for her breasts.

She pushed his hand away.

"Not that old name."

His hands went to her waist. "Monika. Monika. Monika," he said in a teasing voice, stroking her belly.

"That's not my name."

He rolled over on his back, puzzled now. "Big Piroschka calls you Esterka sometimes."

"No, not that."

Angry tears welled up. She'd seen those two people again in a dream, talking and talking. One of them must be her mother. What had she called her? The name had hovered at the edge of her consciousness, but she lost it before she woke up.

"You're crazy," Erik said, turning his back to her.

But she wouldn't let him go. It wasn't that easy. Maybe she was crazy, but there was more. That damned dolls house had started everything roiling in her. She buried her face in his back and sobbed. He turned to her and embraced her.

"Who am I?" she whispered into his chest.

"My very own Mrs. Kasmierski," he said proudly.

Her heart sank, but she let him rock her to sleep.

The next day it snowed heavily, and Lena stayed indoors while Erik went to the fur shop. Piroschka had played with doll's house all morning, Suddenly she appeared in the kitchen.

"Mamma, I'd like a bear," she said.

"Maybe Papa can find one in Krakau."

"Not a new bear. I want the bear that's in your room."

"It's a dirty old thing," Lena said. Besides, it wasn't a toy any more, she thought. It was a traveling companion, a survivor.

The child looked sad. Lena hated to disappoint her, so she went to her bedroom and took the bear from the chest of drawers and wiped it with a wet cloth until it began to come apart at the seams. The foot pads were wearing away, and the feet were leaking their straw stuffing. She'd have to sew it up tomorrow. Then she noticed the corner of a cloth buried in the bear's foot. She pulled on it until it came out. Straw fell on the floor. Carefully stitched into the cotton were three words and a date:

Lena Bernstein, born 1936.

Her face grew hot. *That was the name. In her dream she'd almost found it, but then it had fallen back into the darkness of her memory.* Lena put the cloth into her pocket.

Absentmindedly she gave Little Piroschka the bear, and the child opened her arms and hugged the torn creature. She went down for her nap, holding the bear. In the kitchen Lena sliced cheese and salami, but then she stopped. She wasn't hungry. She took the cloth from her pocket and held it up to the window, read it again against the snow.

When her foster mother arrived to babysit, Lena put on her fur hat and coat, picked up her shopping bag, and set out in the snow. She kept one hand bare and in her pocket, so she could finger the embroidered letters on the cloth. *Lena Bernstein.*

The cold air stung her face, and the sky above appeared swollen with more snow. But inside her, something warm washed over the hard place where she stored the imagined memories of her mother—*She knew she'd sat under a table pretending to be a Chinese princess. The woman who had abandoned her because she was too much trouble was talking, talking. But one day she'd stuffed the cloth into the bear. Why?*

Numb with cold, Lena walked to the edge of the village, where the farms and the smell of animals began. It was snowing again. The air seemed lighter when the flakes finally came down. Suddenly, she understood. She'd sewed a label into little Piroschka's fur coat. If the child left the coat in the park behind the sandbox, the label would help her find it again. Labeling was an act of love.

Walking home, she thought how her foster mother had saved her life, but also how she'd missed living the life meant for Lena Bernstein. She'd been Monika and now Esterka and hardly Lena at all. She'd never used the word for her foster mother. *Mamma.*

During the next weeks, she practiced her new identity in the bathroom with the door closed. She looked in the mirror and addressed herself as Lena Bernstein.

At last, she showed the cloth to her foster mother. A startled look crossed her foster mother's face. "Doesn't mean a thing," Piroschka said.

But it was too late. Lena already knew who she was. She met her foster mother's gaze.

"I'm going to the place for lost people."

"But you're not lost."

The words *I found you* hung on the air between them, but Lena was already halfway out the door.

At the Polish Red Cross, a little man with spectacles at the end of his nose looked at her with kind eyes.

"I'm probably a German Jew. My mother hid me somewhere eighteen or twenty years ago."

He looked interested. But it occurred to Lena that most such searches ended nowhere.

"Do you have any idea where she hid you?" he asked.

It was a stupid question, but he spoke in a gentle way, unlocking something in her. She couldn't distinguish dream from memory, but she was back on the train with her mother, leaning against her bosom, breathing in the rose fragrance of her soap. She wiped her cheeks with the back of her hand.

"No."

"Then go to the Berlin Red Cross."

She nodded solemnly.

"Did you say you're Jewish?"

She showed him the cloth.

"Name could be Berlin Jewish," he said.

The next day she took the train to Berlin. Farms and woodland rushed by the window. She'd missed the view on the way out to Poland years ago. The thought chilled her. Why was she doing this? Traveling in the wrong direction? Back to Germany? She could have taken the train to Krakau instead, spent the day downtown, shopping.

In Berlin, she found the address the Polish Red Cross had given her. She entered what appeared to be a large lobby. On the walls hung photos, some curled at the edges. When she approached the counter asking for help in Polish, the clerk gestured to a woman with short hair to come to the front.

Lena took the cloth from her pocket. The woman glanced at it and raised her eyebrows. She disappeared into the back room, returned with a sheet of paper and a photo, gestured for Lena to sit down at a table. The photo was of a girl of about five with curly hair. She resembled little Piroschka. Lena glanced at the paper and read her new name there.

The woman explained that an older woman had come looking for a granddaughter named Lena, that the woman's daughter, the mother, was living in another country, that she'd never come back to Germany. She'd left just after the war.

Lena's heart sank. Not only had her mother dumped her Jewish baby, but she'd left the country so she could forget all about her. She felt like getting back on the train. But the clerk was smiling now, handing her some German coins, writing down an address and directions for the bus to Wilmersdorferstrasse.

Outside again, Lena felt dizzy and confused. A gloomy winter darkness had already crept into the weak daylight. She boarded a bus, and held her stomach as the vehicle rumbled through the city streets. By the time they got to the designated neighborhood, she was the last person on the bus.

The driver stopped. She got up from her seat and showed him the address. He pointed out the window.

Left, then right, then right again.

She found it difficult to follow his directions. Her head spun with the complexity of traveling back in time to visit people who hadn't wanted her. Her foster mother's words wrapped themselves around her heart.

People who had children with Jews abandoned them in convents. You're better off staying in Poland with me.

This country gave her a choking feeling. A woman carrying groceries walked by. She was probably one of those who'd watched from the window when they hauled away the Jews next door. Like her mother had done.

She longed to be at home again. Little Piroschka would be asking for a story.

Where's Mamma?

She'd never leave the child.

The driver tapped the steering wheel. He smiled, gestured with his hand to the door. Lena got off the bus. She began walking, turning down streets. She looked up at the numbers on the buildings, tried to recall the driver's instructions.

At last she stood in front of a brick building. Her heart pounding, she pulled open the door and entered a dark stairwell. If this was really her grandmother's building, it should look familiar.

But she'd never been here before. Second floor, first door on the left. She climbed the steps and stopped in front of a large wooden door. Wouldn't she remember a big door like that? A big brass knocker? Was she at the wrong building? But she'd followed the directions precisely, read the house numbers carefully.

Her ear against the door, she listened. For what? The sound of her own grandmother's voice? But there was no sound, not even a radio.

An old man walked down the hall. He stared at her. She raised the brass knocker and rapped hard on the door. The man disappeared down the stairs. Then she waited, listened hard to the silence. She banged on the door with both fists. Nothing. Tears welled in her eyes. She'd come all this way, and nobody was home.

Back at the Red Cross office, she told the Polish speaking woman what had happened.

"She must've gone out shopping," the woman said gently.

"It was the wrong address," Lena said.

The clerk shook her head. "Please leave your address with us."

Lena wrote her Polish address in block letters. She pushed the paper over the counter towards the clerk. Without another word, she walked out the door and hurried to the train station. She found a seat next to the window, kept her eyes closed until the train was well out of the station. As the train rolled over the tracks, she gradually began to breathe evenly.

With Berlin behind her, she felt relieved.

I might not have liked them anyway.

The lights from the city of Krakau glittered through the raindrops on the window. Her heart beat with anticipation as if she'd been away for years, as if she'd nearly lost everything. At last, the train pulled into the village station. At home, she turned the key and pushed the door in. Her foster mother sat asleep on a chair. Little Piroschka must have gone to bed hours ago.

Her foster mother opened her eyes. Lena saw the searching look.

"It was a mistake," Lena said quickly. Gratification crossed her foster mother's face like a skulking goblin.

She went to little Piroschka's room, touched the child's foot.

The little girl opened her eyes, sat up, let her mother hug her. Lena told her the story of the old Russian couple that always slept on top of the oven. They refused to leave their village even when their son sent money from America because they never wanted anything more from life but the warmth of their very own stove in the night.

Little Piroschka was breathing soundly again before the story was done. Lena noticed the bear lying on the floor next to the bed. She picked it up and cradled it in her arms.

In the kitchen, her foster mother was taking off her bathrobe, preparing for bed. Piroschka turned and gazed at Lena with the adoration that both consoled and irritated her. She rolled the word over her tongue without speaking it. *Mamma.* It would always be a label for the mystery woman who lived in her imagination. She kissed Piroschka, then watched her shuffle towards the bed she'd made for herself on the sofa.

Erik did not stir when she got into bed next to him. She brought her knees to her chest, cuddled the bear the way she used to, burying her nose in the thin fur on the bear's head. Breathing in the dusty smell from long ago, she tried to remember a time before Poland. But her memory would not travel beyond the root cellar.

50. Tiny Crows Feet

That spring Charlotte wore the old blue cardigan that her mother had knitted. When it wore out at the elbows, she hadn't bothered to darn the holes. It had pockets—the kind you used for a hanky on runny nose days. In the right pocket was the telegram from her mother. Now she moved her elbow against the pocket, heard the reassuring sound of paper crackling.

Ragnar had brought it back from the village. She'd met him at the door, carried it in both hands into the shed. Under the flickering oil lamp, her feet firmly planted on the dirt floor, she'd told herself that whatever the telegram said didn't matter. What happened beyond the horizon was not her concern. Her roots lay in the earth at Dark Castle—shallow like the Alpine Azalea's—but firm enough to nourish a flower. She envisioned an arc of tomorrows, time measured in units of sheep-shearing, haying, and sheep slaughter. Bored with the pattern, she also feared its disruption.

She ripped open the envelope.

They called me from the Red Cross. A young Polish woman had contacted them. They said she had a cloth with the name Lena Bernstein on it. They gave her my address. She came looking for me, but I wasn't there. She left an address, lives somewhere near Krakau. Do you know about this cloth?

Her heart beat like a captured animal. She walked towards the house, tripping over the familiar stones in the driveway. Back in the house, she entered her bedroom and closed the door. She sat down on the edge of the bed. The cloth. She recalled that she'd sewn the letters into the cloth and pushed it into the bear's foot. Why? Then she remembered. The bear was expensive. It cost more than all the little gifts she'd bought for Max. And if somebody found it—

Now the bear was in Poland with Lena. But Poland was a big country, big enough to obscure a young woman's whim. Her mother would keep looking, but Poland was full of people. Her mother would bump into the wrong ones and miss the slender young woman who looked like Max. She pushed her legs against the bed frame, marking her thighs with the bed's reality, taking in the hard truth that she was *here* not *there.*

She rose to her feet and stood sideways at the window so that she could glimpse the ocean. In the distance she could see the glacier. Deep inside the earth, below the ice, throbbed the fire. Air. She needed air. In the hall, she found her windbreaker. Out on the steps, the wind whipped her hair across her face. Flopping her hood over her head, she pulled on the twine at the neck and tied it in a bow. Hands in her pockets, she walked until she grew warm inside the windbreaker. Just beyond the home field, a small herd of sheep faced the wind, their coats flat against their bodies. The grass flew straight back at the same angle. At the gate that separated the home field from the meadow, the wind flattened her windbreaker against her chest. The old woman looked up from picking angelica at the edge of the field. Charlotte waved to her and pointed to some fence posts, pretending to be looking for broken ones. She lifted the hemp noose from the post. Built of the few wood scraps they could spare from maintaining the shed, the rickety gate shuddered in the wind as she slipped out.

She avoided the turn that led to the village and the shore. Instead, she walked straight until the road curved around a cluster of rocks. The wind shifted slightly, carrying her forward toward the wooden platform where Ragnar placed their canisters of milk for dairy pick-up. It was also the bus stop, where she'd begun this strange life so many years ago.

The oxygen in her lungs helped her imagine her five-year old baby, the one she'd lunged after in the ocean. But somewhere on a Warsaw street, a Polish shop girl teetered on ridiculously high heels. Later she could weep over the loss of Baby Lena. Now she must sniff the air for her grown cub. But she needed a balm to soften the uncertainty. If only she could paint the girl, wrap her in color the way Egill had swathed his son in words.

Later that week she finally began to paint. But Gunnar, not Lena, was her subject. She held the brush loosely as if he would flow into reality through her fingers. This boy, whom she'd never seen, assembled himself. Her brush created his strong shoulders, his thick legs, his eyes lively with a love of mortal danger. Painting Ragnar as a boy took a long time. Surrounded by photos provided by the old woman, she kept changing his face, his hands. It had to be just right. Nobody must mistake Gunnar and Ragnar for her own two sons.

At last the painting hung on the wall. Often she caught Ragnar looking at it. Once she found him tracing with his fingertip the log that bound the boys, from shoulder to shoulder, a bond for one short moment in eternity. She stood behind him and said nothing. He turned around slowly and gazed into her eyes.

"When will you paint Lena?"

And finally she began. But she kept starting over again. That fall during the round-up of the sheep, the slaughter of the lambs, the stirring of the blood sausage, Charlotte did what she had to do and then washed her hands and went to her canvas.

During the dark days of winter, she broke into the Christmas candle supply and studied the canvas in candlelight. The bright light of noon sometimes obscured what she was trying to see. And the more she painted, the more she saw. And whatever she saw, she strove to give back to the canvas.

At Christmas, they made a bonfire in the snow and danced around it singing *Adam had seven sons. Seven sons had Adam.* Laughing at the boys' antics, Charlotte was completely happy. Yet, in the flames, she saw what her oils tried to create, a young woman with a long waist and a graceful neck. She wore white and tossed her hair.

Catch me if you can.

And now when her mother wrote about the deadly cold that gripped the continent, Charlotte worried. Did Lena own a coat?

In the middle of January, Charlotte began yet another portrait of Lena. Each day she visualized the girl differently, so that her skin shaded from a pale freckled complexion to a glowing olive skin. The eyes ranged from periwinkle to sapphire. Henrik often sat at her side, busy with his own painting. He often looked at her work and nodded soberly, as if to affirm that this too might be Lena.

One day, when she rolled her sleeves up to the elbows, Charlotte noted the dryness of her skin, how it furrowed into weather beaten wrinkles. It occurred to her that her skin was over fifty years old. Lena's skin had been downy soft against her own cheek. Today she'd have strong young skin that blushed easily and stretched smoothly over the fine bones of her face. Would she already have tiny crow's feet at her eyes?

Icicles hung hard and uncompromising from the shed roof, frozen like her hopes should be, she told herself.

In the Wilmersdorferstrasse her parents had owned a cat that sat for hours at the entrance to the hole where a mouse had disappeared. But the mouse had probably come out somewhere else. Lena could just as well be in Hungary or East Germany, two other big countries.

51. Capturing their Likeness

With the spring, Charlotte felt a quickening in her blood. The cows cavorted like calves drunk with the smell of growing grass.

The lambing season brought joys and heartaches. A ewe, busy with her sturdier lamb, butted its pitiful undersized brother, then turned her back on him.

"We've got another orphan," she called to Ragnar.

"Make her accept it," he called back.

But Charlotte could not cajole the ewe to allow the rejected animal to suck. Henrik would have to spend the summer giving it milk from the old baby bottle. Still, as the summer wore on, the orphan thrived. When Henrik forgot to close the farmhouse door, they heard the piercing *ack ack* in the hall. Henrik ran for the baby bottle.

The old woman swore as she plucked sheep droppings out of boots and shoes. But Charlotte rejoiced over the animal's plucky survival.

As the days grew longer, Charlotte's dreams changed. One night, she drifted into a café in a foreign city and took a table next to the window. Sitting alone, she could devote herself to watching pedestrians. A tall girl with a bouncing step passed by. Charlotte didn't recognize Lena, simply sensed that this might be her daughter. From the girl's backpack peered a worn, one-eyed teddy bear.

When she awoke, she punched the mattress to shake Ragnar out of his snoring, then lay back, feeling a new sense of peace. At its core was a new feeling about Lena. She called it Lena's *knowing*. If she concentrated hard enough, she felt she could let Lena know that she was thinking about her. The old woman had sung the words to the thrush.

O greet most fondly, if you chance to see
An angel whom—

The next day, Charlotte looked out over the meadow. Wildflowers bloomed in pink and yellow and blue clusters. That evening, when she was filtering the milk, Ragnar touched her arm.

"I liked the cluster of wild geraniums in the painting of me and Gunnar. Can you fill a whole canvas with those flowers. We could have them to look at all year around."

A warmth flooded her cheeks.

The next day she placed her sketchpad and colors in her backpack. She stroked Red's flaxen forelock, touched her cheek to the horse's velvety muzzle, and breathed in his smell.

"One day I'll paint the way you feel and smell," she promised, swinging herself into the saddle.

The old woman helped Henrik clamber up into the saddle in front of her. She touched the horse's withers with her stirrups, and Red moved eagerly out of the homefield and down the hillside. She was glad Ragnar had taught her to ride if only for the squeak of the saddle and the rich smell of horse. On some of the farms, they ate horse flesh, serving it with a rich sauce and wild berries. But Charlotte had never been able to do that. Rotten horse flesh was a favorite form of bait among those who rowed out alone on tiny boats.

The dog, Sam, ran ahead as Red trotted slowly across the meadow towards the valley.

The pattern of blue wild geraniums and yellow marsh marigolds blanketed the hillside all the way down to the stream. She nosed Henrik's hair. The earthy smell stirred an old melancholy.

Below, Sam skipped through the icy stream and shook himself on the mossy rocks on the other side. A frightened godwit fluttered up out of the water and flew towards the ocean, the sun gleaming on its rust-colored neck. The graceful Modigliani of birds always reminded her of Max.

Charlotte turned Red away from the ocean towards the hill on the other side. She dismounted and left him to graze by the stream. The wind was cool, but the sun warmed her. Halfway up the hill, Charlotte stopped. Lava rocks formed a sheltering ridge, and the heather smelled sweet. Sheep pellets littered the ground like tiny black pebbles, and yellow fleece clung to the rocks. She sat on a tuft of gray-green moss, and Henrik joined her. He leaned back and stretched his legs until his toes touched a rock covered with orange and rust-colored lichen.

He placed his fingers on his lips.

"A secret place."

"Why secret?" she asked.

But then she saw it, the place where the gentian had bloomed last summer. No sign of it now. A holy place for those who saw what others missed. She rolled up her sleeves and felt the warmth of the sun on her skin.

Drowsiness overcame her, and the brown and golden lichens took on new shape. They blended, pulled apart, changed their colors to amber and red. Their apricot- and marmelade-colored bodies wrapped themselves around one another.

Without taking her eyes off the rock lovers, she sketched this eternal life-giving embrace of the fungus and algae. She worked on the drawing until her hand hurt and her neck ached. Examining the drawing, she stretched out her arm, looked away, then back. In it she recognized the familiar hawk-like profile. It had been a long time, but it was definitely he.

She set down the sketchpad and lay back against the moss. His face, yellow and brown like the lichen lovers, appeared above her. Her fingers reached for his tangled curls of ginger and chestnut and drew him to her. His hair tickled her face, warmed her neck. The thirst began in her mouth.

Apollo held a silver cup of divine nectar to her lips, but a rumbling sound disturbed her rapture, and red-headed Thor, the clumsy Norse god of thunder, pressed a drinking horn of foaming mead to her lips. She laughed. There was no accounting for gods. The copper-colored hair of Thor's chest brushed across her bare breasts. The familiar smell of Max's sweat sent a ripple of pleasure through her.

Her lips brushed his navel, and her nose moved ever so slightly against his hardness. The tiny hairs tickled her nostrils. Somewhere above her he sighed. She parted her lips and tasted him. Finally, he was no longer the wounded Jew, torn to shreds because she hadn't saved him. She gave herself over to his pleasure. Afterwards, he did not leave her. His head on her breast, he spoke in a voice so low that she could barely hear him.

You see how happy I am.

He was gone, but this time she did not feel the pain of losing him. A sense of peace came over her. Another being came into her arms, and she knew the smell of her cub, stroked its soft birth hairs, hugged its warm little body.

When she woke up, the sun was gone. The fog climbed the hill towards her like a veil, and everything beyond it was invisible. She looked at her sketch of Max and knew that he was finally gone.

But where was her cub?

"Henrik," she called.

Silence.

The stream beyond gurgled. She stood and walked into the veil itself, all the time calling his name. The woman's voice spoke first, followed by Henrik's high-pitched voice. They were climbing the hill towards her. But who? Charlotte instinctively withdrew, but it was too late. She could see them now.

The woman had short brown hair and wore a white dress. She held the hand of a small girl with copper-colored hair. The child also wore white. Charlotte cursed herself for drinking the old woman's tea that morning. It made her see things in the fog. People who saw these hidden creatures were usually loners like Henrik who walked alongside the earth's crevices. On foggy days, the hidden people crawled up out of the earth. The women were always beautiful. They wore white.

Henrik ran ahead of them, then back, a herding dog who's finally found his sheep.

Suddenly it was too much. Her heart felt like it would burst. Charlotte closed her eyes and turned her back on them. That would make them disappear. But they wouldn't go away. Instead, they came closer. She could see the pink in their cheeks, the tiny wrinkles around the eyes of the woman.

Hadn't the old woman warned her?—don't fall in love with the hidden people or you'll go mad. She wouldn't look at them, just at Henrik. But out of the corner of her eye she saw the shape of the girl's cheek, just like—and the eyes. Henrik's eyes. The same eyes that she'd seen in the ocean. But they'd turned out to be seal's eyes. She wouldn't be fooled again. She stepped back, ran her fingers over the abrasive lichens on the rock. When you faced hidden people, you had to hold onto something real. The woman came closer. Her skin had an olive tone. Her eyes were locked on hers.

"Mamma," a voice said.

Charlotte glanced at the child. But it was the woman, not the child, who had spoken.

Then their outlines began to blur. Was her eyesight fading? Quickly she took up her pencil and began to draw them, following them when they moved, pursuing them between rocks, chasing them among the heather. Looking quickly from them to her paper, she added colors, making their faces ochre and orange against sun-colored lichens.

At last, exhausted, she looked up from her work. The sun had slid behind the hillside. The cool breeze stung her, emphasizing her loss. She rose to her feet and began to run.

Let me see you just one more time.

She discovered them nestled in the moss, their faces soft and gray and gentle. She started a new drawing with different colors. Her arm moved in different ways, quickly without stopping, until she'd filled the whole page.

Her heart beat fast, and her breath came rapidly. Wisps of fog streaked the hillside now, and she could barely see the meadow beyond. She looked everywhere. The figures had blended back into the moss and flowers. But she knew she'd captured their essence in her drawings. It was the only way to ensure they were hers forever.

Charlotte lay in bed, drifting between sleep and waking. Somebody touched her hand. Henrik's face was lively with enthusiasm.

"I want to go to the ocean today," he said.

"Why?"

"You said we should think of others."

"Yes."

Then she saw them on the chair behind him, his bones, white and dry, lying in a pile, waiting.

"It's for them. They want to see the ocean."

She sat up, reached for her bathrobe. In the back of her mind a question sharpened its tiny teeth. *Was he stranger than other children?*

She searched her mind for a comparison and remembered a time at the lake. It was after Max had been transported. Lena had brought her bear with her to let it swim. When it sank, Charlotte had closed her eyes and held her nose. Swimming below the surface, she had felt along the muddy bottom until she put her hands on the bear. But a bear was practically a living thing, not a pile of bones.

Henrik bent over the bones, picked them up and embraced

them. He fixed her with his wide eyes. She pulled on her pants, hunted for a sweater. Tryggvi and Ragnar were at Butterdale leveling Nonni's field of tussocks. Soon they would do the same at Dark Castle.

The truck rolled down the hill like a horse that knew the way. Charlotte's occasional tap of the brake was the bridle. Henrik hugged the bones to his chest.

"You will like this more than anything you ever did before," he told them.

At the edge of the sand, Charlotte stopped the car. The wind blew in off the ocean, and the water shone like green glass under the sun. The briny sea smell filled her nostrils, and she felt the pull of the tide in her blood stream. The sand was loose under her feet. She placed her hand on the back of Henrik's neck, felt the warmth of his skin. They walked to the ocean's edge.

The sea foam curled over the toes of Henrik's boots.

"What do the bones want here?" she asked.

"This."

He leaned forward and flung his arms open so that the bones fell into the sea.

Something tightened around Charlotte's heart as a greedy wave pulled the bones into its center, then released them, exposing the bones where they had sunk into the sand. The next wave swallowed them completely. But she breathed in an easy, steady manner and felt no urge to go in after them. She glanced at Henrik.

He looked up at her.

"Can they swim?" she asked.

"No. But they'll come back."

She saw the faith in his eyes. Could he stand the disappointment? She must prepare him.

"What if they don't come back?"

"That's all right. I've got more at home in the tussocks."

She placed an arm over his shoulders, gently squeezed his

upper arm. Her gaze traveled up the dark curve of the next mounting wave, over its white crest, down into the emerald green valley between the waves, then up again, moving onwards, all the way to the horizon. She fixed on a tiny dot that grew under her eyes until she could read it from left to right—the fulfillment of her promise to Max to keep his daughter safe. And along the entire line where the ocean met the sky, she saw all the years tumbling forward into the future, forward from Henrik's sixth year, forever and ever until she was gone, and Henrik was still here.

CPSIA information can be obtained at www.ICGtesting.com
Printed in the USA
BVOW03s1842130314

347583BV00001B/61/P